WITH THE SUN'S LIGHT AS FUEL,
THE STARS ARE THEIR DESTINATION

From a space-sailing race both fueled and threatened by the power of our sun . . . to a visit by alien traders who would determine whether humanity was entitled to survive . . . to a long-colonized Mars where even Santa travels by solar power, here are tales to send the imagination soaring free of planet Earth.

And with articles that explore the current status of light-sail research and the future directions of its development, the stories, poems, and illustrations included in this visionary collection reveal the whole spectrum of possibilities which await us as we prepare to launch our first lightships on exploratory missions through the solar system and beyond. . . .

PROJECT SOLAR SAIL

PROJECT SOLAR SAIL

Edited by
Arthur C. Clarke

Managing editor:
David Brin

A ROC BOOK

ROC

Published by the Penguin Group Penguin Books USA Inc.,
375 Hudson Street, New York, New York 10014, U.S.A.
Penguin Books Ltd, 27 Wrights Lane, London W8 5TZ, England
Penguin Books Australia Ltd, Ringwood, Victoria, Australia
Penguin Books Canada Ltd, 2801 John Street, Markham, Ontario, Canada L3R 1B4
Penguin Books (N.Z.) Ltd, 182-190 Wairau Road, Auckland 10, New Zealand

Penguin Books Ltd, Registered Offices: Harmondsworth, Middlesex, England

First Published by Roc, an imprint of Penguin Books USA Inc.

First Printing, April, 1990
10 9 8 7 6 5 4 3 2 1

ROC Roc is a trademark of Penguin Books USA Inc.

Printed in the United States of America

To Konstantin Tsiolkovsky, Fridrikh Tsander, and Carl Wiley, and those who came before them.

Contents

Foreword: The Winds of Space

Two very different kinds of wind blow forever from the sun. One is the gale of charged particles that shapes the tails of comets, whipping them across hundreds of mega-miles like pennants in a breeze. It is as inconstant and un-predictable as the hurricanes of Earth; sometimes it is a gentle zephyr, but it may rage with cyclonic violence dur-ing the peaks of the solar cycle. Then the ghostly aurora folds its curtains around Earth's magnetic field, and tor-rents of incoming electrons paint flickering images as the ionosphere becomes a gigantic cathode ray tube in the sky.

The other wind is a far gentler one, scarcely varying from eon to eon. It is a wind not of particles, but of pure radiation—light itself. Feeble though it is, we may one day learn to harness it, as since the beginning of history we have enslaved the winds of Earth.

The great sailing ships of the past—tea-clippers like *Cutty Sark,* and the splendid windjammers of the New En-gland master builders—were among the most beautiful achievements of human engineering. They reached one level of perfection just before the advent of steam and oil swept them from the seas—but they may return in a new, environmentally conscious age, with technologies based on composite materials, computer control, and satellite navigation.

This book is about a closely related idea whose time has yet to come. What a delightful irony it will be if the *real* age of sail has yet to dawn—not only on the oceans of Earth, but also in the far wider seas of space.

What is especially nice is that *you've* helped bring the age of interplanetary sailing closer, just by buying this book! I'll come back in the final pages to tell you about an exciting opportunity to participate even more dramatically. But right now I'll pass you on to some colleagues of mine, who volunteered their time and creativity to contribute to this unique volume about the adventure awaiting us tomorrow.

—Arthur C. Clarke
London, October 12, 1989

Introduction:
Sailing the Void

by
Isaac Asimov

In the early days of civilization, human beings discovered the use of sails. Woven sheets or rough textile caught the wind, and the momentum of that moving air was transferred to the floating ship, which then moved without a water current, and even against one. It was a wondrous advance. Until this innovation, ships could move upstream only by the unending application of human muscle. Of course, the wind might not always blow, or if it did, it might not blow in the right direction. Nevertheless, sail technology advanced steadily, so that feebler and feebler gusts could be used, even gusts that were in the wrong direction.

By the 1850s, Yankee clippers were the speediest and most beautiful vessels the world had ever seen. The steamships that replaced them were larger and, eventually, faster, but they were also uglier, dirtier, and noisier and always greedy for a steady stream of fuel. Sailing ships (except for pleasure vessels) have now disappeared from the world's oceans, but humanity faces another ocean today, an infinitely vaster and emptier one. Our water ocean spans tens of thousands of miles, but the ocean of outer space stretches for billion of trillions of miles.

Now, with fossil fuels growing scarce, there is new interest in cutting this umbilical again. Research into renewable power includes experiments in ultramodern sails for cargo ships and even cruise liners at sea.

We've begun the navigation of outer space with the equivalent of steamship races—the use of raw power, incredibly noisy power. Rockets. Nothing else will do, perhaps, to break through Earth's atmosphere and the lower reaches of its gravitational field.

Once a ship is in space, however, and is moving through a vacuum in orbit about Earth, is there anything quieter? Gentler? Better? More important, is there a way to move out there without being tied forever to an earthly supply of fuel? A wind would fit the bill, certainly, but outer space is a vacuum. What is there in space that can form a wind?

Two things, actually—at least in the neighborhood of a star like our sun. As my esteemed friend Arthur has told you, the sun emits two types of radiation: high-energy charged particles—mostly protons and electrons—and, of course, light. The first of these flows, the stream of high-speed particles, is what's referred to as the "solar wind." The name may be misleading, especially for the purposes of this book, as this is *not* the wind that drives a solar sail. The charged protons of the solar wind do possess momentum, and this momentum can be transferred to other charged objects in space. But we won't be discussing it much here.

The second "wind" in space is the sun's torrential output of light, which also possesses momentum, and which exerts a minuscule pressure on anything it strikes. Like the solar wind, it grows weaker with increasing distance from the sun. As it turns out, sunlight itself is more than a thousand times stronger than the solar wind from our sun.

A good example of these two streams at work can be seen during the active phase of a comet. A comet, as it approaches the sun, is partially vaporized. The rocky dust frozen in its outer layer then rises to surround the still-frozen nucleus in a haze. The tiny grains have large surface area per mass and so get swept away by light pressure alone. This dust is swept outward from the sun by sunlight to form the long "dust tail." There is a second comet tail as well, the *ion* tail, which consists of charged particles interacting with the protons and electrons of the solar wind, shining like neon lamps across millions of miles.

Scientists have long known about these two outward forces from the sun. However, they seemed so weak that it was long before serious consideration was given to how they might somehow prove useful. Except for the predictions of a few visionaries, it wasn't until the advent of spaceflight that plans began to be made to use these winds of space.

So far, of the two, it is sunlight which has received the most attention. Because light interacts with matter on a shorter scale than charged particles do, we can manipulate light more easily than the charged particles. Radiation pressure is much weaker than the sun's gravitational pull unless you mimic the dust grains . . . increase your surface area compared to mass. This can be done by spreading a thin collecting area—a reflecting sail—over vast tracts of space.

Fortunately, the free-fall conditions of space mean you don't need a lot of mass to support your reflector. You don't need the heavy masts or sturdy canvas sails of an earthly sailing ship. The result is a gossamer wonder, the lightsail, which has inspired this book.

While lightsails cannot do the grunt work, the heavy lifting from ground to orbit, they do appear to offer some wondrous opportunities for getting around once you're up there. What's more, they also appear to be *cheap*. By that I mean they may open the door for smaller groups to play a role in space than just the club of big national governments that now run the show.

Many grand ideas have been proposed for how photon sails might help us maneuver in, and make use of, interplanetary space. I will leave the experts to tell you of them.

I just want to mention, before I stop, one special application of light pressure—as a way to reach the stars. There are ways of converting the ordinary light of the sun into a laser beam, which is a wave of "coherent" light. This is light in which all the waves are the same length and move in the same direction. Whereas ordinary sunlight spreads out rapidly, so that far from the sun its pressure weakens into utter uselessness, a laser beam spreads out only very slightly, so its pressures, and its ability to move a ship, can remain constant over a very long distance.

A laser beam from Earth could drive such a ship through space by solar energy, burning no fuel and never running out of energy. Such a ship could be driven to the nearest star, Alpha Centauri, in just a few years.

It might seem that such a laser beam could drive the ship only outward, never to return; but with the use of still larger sails and ingenious ways of extending electrically charged systems, such ships could be brought to a halt in the neighborhood of Alpha Centauri and might even be made to take up the return journey. The requisite technology is a bit beyond us today, but a hundred years from now it may not be, and sailing vessels more magnificent than any we have ever seen may navigate distances vaster and emptier than anything our ancestors would have dreamed of.

This concept, and many others, await you in the pages ahead, as eminent scientists and gifted writers take you on a tour of the future. In fact and fiction, in essays and stories, you will catch glimpses of a tomorrow filled with wonder and possibility, as we and our descendants spread our sails and head forth, the wind at our backs, to the stars.

Isaac Asimov says: "My life is incredibly dull since I do nothing but write and have done nothing but write for fifty years. All I have to show for it is a number. Leaving quality aside as something that is moot, I have published to date 434 books, and have some 25 or 26 in press. I have written thousands of short pieces, both fiction and nonfiction, some, but not all, of which are included in

the books. I might add that, dullness or not, it has
been a very happy life."

And let me add that Isaac has been a friend for
a very long time. Thank you for the typically in-
cisive introduction, Isaac. Now it's my turn.

The Wind from the Sun

by
Arthur C. Clarke

The enormous disk of sail strained at its rigging, already filled with the wind that blew between the worlds. In three minutes the race would begin, yet now John Merton felt more relaxed, more at peace, than at any time for the past year. Whatever happened when the Commodore gave the starting signal, whether *Diana* carried him to victory or defeat, he had achieved his ambition. After a lifetime spent in designing ships for others, now he would sail his own.

"T minus two minutes," said the cabin radio. "Please confirm your readiness."

One by one, the other skippers answered. Merton recognized all the voices—some tense, some calm—for they were the voices of his friends and rivals. On the four inhabited worlds, there were scarcely twenty men who could sail a sun yacht; and they were all here, on the starting line or aboard the escort vessels, orbiting twenty-two thousand miles above the equator.

"Number One, *Gossamer*—ready to go."

"Number Two, *Santa Maria*—all O.K."

"Number Three, *Sunbeam*—O.K."

"Number Four, *Woomera*—all systems go."

Merton smiled at that last echo from the early, primitive days of astronautics. But it had become part of the tradition of space; and there were times when a man needed to evoke the shades of those who had gone before him to the stars.

"Number Five, *Lebedev*—we're ready."

"Number Six, *Arachne*—O.K."

Now it was his turn, at the end of the line; strange to think that the words he was speaking in this tiny cabin were being heard by at least five billion people.

"Number Seven, *Diana*—ready to start."

"One through Seven acknowledged." The voice from the judge's launch was impersonal. "Now T minus one minute."

Merton scarcely heard it; for the last time, he was checking the tension in the rigging. The needles of all the dynamometers were steady; the immense sail was taut, its mirror surface sparkling and glittering gloriously in the sun.

To Merton, floating weightless at the periscope, it seemed to fill the sky. As it well might—for out there were fifty million square feet of sail, linked to his capsule by almost a hundred miles of rigging. All the canvas of all the tea-clippers that had once raced like clouds across the China seas, sewn into one gigantic sheet, could not match the single sail that *Diana* had spread beneath the sun. Yet it was little more substantial than a soap bubble; that two square miles of aluminized plastic was only a few millionths of an inch thick.

"T minus ten seconds. All recording cameras *on.*"

Something so huge, yet so frail, was hard for the mind to grasp. And it was harder still to realize that this fragile mirror could tow them free of Earth, merely by the power of the sunlight it would trap.

". . . five, four, three, two, one, *cut!*"

Seven knifeblades sliced through the seven thin lines tethering the yachts to the motherships that had assembled and serviced them.

Until this moment, all had been circling Earth together in a rigidly held formation, but now the yachts would begin to disperse, like dandelion seeds drifting before the breeze. And the winner would be the one that first drifted past the moon.

Aboard *Diana*, nothing seemed to be happening. But Merton knew better; though his body would feel no thrust, the instrument board told him he was now accelerating at almost one thousandth of a gravity. For a rocket, that figure would have been ludicrous—but this was the first time any solar yacht had attained it. *Diana*'s design was sound; the vast sail was living up to his calculations. At this rate, two circuits of Earth would build up his speed to escape velocity—then he would head out for the moon, with the full force of the sun behind him.

The full force of the sun. He smiled wryly, remembering all his attempts to explain solar sailing to those lecture audiences back on Earth. That had been the only way he could raise money, in those early days. He might be Chief Designer of Cosmodyne Corporation, with a whole string of successful spaceships to his credit, but his firm had not been exactly enthusiastic about his hobby.

"Hold your hands out to the sun," he'd said. "What do you feel? Heat, of course. But there's pressure as well—though you've never noticed it, because it's so tiny. Over the area of your hands, it only comes to about a millionth of an ounce.

"But out in space, even a pressure as small as that can be important—for it's acting all the time, hour after hour, day after day. Unlike rocket fuel, it's free and unlimited. If we want to, we can use it; we can build sails to catch the radiation blowing from the sun."

At that point, he would pull out a few square yards of sail material and toss it toward the audience. The silvery film would coil and twist like smoke, then drift slowly to the ceiling in the hot-air currents.

"You can see how light it is," he'd continue. "A square mile weighs only a ton, and can collect five pounds of radiation pressure. So it will start moving—and we can let it tow us along, if we attach rigging to it.

"Of course, its acceleration will be tiny—about a thousandth of a g. That doesn't seem much, but let's see what it means.

"It means that in the first second, we'll move about a

fifth of an inch. I suppose a healthy snail could do better than that. But after a minute, we've covered sixty feet, and will be doing just over a mile an hour. That's not bad, for something driven by pure sunlight! After an hour, we're forty miles from our starting point, and will be moving at eighty miles an hour. Please remember that in space there's no friction, so once you start anything moving, it will keep going forever. You'll be surprised when I tell you what our thousandth-of-a-g sailing boat will be doing at the end of a day's run. *Almost two thousand miles an hour!* If it starts from orbit—as it has to, of course—it can reach escape velocity in a couple of days. And all without burning a single drop of fuel!''

Well, he'd convinced them, and in the end he'd even convinced Cosmodyne. Over the last twenty years, a new sport had come into being. It had been called the sport of billionaires, and that was true—but it was beginning to pay for itself in terms of publicity and television coverage. The prestige of four continents and two worlds was riding on this race, and it had the biggest audience in history.

Diana had made a good start; time to take a look at the opposition. Moving very gently. Though there were shock absorbers between the control capsule and the delicate rigging, he was determined to run no risks. Merton stationed himself at the periscope.

There they were, looking like strange silver flowers planted in the dark fields of space. The nearest, South America's *Santa Maria*, was only fifty miles away; it bore a resemblance to a boy's kite—but a kite more than a mile on its side. Farther away, the University of Astrograd's *Lebedev* looked like a Maltese cross; the sails that formed the four arms could apparently be tilted for steering purposes. In contrast, the Federation of Australasia's *Wommera* was a simple parachute, four miles in circumference. General Spacecraft's *Arachne*, as its name suggested, looked like a spiderweb—and had been built on the same principles, by robot shuttles spiraling out from a central point. Eurospace Corporation's *Gossamer* was an identical design, on a slightly smaller scale. And the Republic of Mar's *Sunbeam* was a flat ring, with a half-mile-wide hole in the center, spinning slowly so that centrifugal force gave it stiffness. That was an old idea, but no one had ever made it work. Merton was fairly sure that the colonials would be in trouble when they started to turn.

That would not be for another six hours, when the yachts had moved along the first quarter of their slow and stately twenty-four-hour orbit. Here at the beginning of the race, they were all heading directly away from the sun—running, as it were, before the solar wind. One had to make the most of this lap, before the boats swung round to the other side of Earth and then started to head back into the sun.

Time for the first check, Merton told himself, while he had no navigational worries. With the periscope, he made a careful examination of the sail, concentrating on the points where the rigging was attached to it. The shroud lines—narrow bands of unsilvered plastic film—would have been completely invisible had they not been coated with fluorescent paint. Now they were taut lines of colored light, dwindling away for hundreds of yards toward that gigantic sail. Each had its own electric windlass, not much bigger than a game fisherman's reel. The little windlasses were continually turning, playing lines in or out, as the autopilot kept the sail trimmed at the correct angle to the sun.

The play of sunlight on the great flexible mirror was beautiful to watch. It was undulating in slow, stately oscillations, sending multiple images of the sun marching across the heavens, until they faded away at the edges of the sail. Such leisurely vibrations were to be expected in this vast and flimsy structure; they were usually quite harmless, but Merton watched them carefully. Sometimes they could build up to the catastrophic undulations known as the wriggles, which could tear a sail to pieces.

When he was satisfied that everything was shipshape, he swept the periscope around the sky, rechecking the positions of his rivals. It was as he had hoped; the weeding-out process had begun, as the less efficient boats fell astern. But the real test would come when they passed into the shadow of Earth; then maneuverability would count as much as speed.

It seemed a strange thing to do, now that the race had just started, but it might be a good idea to get some sleep. The two-man crews on the other boats could take it in turns, but Merton had no one to relieve him. He must rely on his physical resources—like that other solitary seaman Joshua Slocum, in his tiny *Spray*. The American skipper had sailed *Spray* single-handed round the world; he could never have dreamed that, two centuries later, a man would be sailing single-handed from Earth to moon—inspired, at least partly, by his example.

Merton snapped the elastic bands of the cabin seat around his waist and legs, then placed the electrodes of the sleep-inducer on his forehead. He set the timer for three hours, and relaxed.

Very gently, hypnotically, the electronic pulses throbbed in the frontal lobes of his brain. Colored spirals of light expanded beneath his closed eyelids, widening outward to infinity. Then—nothing . . .

The brazen clamor of the alarm dragged him back from his dreamless sleep. He was instantly awake, his eyes scanning the instrument panel. Only two hours had passed—but above the accelerometer, a red light was flashing. Thrust was falling; *Diana* was losing power.

Merton's first thought was that something had happened to the sail; perhaps the antispin devices had failed and the rigging had become twisted. Swiftly, he checked the meters that showed the tension in the shroud lines. Strange, on one side of the sail they were reading normally—but on the other, the pull was dropping slowly even as he watched.

In sudden understanding, Merton grabbed the periscope, switched to wide-angle vision, and started to scan the edge of the sail. Yes—there was the trouble, and it could have only one cause.

A huge, sharp-edged shadow had begun to slide across the gleaming silver of the sail. Darkness was falling upon *Diana*, as if a cloud had passed between her and the sun. And in the dark, robbed of the rays that drove her, she would lose all thrust and drift helplessly through space.

But, of course, there were no clouds here, more than twenty thousand miles above Earth. If there was a shadow, it must be made by man.

Merton grinned as he swung the periscope toward the sun, switching in the filters that would allow him to look full into its blazing face without being blinded.

"Maneuver 4a," he muttered to himself. "We'll see who can play best at *that* game."

It looked as if a giant planet was crossing the face of the sun. A great black disk had bitten deep into its edge. Twenty miles astern, *Gossamer* was trying to arrange an artificial eclipse—specially for *Diana*'s benefit.

The maneuver was a perfectly legitimate one; back in the days of ocean racing, skippers had often tried to rob each other of the wind. With any luck, you could leave your rival becalmed, with his sails collapsing around him— and be well ahead before he could undo the damage.

Merton had no intention of being caught so easily. There was plenty of time to take evasive action; things happened very slowly when you were running a solar sailing boat. It would be at least twenty minutes before *Gossamer* could slide completely across the face of the sun, and leave him in darkness.

Diana's tiny computer—the size of a matchbox, but the equivalent of a thousand human mathematicians— considered the problem for a full second and then flashed the answer. He'd have to open control panels three and four, until the sail had developed an extra twenty degrees of tilt; then the radiation pressure would blow him out of *Gossamer*'s dangerous shadow, back into the full blast of the sun. It was a pity to interfere with the autopilot, which had been carefully programmed to give the fastest possible run—but that, after all, was why he was here. This was what made solar yachting a sport, rather than a battle between computers.

Out went control lines one to six, slowly undulating like sleepy snakes as they momentarily lost their tension. Two miles away, the triangular panels began to open lazily, spilling sunlight through the sail. Yet, for a long time, nothing seemed to happen. It was hard to grow accustomed to this slow-motion world, where it took minutes for the effects of any action to become visible to the eye. Then Merton saw that the sail was indeed tipping toward the sun—and that *Gossamer*'s shadow was sliding harmlessly away, its cone of darkness lost in the deeper night of space.

Long before the shadow had vanished and the disk of the sun had cleared again, he reversed the tilt and brought *Diana* back on course. Her new momentum would carry her clear of the danger; no need to overdo it, and upset his calculations by side-stepping too far. That was another rule that was hard to learn. The very moment you had started something happening in space, it was already time to think about stopping it.

He reset the alarm, ready for the next natural or manmade emergency; perhaps *Gossamer,* or one of the other contestants, would try the same trick again. Meanwhile, it was time to eat, though he did not feel particularly hungry. One used little physical energy in space, and it was easy to forget about food. Easy—and dangerous; for when an emergency arose, you might not have the reserves needed to deal with it.

He broke open the first of the meal packets, and inspected it without enthusiasm. The name on the label—SPACETASTIES—was enough to put him off. And he had grave doubts about the promise printed underneath. Guaranteed Crumbless. It had been said that crumbs were a greater danger to space vehicles than meteorites. They could drift into the most unlikely places, causing short circuits, blocking vital jets that were supposed to be hermetically sealed.

Still, the liverwurst went down pleasantly enough; so did the chocolate and the pineapple purée. The plastic coffee bulb was warming on the electric heater when the outside world broke in on his solitude. The radio operator on the Commodore's launch routed a call to him.

"Dr. Merton? If you can spare the time, Jeremy Blair would like a few words with you." Blair was one of the more responsible news commentators, and Merton had been on his program many times. He could refuse to be interviewed, of course, but he liked Blair, and at the moment he could certainly not claim to be too busy. "I'll take it," he answered.

"Hello, Dr. Merton," said the commentator immediately. "Glad you can spare a few minutes. And congratulations—you seem to be ahead of the field."

"Too early in the game to be sure of that," Merton answered cautiously.

"Tell me, doctor—why did you decide to sail *Diana* yourself? Just because it's never been done before?"

"Well, isn't that a very good reason? But it wasn't the only one, of course." He paused, choosing his words carefully. "You know how critically the performance of a sun yacht depends on its mass. A second man, with all his supplies, would mean another five hundred pounds. That could easily be the difference between winning and losing."

"And you're quite certain that you can handle *Diana* alone?"

"Reasonably sure, thanks to the automatic controls I've designed. My main job is to supervise and make decisions."

"But—two square miles of sail! It just doesn't seem possible for one man to cope with all that!"

Merton laughed.

"Why not? Those two square miles produce a maximum

pull of just ten pounds. I can exert more force with my little finger.''

"Well, thank you, doctor. And good luck.''

As the commentator signed off, Merton felt a little ashamed of himself. For his answer had been only part of the truth; and he was sure that Blair was shrewd enough to know it.

There was just one reason why he was here, alone in space. For almost forty years he had worked with teams of hundreds or even thousands of men, helping to design the most complex vehicles that the world had ever seen. For the last twenty years he had led one of those teams, and watched his creations go soaring to the stars. (But there were failures that he could never forget, even though the fault had not been his.) He was famous, with a successful career behind him. Yet he had never done anything by himself; always he had been one of an army.

This was his very last chance of individual achievement, and he would share it with no one. There would be no more solar yachting for at least five years, as the period of the quiet sun ended and the cycle of bad weather began, with radiation storms bursting through the solar system. When it was safe again for these frail, unshielded craft to venture aloft, he would be too old. If, indeed, he was not too old already. . . .

He dropped the empty food containers into the waste disposal, and turned once more to the periscope. At first, he could find only five of the other yachts; there was no sigh of *Woomera*. It took him several minutes to locate her—a dim, star-eclipsing phantom, neatly caught in the shadow of *Lebedev*. He could imagine the frantic efforts the Australasians were making to extricate themselves, and wondered how they had fallen into the trap. It suggested that *Lebedev* was unusually maneuverable; she would bear watching, though she was too far away to menace *Diana* at the moment.

* * *

Now Earth had almost vanished. It had waned to a narrow, brilliant bow of light that was moving steadily toward the sun. Dimly outlined within that burning bow was the night side of the planet, with the phosphorescent gleams of great cities showing here and there through gaps in the clouds. The disk of darkness had already blanked out a huge section of the Milky Way; in a few minutes, it would start to encroach upon the sun.

The light was fading. A purple, twilight hue—the glow of many sunsets, thousands of miles below—was falling across the sail, as *Diana* slipped silently into the shadow of Earth. The sun plummeted below that invisible horizon. Within minutes, it was night.

Merton looked back along the orbit he had traced now a quarter of the way around the world. One by one he saw the brilliant stars of the other yachts wink out, as they joined him in the brief night. It would be an hour before the sun emerged from that enormous black shield, and through all that time they would be completely helpless, coasting without power.

He switched on the external spotlight and started to search the now darkened sail with its beam. Already, the thousands of acres of film were beginning to wrinkle and become flaccid; the shroud lines were slackening, and must be wound in lest they become entangled. But all this was expected; everything was going as planned.

Forty miles astern, *Arachne* and *Santa Maria* were not so lucky. Merton learned of their troubles when the radio burst into life on the emergency circuit.

"Number Two, Number Six—this is Control. You are on a collision course. Your orbits will intersect in sixty-five minutes! Do you require assistance?"

There was a long pause while the two skippers digested this bad news. Merton wondered who was to blame; perhaps one yacht had been trying to shadow the other, and had not completed the maneuver before they were both caught in darkness. Now there was nothing that either could do; they were slowly but inexorably converging, unable to change course by a fraction of a degree.

Yet, sixty-five minutes! That would just bring them out into sunlight again, as they emerged from the shadow of Earth. They still had a slim chance, if their sails could snatch enough power to avoid a crash. There must be some frantic calculations going on, aboard *Arachne* and *Santa Maria*.

Arachne answered first; her reply was just what Merton had expected.

"Number Six calling Control. We don't need assistance, thank you. We'll work this out for ourselves."

I wonder, thought Merton. But at least it will be interesting to watch. The first real drama of the race was approaching—exactly above the line of midnight on sleeping Earth.

For the next hour, Merton's own sail kept him too busy to worry about *Arachne* and *Santa Maria*. It was hard to keep a good watch on that fifty million square feet of dim plastic out there in the darkness, illuminated only by his narrow spotlight and the rays of the still distant moon. From now on, for almost half his orbit around Earth, he must keep the whole of this immense area edge-on to the sun. During the next twelve or fourteen hours, the sail would be a useless encumbrance; for he would be heading into the sun, and its rays could only drive him backward along his orbit. It was a pity that he could not furl the sail completely, until he was ready to use it again. But no one had yet found a practical way of doing this.

Far below, there was the first hint of dawn along the edge of Earth. In ten minutes, the sun would emerge from its eclipse; the coasting yachts would come to life again as the blast of radiation struck their sails. That would be the moment of crisis for *Arachne* and *Santa Maria*—and, indeed, for all of them.

Merton swung the periscope until he found the two dark shadows drifting against the stars. They were very close together—perhaps less than three miles apart. They might, he decided, just be able to make it. . . .

Dawn flashed like an explosion along the rim of Earth, as the sun rose out of the Pacific. The sail and shroud lines glowed a brief crimson, then gold, then blazed with the pure white light of day. The needles of the dynamometers began to lift from their zeros—but only just. *Diana* was still almost completely weightless, for with the sail pointing toward the sun, her acceleration was now only a few millionths of a gravity.

But *Arachne* and *Santa Maria* were crowding on all the sail they could manage, in their desperate attempt to keep apart. Now, while there was less than two miles between them, their glittering plastic clouds were unfurling and expanding with agonizing slowness, as they felt the first delicate push of the sun's rays. Almost every TV screen on Earth would be mirroring this protracted drama; and even now, at this very last minute, it was impossible to tell what the outcome would be.

The two skippers were stubborn men. Either could have cut his sail, and fallen back to give the other a chance; but neither would do so. Too much prestige, too many millions, too many reputations were at stake. And so, silently and softly as snow-flakes falling on a winter night, *Arachne* and *Santa Maria* collided.

The square kite crawled almost imperceptibly into the circular spider's web; the long ribbons of the shroud lines twisted and tangled together with dreamlike slowness. Even aboard *Diana*, busy with his own rigging, Merton could scarcely tear his eye away from this silent, long-drawn-out disaster.

For more than ten minutes the billowing, shining clouds continued to merge into one inextricable mass. Then the crew capsules tore loose and went their separate ways, missing each other by hundreds of yards. With a flare of rockets, the safety launches hurried to pick them up.

That leaves five of us, thought Merton. He felt sorry for the skippers who had so thoroughly eliminated each other, only a few hours after the start of the race; but they were young men, and would have another chance.

Within minutes, the five had dropped to four. From the very beginning, Merton had had doubts about the slowly rotating *Sunbeam*. Now he saw them justified.

The Martian ship had failed to tack properly; her spin had given her too much stability. Her great ring of a sail was turning to face the sun, instead of being edge-on to it. She was being blown back along her course at almost her maximum acceleration.

That was about the most maddening thing that could happen to a skipper—worse even than a collision, for he could blame only himself. But no one would feel much sympathy for the frustrated colonials, as they dwindled slowly astern. They had made too many brash boasts before the race, and what had happened to them was poetic justice.

Yet it would not do to write off *Sunbeam* completely. With almost half a million miles still to go, she might still pull ahead. Indeed, if there were a few more casualties, she might be the only one to complete the race. It had happened before.

However, the next twelve hours were uneventful, as Earth waxed in the sky from new to full. There was little to do while the fleet drifted around the unpowered half of its orbit, but Merton did not find the time hanging heavily on his hands. He caught a few hours' sleep, ate two meals, wrote up his log, and became involved in several more radio interviews. Sometimes, though rarely, he talked to the other skippers, exchanging greetings and friendly taunts. But most of the time he was content to float in weightless relaxation, beyond all the cares of Earth, happier than he had been for many years. He was—as far as any man could be in space—master of his own fate, sailing the ship upon which he had lavished so much skill, so much love, that she had become part of his very being.

The next casualty came when they were passing the line between Earth and sun, and were just beginning the powered half of the orbit. Aboard *Diana*, Merton saw the great sail stiffen as it tilted to catch the rays that drove it. The acceleration began to climb up from the microgravities, though it would be hours yet before it would reach its maximum value.

It would never reach it for *Gossamer*. The moment when power came on again was always critical, and she failed to survive it.

Blair's radio commentary, which Merton had left running at low volume, alerted him with the news: "Hello, *Gossamer* has the wriggles!" He hurried to the periscope, but at first could see nothing wrong with the great circular disk of *Gossamer*'s sail. It was difficult to study it, as it was almost edge-on to him and so appeared as a thin ellipse; but presently he saw that it was twisting back and forth in slow, irresistible oscillations. Unless the crew could damp out these waves, by properly timed but gentle tugs on the shroud lines, the sail would tear itself to pieces.

They did their best, and after twenty minutes it seemed that they had succeeded. Then, somewhere near the center of the sail, the plastic film began to rip. It was slowly driven outward by the radiation pressure like smoke coiling upward from a fire. Within a quarter of an hour, nothing was left but the delicate tracery of the radial spars that had supported the great web. Once again there was a flare of rockets, as a launch moved in to retrieve the *Gossamer*'s capsule and her dejected crew.

"Getting rather lonely up here, isn't it?" said a conversational voice over the ship-to-ship radio.

"Not for you, Dimitri," retorted Merton. "You've still got company back there at the end of the field. I'm the one who's lonely, up here in front." It was not an idle boast. By this time *Diana* was three hundred miles ahead of the next competitor, and his lead should increase still more rapidly in the hours to come.

Aboard *Lebedev*, Dimitri Markoff gave a good-natured chuckle. He did not sound, Merton thought, at all like a man who had resigned himself to defeat.

"Remember the legend of the tortoise and the hare,"

answered the Russian. "A lot can happen in the next quarter-million miles."

It happened much sooner than that, when they had completed their first orbit of Earth and were passing the starting line again—though thousands of miles higher, thanks to the extra energy the sun's rays had given them. Merton had taken careful sights on the other yachts, and had fed the figures into the computer. The answer it gave for *Woomera* was so absurd that he immediately did a recheck.

There was no doubt of it—the Australasians were catching up at a fantastic rate. No solar yacht could possibly have such an acceleration, unless—

A swift look through the periscope gave the answer. *Woomera*'s rigging, pared back to the very minimum of mass, had given way. It was her sail alone, still maintaining its shape, that was racing up behind him like a handkerchief blown before the wind. Two hours later it fluttered past, less than twenty miles away. But long before that, the Australasians had joined the growing crowd aboard the Commodore's launch.

So now it was a straight fight between *Diana* and *Lebedev*—for though the Martians had not given up, they were a thousand miles astern and no longer counted as a serious threat. For that matter, it was hard to see what *Lebedev* could do to overtake *Diana*'s lead. But all the way around the second lap—through eclipse again, and the long, slow drift against the sun—Merton felt a growing unease.

He knew the Russian pilots and designers. They had been trying to win this race for twenty years, and after all, it was only fair that they should, for had not Pyotr Nikolayevich Lebedev been the first man to detect the pressure of sunlight, back at the very beginning of the twentieth century? But they had never succeeded.

And they would never stop trying. Dimitri was up to something—and it would be spectacular.

Aboard the official launch, a thousand miles behind the

racing yachts, Commodore van Stratten looked at the radiogram with angry dismay. It had traveled more than a hundred million miles, from the chain of solar observatories swinging high above the blazing surface of the sun, and it brought the worst possible news.

The Commodore—his title, of course, was purely honorary; back on Earth he was Professor of Astrophysics at Harvard—had been half expecting it. Never before had the race been arranged so late in the season; there had been many delays, they had gambled, and now it seemed they might all lose.

Deep beneath the surface of the sun, enormous forces were gathering. At any moment, the energies of a million hydrogen bombs might burst forth in the awesome explosion known as a solar flare. Climbing at millions of miles an hour, an invisible fireball many times the size of Earth would leap from the sun and head out across space.

The cloud of electrified gas would probably miss Earth completely. But if it did not, it would arrive in just over a day. Spaceships could protect themselves, with their shielding and their powerful magnetic screen. But the lightly built solar yachts, with their paper-thin walls, were defenseless against such a menace. The crews would have to be taken off, and the race abandoned.

John Merton still knew nothing of this as he brought *Diana* around Earth for the second time. If all went well, this would be the last circuit, both for him and for the Russians. They had spiraled upward by thousands of miles, gaining energy from the sun's rays. On this lap, they should escape from Earth completely—and head outward on the long run to the moon. It was a straight race now. *Sunbeam*'s crew had finally withdrawn, exhausted, after battling valiantly with their spinning sail for more than a hundred thousand miles.

Merton did not feel tired; he had eaten and slept well, and *Diana* was behaving herself admirably. The autopilot, tensioning the rigging like a busy little spider, kept the great sail trimmed to the sun more accurately than any

human skipper. Though by this time the two square miles
of plastic sheet must have been riddled by hundreds of
micrometeorites, the pin-head-sized punctures had produced no falling off to thrust.

He had only two worries. The first was shroud line number eight, which could no longer be adjusted properly.
Without any warning, the reel had jammed; even after all
these years of astronautical engineering, bearings sometimes seized up in vacuum. He could neither lengthen nor
shorten the line, and would have to navigate as best he
could with the others. Luckily, the most difficult maneuvers were over. From now on, *Diana* would have the sun
behind her as she sailed straight down the solar wind. And
as the old-time sailors often said, it was easy to handle a
boat when the wind was blowing over your shoulder.

His other worry was *Lebedev*, still dogging his heels
three hundred miles astern. The Russian yacht had shown
remarkable maneuverability, thanks to the four great panels that could be tilted around the central sail. All her flip-
overs as she rounded Earth had been carried out with
superb precision; but to gain maneuverability she must
have sacrificed speed. You could not have it both ways. In
the long, straight haul ahead, Merton should be able to
hold his own. Yet he could not be certain of victory until,
three or four days from now, *Diana* went flashing past the
far side of the moon.

And then, in the fiftieth hour of the race, near the end
of the second orbit around Earth, Markoff sprang his little
surprise.

"Hello, John," he said casually, over the ship-to-ship
circuit. "I'd like you to watch this. It should be interesting."

Merton drew himself across to the periscope and turned
up the magnification to the limit. There in the field of
view, a most improbable sight against the background of
the stars, was the glittering Maltese cross of *Lebedev*, very
small but very clear. And then, as he watched, the four
arms of the cross slowly detached themselves from the

central square and went drifting away, with all their spars and rigging, into space.

Markoff had jettisoned all unnecessary mass, now that he was coming up to escape velocity and need no longer plod patiently around Earth, gaining momentum on each circuit. From now on, *Lebedev* would be almost unsteerable—but that did not matter. All the tricky navigation lay behind her. It was as if an old-time yachtsman had deliberately thrown away his rudder and heavy keel—knowing that the rest of the race would be straight downwind over a calm sea.

"Congratulations, Dimitri," Merton radioed. "It's a neat trick. But it's not good enough—you can't catch up now."

"I've not finished yet," the Russian answered. "There's an old winter's tale in my country, about a sleigh being chased by wolves. To save himself, the driver has to throw off the passengers one by one. Do you see the analogy?"

Merton did, all too well. On this final lap, Dimitri no longer needed his copilot. *Lebedev* could really be stripped down for action.

"Alexis won't be very happy about this," Merton replied. "Besides, it's against the rules."

"Alexis isn't happy, but I'm the captain. He'll just have to wait around for ten minutes until the Commodore picks him up. And the regulations say nothing about the size of the crew—you should know that."

Merton did not answer. He was too busy doing some hurried calculations, based on what he knew of *Lebedev*'s design. By the time he had finished, he knew that the race was still in doubt. *Lebedev* would be catching up with him at just about the time he hoped to pass the moon.

But the outcome of the race was already being decided, ninety-two million miles away.

On Solar Observatory Three, far inside the orbit of Mercury, the automatic instruments recorded the whole history of the flare. A hundred million square miles of the sun's surface suddenly exploded in such blue-white fury that, by comparison, the rest of the disk paled to a dull glow. Out of that seething inferno, twisting and turning like a living creature in the magnetic fields of its own creation, soared the electrified plasma of the great flare. Ahead of it, moving at the speed of light, went the warning flash of ultraviolet and x-rays. That would reach Earth in eight minutes, and was relatively harmless. Not so the charged atoms that were following behind at their leisurely four million miles an hour—and which, in just over a day, would engulf *Diana, Lebedev,* and their accompanying little fleet in a cloud of lethal radiation.

The Commodore left his decision to the last possible minute. Even when the jet of plasma had been tracked past the orbit of Venus, there was a chance that it might miss Earth. But when it was less than four hours away, and had already been picked up by the moon-based radar network, he knew that there was no hope. All solar sailing was over for the next five or six years until the sun was quiet again.

A great sigh of disappointment swept across the solar system. *Diana* and *Lebedev* were halfway between Earth and moon, running neck and neck—and now no one would ever know which was the better boat. The enthusiasts would argue the result for years; history would merely record: race cancelled owing to solar storm.

When John Merton received the order, he felt a bitterness he had not known since childhood. Across the years, sharp and clear, came the memory of his tenth birthday. He had been promised an exact scale model of the famous spaceship *Morning Star,* and for weeks had been planning how he would assemble it, where he would hang it up in his bedroom. And then, at the last moment, his father had broken the news. "I'm sorry, John—it costs too much money. Maybe next year . . ."

Half a century and a successful lifetime later, he was a heartbroken boy again.

For a moment, he thought of disobeying the Commodore. Suppose he sailed on, ignoring the warning? Even if

the race were abandoned, he could make a crossing to the
moon that would stand in the record books for generations.

But that would be worse than stupidity. It would be suicide—and a very unpleasant form of suicide. He had seen
men die of radiation poisoning, when the magnetic shielding of their ships had failed in deep space. No—nothing
was worth that. . . .

He felt as sorry for Dimitri Markoff as for himself; they
both deserved to win, and now victory would go to neither. No man could argue with the sun in one of its rages,
even though he might ride upon its beams to the edge of
space.

Only fifty miles astern now, the Commodore's launch
was drawing alongside *Lebedev,* preparing to take off her
skipper. There went the silver sail, as Dimitri—with feeling that he would share—cut the rigging. The tiny capsule
would be taken back to Earth, perhaps to be used again—
but a sail was spread for one voyage only.

He could press the jettison button now, and save his
rescuers a few minutes of time. But he could not do so.
He wanted to stay aboard to the very end, on the little boat
that had been for so long a part of his dreams and his life.
The great sail was spread now at right angles to the sun,
exerting its utmost thrust. Long ago it had torn him clear
of Earth—and *Diana* was still gaining speed.

Then, out of nowhere, beyond all doubt or hesitation,
he knew what must be done. For the last time, he sat down
before the computer that had navigated him halfway to the
moon.

When he had finished, he packed the log and his few
personal belongings. Clumsily—for he was out of practice,
and it was not an easy job to do by oneself—he climbed
into the emergency survival suit.

He was just sealing the helmet when the Commodore's
voice called over the radio. "We'll be alongside in five
minutes, Captain. Please cut your sail so we won't foul
it."

John Merton, first and last skipper of the sun yacht *Diana,* hesitated for a moment. He looked for the last time around the tiny cabin, with its shining instruments and its neatly arranged controls, now all locked in their final positions. Then he said to the microphone: "I'm abandoning ship. Take your time to pick me up. *Diana* can look after herself."

There was no reply from the Commodore, and for that he was grateful. Professor van Stratten would have guessed what was happening—and would know that, in these final moments, he wished to be left alone.

He did not bother to exhaust the airlock, and the rush of escaping gas blew him gently out into space; the thrust he gave her then was his last gift to *Diana.* She dwindled away from him, sail glittering splendidly in the sunlight that would be hers for centuries to come. Two days from now she would flash past the moon; but the moon, like Earth, could never catch her. Without his mass to slow her down, she would gain two thousand miles an hour in every day of sailing. In a month, she would be traveling faster than any ship that man had ever built.

As the sun's rays weakened with distance, so her acceleration would fall. But even at the orbit of Mars, she would be gaining a thousand miles an hour in every day. Long before then, she would be moving too swiftly for the sun itself to hold her. Faster than any comet that had ever streaked in from the stars, she would be heading out into the abyss.

The glare of rockets, only a few miles away, caught Merton's eye. The launch was approaching to pick him up at thousands of times the acceleration that *Diana* could ever attain. But engines could burn for a few minutes only, before they exhausted their fuel—while *Diana* would still be gaining speed, driven outward by the sun's eternal fires, for ages yet to come.

"Goodbye, little ship," said John Merton. "I wonder what eyes will see you next, how many thousand years from now."

At last he felt at peace, as the blunt torpedo of the launch nosed up beside him. He would never win the race to the moon; but his would be the first of all man's ships to set sail on the long journey to the stars.

Arthur C. Clarke is from Somerset in England, although he now makes his home in Sri Lanka on the other side of the world. He is well known for his television appearances commenting on the moon flights, as well as for the motion pictures *2001: A Space Odyssey* and *2010: Odyssey Two.* Yet his reputation rests first upon his excellent science fiction novels like *A Fall of Moondust* and *Childhood's End,* as well as classic short stories such as "The Billion Names of God" and "The Star."

When it first appeared, this story was entitled "Sunjammer." (I didn't know about the Poul Anderson story of the same title. Besides, I like "The Wind from the Sun" better now.) Many of the bright men and women working to develop solar sails have told me that their lifelong interest began when they first read this story back in the 1960s. Flatterers!

To Sail Beyond the Sun
(A Luminous Collage)

by Ray Bradbury
and Jonathan V. Post

We all are solar sails
in the tree of heaven climbing free
And yet in looking back I see
From topmost part of farthest tree
A land as bright, beloved, and blue
As any Yeats found to be true
home-planet Earth
As bright as all the summer air

And in the solar-system's body, where
I circumnavigate each cell in you
Your merest molecule is right and true
Your moons and planets passing fair

And so we earn what we shall dare
Tossed from the central sun
We with our own concentric fires
Blaze and burn.
Burn and blaze, Until we feel
Once at the hub of wakening
the vast starwheel

Of solar system's body
A Pegasus of cometary hair
tended by
comet grooms like Kepler and
Galileo Galilei

Whose short-sight probing light-years
saw the way for solar sails to go
To change tomorrow's clime, its meteor snows.
Our rocket selfhood grows
and, rocket-less, more elegantly knows

And claim from Heaven
The Garden we were shunted from,
For now, space-driven
We fit, fix, force and fuse,
Re-hub the system vast
On wings of sunlight, travel fast,
on vector axle, over vacuum's floor

Respoke starwheel
And at the spiraled core
Plant foot, full fire-shod
and stride the stride of God
whose name is spelled in stars,
and in whose name
We clothe ourselves in flame

Why do we, the solar sails,
fragile as a feather's frond,
silently seek to sail so far?
We walk the air from here to planet out beyond
Because we're more than fond of life and what we are.

We are the energy of Shakespeare's verse,
we are what mathematics wants to be—
The Life Force in the Universe
That longs to See!
That would Become
and give a voice to matter that was dumb.

We are, to the gates of gravity, the keys
We are the Abyss Light that comes from Pleiades
We are the melody of futures flying soon

And what the song, the tune?
To fashion fires and thus outrace the Moon
West is West, and East is East,
but we sail on perpendiculars
To grow man ten ways tall to feast
On Universe and stars

And why did Engineering bend
the force of light to give us play?
To landfall Time, give man Forever's Day
And free us from well-bottom's cave
Unlock the doors of light-year grave
Fling wide the portal;
Give man the gift of stars

And so, as solar sail, while children sleep
in atmospheric blanket curled
I bury all the stars in Cosmic Deep
So, listen, world . . .

Is this the setting of the sun of Earth?
No, this is what the future brings:
A million-dozen multitudes of summer things!

O child, they said, avert your eyes.
What does a solar sailor feel?
Avert my eyes? I said, what, from wild skies
Where stars appear and wheel.

And so a sail takes flight
beyond the airy skirts of old Earth-mother
And fills my heart and make me feel as if I might
This night and then another and another
Live forever and not die.

This is life itself, to onward fly
A boy alone with Universe
who knows that he must go into the dark.

God minds me to be so. He put the bright sparks
  in my blood
and taught me to run,
and run again after I fall

Small sparks, large sun—
All one, it is the same.
Large flame or small
as long as my heart is young
the flavor of the night lies on my tongue . . .

The Universe is thronged with fire and light,
And we but smaller suns which, skinned, trapped and
  kept
where we have dreamed, and laughed, and wept
Enshrined in blood and precious bones,
with heartbeat's rhythms, passion's tones
Hold back the night

Somewhere a band is playing
Where the moon never sets in the sky
And the sun sets never
And Time . . . goes on forever
And hearts then continue to beat
to the pulse of the future coming
To the sound of the old moon-drum drumming
And the glide of Eternity's feet

Infinity my destination,
until my course is run,
Light hierarchies of Time and, one by one,
With mighty Ra, fall in that final sun

Billions of years ago, Big Bang began the flight
of galaxy from galaxy that was to be
A thousand tigers' eyes fireworked the night
Quadrillions of years hence,
the suns burnt out, we solar sails still drift

Gone blind from stars and dark of moon
thinned by evaporation from our metal flesh
And saw in X-ray warp and mesh
A sigh of polar-region breath

At first there was but sea and tides by night
fingerboard space with silver starlight frets
and souls' pure jets.
At first, we dandelion sails were still as death
At first there was no captain to the ship
But: God obtruded, rose and blew his breath
and we went spinning outward from His lip
Sailed . . . through wild dreams
In free-fall fell
God, Nature, Space, all Time, now stand aside we said
Illumine Heaven and relight the coals of Hell
Past Uranus we sailed, that tilted planet saw
And knocked the world half off its axis into awe

What size is Space? A thimble!
No! outside of a sun!
pocked by sun-spots in which gods
could bathe themselves in ion streams
and sleep in plasma magnet dreams . . .
What is this dream of Cosmos
Born from a senseless yearning
Of molecules for form,
Birthed from a mindless burning
Of solar fire-storm—
The Universe, in Needing,
Made flesh of empty space,
And with a mighty seeding
Made pygmy human race . . .

Which now on fires striding
the solar sails to give
on solar lightbeams riding
Wakes up the stars to live

Then off they glide on rafters
of centripetal force
with sails as light as laughters
Of stars like skating ponds.
The ice between the stars
is gravity's weak bonds
Twin mirror selves of seeing,
each soul to soul responds.
We dance, and spin, and play
We live Forever's Day
And spawn the Cosmic rivers,
in billions celebrate
with out-from-sunward spinning
No Ending or beginning
Behold! The Mystery stirring . . .

Here in space our dreams are truly ours
Here they lie—in countries where the spacemen
Flow in fire and much desire the Moon
And reach for Mars
on thin metallic wing
And teach the firey atoms how to sing
Mind's quest makes footfall here
leaving cradle Earth behind
To transfer across Space to lift Mankind
beyond the reach of ancient fear
The thought that birthed itself to Space
is the thought that knows it knows it knows
Across the solar system's face
Where now Man goes
Grand Things to Come? Yes! Things to Come!
Starlings, eagles, falcons, larks
we sing from throats no longer dumb
and spread our wings, and soar in arcs
Of wheeling orbs and sparks

From graveyard dirt he shapes a striding man
To jig the stars and go where none else can.

What pulls him there in arrow flight of ships?
A birth of suns that burn from Shakespeare's flaming
    lips
From Stratford's fortress mind we build and go
And strutwork catwalk stars across abyss
The Universe itself is our stage
and our script reads something close to this:
Stand here, grow tall, rehearse
and then surpass the plan.
Be God-grown-Man.
Act out the Universe!
Across the waters of galactic Babylon
We sail, we solar sails, and sing of Zion.
Our golden song goes on and on
The sun whose light we sail upon:
A blazing summer dandelion.

What can I say?
    We can follow this dream, and so many others
like it, if we only lift our heads and go!

The Canvas of the Night

by
K. Eric Drexler

As the sun sinks from sight one summer evening, a spark appears in the fading light, rising and moving east. Faint at first, it climbs toward the zenith, shrinks to a line, then opens to a hexagon of brilliance slowly turning, sweeping across the sky to redden and vanish in the shadows of the horizon. The next night, it comes again.

As night follows night, the hexagon shrinks to a dot, then to a point drifting slowly across the starry vault circling higher and higher, now above both Earth and its cone of shadow. At last it vanishes, no longer circling, a fading glint among the constellations.

Five centuries after Columbus, the hope of treasure calls once more and a ship sets sail for distant shores. And again, the ship has sails.

Why, one may ask, should a spaceship use sails? On the seas of Earth, engines replaced sails generations ago, and engines of awesome power launch our spacecraft today. Sails will work in space: Einstein showed that energy has mass, and light exerts force when it bounces off a mirror. The pressure of sunlight, however, is terribly weak; using sails to replace rockets in space may seem a step backward.

In fact, the two could prove natural partners, each enabling the other to achieve its potential. To understand this, however, we need to skim a little history.

Rockets are as old as Chinese fireworks. They are compact, powerful, and useful. Unlike sails, they can punch through air and fight strong gravity. Even in the 1930s a

41

few visionaries knew that rockets could lift people to the moon. Rockets were needed for the first big step in space travel, the step off our planet.

Project Apollo with its first "Moonwalk" was a triumph so great that it seemed to be what "the space program" was all about, yet the triumph was not followed up. The voyage of Columbus opened a frontier by sailing to new lands in a reusable ship. Apollo virtually closed a frontier by surveying a wasteland in a machine built at great expense and then thrown away.

Beyond the moon, robots with cameras, launched to the planets, replaced the dream of a jungle-clad Venus with the reality of a vast oven of high-pressure poison; they erased the network of lines drawn by wishful earthbound astronomers on the deserts of Mars, and with them went both canals and Martians.

Many scientists believe Mars does possess water, buried in its dusty permafrost. Some consider it the next logical step for manned exploration, though not at once for conquest or settlement. Rather, we may find ourselves going there for reasons having to do with earthly concerns . . . to seal a place between East and West, for instance, or to lift our spirits with a common goal.

But it will be next to impossible to go to Mars the way we went to the moon, using wasteful, throwaway rockets. At least not with rockets alone. The crew themselves may travel that way, but the hundreds of tons of supplies they will need, for a mission lasting two years or more, may be shipped by cheaper means, or the trip may not be made at all. Explorers and scientists will not leave footprints in the red soil until, first, robot freighters have hauled there the means of sustaining life.

Anyway, to practical men and women, a Mars expedition would be at best a start. Symbolic gestures are less important than winning riches from space.

Even as the old space program was shriveling and planetary launches had ground to a halt, new opportunities were coming into sight. Today, we have a shuttle and, better, the beginnings of a private launch industry, and we know more about space and our own abilities. There is talk of building important industries in space, where sunlight and vacuum are free and weightlessness offers novel opportunities. Where attention once focused on planets because they were big and bright and somewhat like Earth, people now realize that an asteroid or two could fill a world's factories and launch a whole new economic frontier.

Between these two poles lies a common problem. The romance of a Mars mission and the gritty practicality of space industry share one attribute, a need for inexpensive propulsion to supplement flashy, inefficient rockets, a need for systems able to haul great cargos, slowly but surely, across vast reaches of space. Although rockets have been used for centuries, light pressure has been known for scarcely a century.

Carl Wiley, in his 1951 factual article on solar sailing, "Clipper Ships of Space," in the May 1951 issue of *Astounding Science Fiction,* looked to a day when sails would be built in space itself. However, the technical literature since Sputnik has followed an understandable direction. Since the only way to get into space is in the nose of a rocket, most sail designers aimed to stuff a sail into a small, rugged package, and to have it spring unaided to full size in space.

Since the force of sunlight on a mirror the size of a football field amounts to the weight of a small marble, a sail must be both big and light to give a useful cargo a reasonable acceleration. To survive packaging, launch, and deployment, the reflector for such a sail must be flexible and tough. Designers settled on aluminized plastic as the best choice. Workable designs emerged. Their projected performance improved with time. They were no use, however, in a crash program to reach the moon, and available rockets could always launch the next robot toward the next planet. Interest waxed and waned, but no sails were built.

JPL studies in the mid 1970s brought positive indications that the sail could not only satisfy many of the energy requirements for inner solar system exploration, but that a sail 640,000 square meters (a square 800 meters or one-half mile, on a side) could take a 1,500-kilogram scientific payload to a rendezvous with the comet named for Edmund Halley. The propellant to add that much speed to a conventional rocket would be over ten billion tons per ton of payload. Yet a single solar sail launched aboard a shuttle and weighing about five tons could develop a small but steady acceleration to accomplish the rendezvous in less than four years.

Meanwhile, others interested in the Halley mission designed a competing system using electrically powered rockets. The two systems (both to be launched by conventional boosters) had comparable performance, but the National Aeronautics and Space Administration finally had to scrap the entire mission for lack of funds.

This time, however, interest did not fade—it shifted. After years of trying to get NASA and Congress to support a program to develop a sail, designers and their supporters have decided to go private and build one themselves.

The Solar Sail Project of the nonprofit World Space Foundation has begun construction of a kitelike plastic-film sail. Project members, mostly space engineers donating their free time, have built spars and sail material on special machines and have tested deployment procedures. Their first prototype, unveiled in a demonstration in 1981, was about 14 meters on a side, the second is planned at 28 meters.

In addition to the World Space Foundation, other groups have expressed interest in building and launching prototype sails. This may really take off if plans for a Columbus Quincenery Regatta are realized (see the chapter on ''Rebel Technology'').

Another approach, which I have proposed, is to build a kind of solar sail, called a lightsail, directly in space. If you imagine a network of carbon-fiber strings, a spinning spiderweb kilometers across with gaps the size of football fields between the strands, you will be well on your way to imagining the structure of a lightsail.

Imagine the gaps bridged by reflecting panels built of aluminum foil thinner than a soap bubble, tied close together to make a vast, rippled mosaic of mirror. Now picture a load of cargo hanging from the web like a dangling parachutist, while centrifugal force holds the spinning, web-slung mirror taut and flat in the void.

Lightsails are what solar sails seem likely to become when we build them in space. They differ considerably from the deployable, plastic-film sails designed for launch by rocket from the ground. Not needing the toughness to survive folding, launch and deployment, lightsail reflectors need no plastic backing tens of thousands of atoms thick: they can be unbacked aluminum films just a few hundred atoms thick. Such thin foil cannot be made by smashing a bar of aluminum between rollers, as kitchen foil is made. Instead, thin films are made by piling up atoms on a smooth surface.

A simple process starting with a little detergent . . .

To make a thin metal film, first take a glass microscope slide and smear it with detergent. Let it dry, then wipe off all that is visible, leaving behind an invisible film. Then place the slide in a vacuum chamber and pump out the air. Next, run current through a tantalum strip in the chamber, until it glows white, to vaporize a bead of aluminum from its surface. This turns the slide and the vacuum-chamber window into instant mirrors. Finally, remove the slide and dip it slowly in water, which will creep under the metal film, following the detergent, floating the film off to turn a rectangular area of water into a smooth, rippling reflector.

Such films have less mass than a slice of air a third of a millimeter thick. A piece of film rubbed between fingers coats them with sparkling dust.

Lightsails have little mass because they use unbacked reflectors and a structure of tension members. Tension members are lighter and slimmer that compression members of similar strength: compare a tower twenty stories high with a rope twenty stories long, if each supports a ton. This combination of reflectors and structure makes lightsails twenty to eighty times lighter than deployable plastic-film sails. This low mass increases the sail's top acceleration by the same factor. One shuttle payload could supply materials enough to build a hundred square kilometers of reflector and structure, divided among a few dozen sails.

Concerns such as heating and micrometeroid damage have been examined and pose no threat to a properly designed sail. The manufacturing facility is small and simple compared to existing factories on Earth. If we plan to use space, we must learn to build in space; building lightsails may be a good way to start because lightsails can help open up the solar system.

Compare a lightsail with an ordinary rocket, operating in deep space. A 1-ton rocket could push a cargo pod weighing more than a ton to a speed of one kilometer per second in a few minutes. A 1-ton sail (more than a mile wide) would take all day to reach the same speed with the same cargo. But the next day the rocket would coast, drained of fuel, while the sail would add another kilometer per second to its speed. Accelerating just over one-thousandth as fast as a falling brick, it would pass twenty times the speed of sound in less than a week.

Worse yet for the rockets, a 2-ton rocket cannot double the speed of the 1-ton rocket because the extra fuel would burden it. Indeed, every 3 kilometers per second added to the final speed of the cargo roughly doubles the mass of the required rocket, but adds just three days to the acceleration time using a sail.

Since solar system journeys, by rocket or sail, will generally take months to years, lightsails have a strong advantage for long voyages: not only is the sail reusable for decades, and never in need of refueling, but also on any given flight around the solar system it will generally be both lighter and faster than the competing rocket. Rockets eat sails at giving swift kicks, but in the long haul they run out of gas and then can only coast along.

Sails in space also have advantages over their relatives below. At sea, the winds shift, stop and storm unpredictably. In space, the "wind" is sunlight, and holds quite steady. At sea, winds can drive a ship only to a modest speed. In space, the "wind" blows at the speed of light and the "hull" has no drag; thus, speed can increase enormously. High velocities are essential, circling the sun along Earth's orbit would take more than a century at the speed of a jet liner.

At sea, mere sails are not enough; seagoing ships have keels so they can tack to go upwind. Lightsails have no keels and do not tack, yet they can manage to navigate in any direction. Light pressure can never pull a sail toward the sun, but the direction it pushes can be steered from side to side by tilting the sail, while gravity provides a steady pull inward. This steerable push and steady pull combine to move the sail in any direction chosen, from any orbit to any other, so long as it remains beyond reach of an atmosphere or the roasting of a close solar approach. At sea, ships have wind and water; in space, sails have light and gravity.

This type of lightsail (unlike some others you'll read about) spins like a gyroscope, and therefore it requires a steady twisting force to turn it to a new orientation. The sail can turn itself in two ways: it can shift the cargo off axis by reeling and unreeling the connecting lines, or it can tilt its reflecting panels to shift the distribution of light pressure. The first turns the sail swiftly, for maneuvers near planets; the second turns it slowly, for maneuvers in orbit around the sun. In solar orbit, the sail can spin in one orientation for weeks at a time without moving a motor. Any panel can jam in any position with little effect, since there are so many of them; thus sails should run for decades without repair.

* * *

Lightsails can change the way humanity uses space because they open new opportunities there. They can carry robots to the planets in record time or haul satellites from low to high orbits. They can do far more, however, because, for a given propulsion capability, they should cost far less to use than any rocket on the drawing boards.

Eventually, even the sophisticated techniques described above will be outstripped by our needs and our ambitions. But now we can see, on the horizon, ways to build even lighter, more powerful lightsails. Before we launch vast sails to the stars, for instance, we may learn a more subtle trick—arranging atoms one by one using "nanotechnology." Nature shows how atom-arranging can be done using molecular machines like those in cells. Novel molecular machines can convert raw materials into better sails.

Freeman Dyson points out that the best sails aren't films at all, but meshes fine enough to catch photons. Mesh sails would be lighter and faster. And because they would catch less air, they would have less drag, letting them dip lower into the fringes of planetary atmospheres. Adding thin spines to the back of a mesh sail would help it radiate heat, letting it tolerate brighter light, hence greater force, hence greater acceleration. This could help laser-driven sails on their way to the stars. The molecular machines of nanotechnology, building atom by atom, could build such sails by the mile. (They will build much, much more than that, but that is a different story).

Sailing the Solar System

Today, the solar system seems vast and inaccessible. But our sense of distance reflects, in part, our experience and the cost of going places with rockets. From this viewpoint, developing lightsails would be somewhat like moving everything in the inner solar system to a 2,000-kilometer orbit above Earth, just outside the fringe of the atmosphere.

Among the most important changes would be access to asteroids. The planets themselves might remain deadly deserts, their gravity blocking access by lightsails and handicapping industry. Planetary atmospheres block solar energy, spread dust, corrode metals, warm refrigerators, cool ovens and blow things down. Even the airless moon rotates, blocking sunlight half the time, and has gravity enough to ground a lightsail beyond hope of escape.

The asteroids, however, are different. They are tiny by planetary standards, and their orbits crisscross the solar system. Some cross the orbit of Earth, and some have hit it. Since the asteroids are small, their gravity is easy to overcome or ignore. They hold no atmosphere to interfere with industry (or to be polluted by it), and the steady sunlight of free space lies near at hand to power equipment and heat furnaces. There, too, lightsails can stop to retrieve precious cargos, for many asteroids hold more than mere rock.

While this notion is controversial at present, many scientists believe asteroids contain abundant supplies of metals of kinds made scarce here on Earth ages ago, elements that sank in the formation of Earth's metal core. Meteoritic steel, for example, is a strong, tough alloy containing nickel, cobalt, platinum-group metals, and gold. Raw materials from the asteroids can provide most of the needs of an industrial civilization in space.

Lightsails could bring robots and refining equipment to an asteroid and return treasure beyond the dreams of Cortez. Since it makes scarcely more sense to bring back a whole asteroid than to bring back the moon, the chunks should be small.

Most of this great wealth need never be returned to the Earth's surface at all. It can be kept in space and used in orbit, aiding us in the creation of industries out where they can do no harm to the environment and where solar power is free, twenty-four hours a day. With proper planning, this wealth can benefit all mankind.

Ironically, the first lightsail mining expeditions may ignore steel and platinum and be sent instead to other asteroids, those rich in volatiles such as water, the key to life support in space, and to making rocket fuel. Brought to Earth, water would be useless, of course. But kept in space, water would be precious. Water from asteroids could make living and working in space economical.

A lightsail program could build on itself. With asteroidal metal, the fabrication facility could build cheap freighter sails using little material hauled up from Earth. Such sails might cut the cost of space transportation so low that eventually asteroids could be mined for ordinary steel.

So far, we have been discussing projects that have already received serious study. Scientists argue over *when* such things might happen, but not whether they are possible. What next, though? In time, principles used for hauling a satellite could serve in a sail large enough to haul an "ocean liner" to Mars in less than a year. But that's only the beginning of the extravagant possibilities.

Eventually, we may be able to pack human-level intelligence into a chip the size of a postage stamp. If so, our first interstellar probes may be sent to neighboring stars by the thousands, tiny ambassadors blown out on miniature sails, like grains of pollen before the wind.

In time, lightsails could be used to drive real starships. A sail pushed by sunlight can leave the solar system in less than two years, its speed climbing past 100 kilometers per second before the sun fades astern. But there are ways to improve on this. As hinted by Isaac Asimov in his introduction, a large laser orbiting the sun could absorb solar energy and convert it into a narrow beam of light. Directed at a sail, such a megalaser could drive a ship far out into the interstellar darkness, pushing it toward the speed of light.

The only problem then is stopping when you get to your

destination. Freeman Dyson of the Institute for Advanced Study in Princeton proposes drag brakes using the interstellar plasma; Robert Forward at the Hughes Research Laboratory in California suggests using light from the laser bounced off the sail as a "brake" to decelerate a smaller mirror. (Many of these ideas will be covered later in the course of this book, especially in the essay by Forward and Davis.) One way or another the stars themselves lie within reach of sails.

The Prospect

Today, despite some recent moves toward peace, earthbound governments still growl at each other, threatening war over the limited resources of a single planet. Perhaps the greatest promise of space is the perspective it provides: that to fight over the resources of Earth is to fight over crumbs.

For a nation interested in prosperity and in peace, the challenge of space cannot be ignored. European, Soviet, and Japanese efforts in space have grown while the U.S. space effort has floundered, and even the leaders of these countries still act as if the Earth were the whole world. Perhaps, after five hundred years, it is time the Copernican revolution came to global politics. Perhaps, five hundred years after Columbus's ships opened a new frontier, it is time to spread our sails and to once again challenge the stars.

K. Eric Drexler is a researcher concerned with emerging technologies and their consequences for the future. This interest led him to study space technology and to design (and patent) structures and fabrication techniques for a class of high-performance, thin metal film solar sails. He later performed ground-breaking studies in the field of nanotechnology—based on molecular machines able to build objects to complex specifications. Now a Visiting Scholar at Stanford University, he discussed the future of both space technology and nanotechnology in his book *Engines of Creation*.

And now our modest, unassuming (and hard-working) young managing editor comes on stage with a story illustrating some intriguing possibilities for the practical use of solar sails.

Ice Pilot

by
David Brin

FROM: Jeminalte Smythe   June 12, 2092
North Intellectual Commune
Semi-Anarchy of Vesta
Middle Belt

TO: Akiro Hsien-Fu
Sovereign Federation of
   Asiatic Historians
Offshore Shanghai
Coastal China Post Zone

Dear Akiro,

Thanks so much for that bit-burst of old records you transmitted up to me last month. Six gigabytes of old U.S. Congress records. (Kwak, but they could *talk* back then, even more than now!) It was an intimidating morass. Even with the help of an expensive software librarian-persona, it took some time to track down what I was looking for.

Found it at last, though. Secret, closed-door committee testimony that was declassified decades ago, but by then, who cared anymore, you know?

You asked what it was I was looking for. Well, scan this excerpt for yourself.

TESTIMONY of QUENTIN R. LEWIS
BEFORE THE SELECT COMMITTEE ON SPACE
RESOURCES
UNITED STATES SENATE
AUGUST 25, 2013

SENATOR MURCHISON: Please state your name and oc-
cupation.

QL: My name is Quentin Lewis, Senator. And at present
      I occupy a cell in the federal holding facility in Ros-
      slyn, Virginia.

SM: You know what I mean, Mr. Lewis. Get on with it,
      please.

QL: If you're asking what I did before your marshals
      plunked me into solitary, I was director of cislunar
      space traffic for the Moonmine Operation: United
      States Extension.

SM: Order! Stop that laughter in the galleries! Unlike
      some of my colleagues, Mr. Lewis, I am not amused
      by that unofficial acronym. This is very serious
      business. It's alleged that you were responsible for
      the untimely loss of a cargo worth on the order of
      one hundred million dollars to the taxpayers of this
      country. Sabotage and treason are not charges to be
      taken lightly.

QL: I am aware of the seriousness of these proceedings,
      Senator. And I willingly take responsibility for my
      role in the affair. I just find your choice of words
      misleading, if not to say amusing.

SENATOR CESARONE: Well, then, Mr. Lewis, how would
      you characterize your actions on the day in question?
      As a "timely and effective rescue operation"?

QL: That does sum it up pretty well. Thank you, Senator.

SC: An interesting point of view. Do you live in the same universe as the rest of us? Let me see if I can refresh your memory. [Reads from a printout.] At 04:20 hours UMT, on the fifth of May, year 2012, you were awakened by your assistant, Ms. Arjanian, with the news that the *Gaucho* tether-retrieval system had been sabotaged.

QL: To be precise, she told me somebody'd planted a bomb on the *Gaucho*. Six-hundred kilometers of bolo-tether were shredded, throwing slivers all over cislunar space. The *Gaucho* was completely destroyed, and with it our elevator off the moon.

SC: You leave out the cargo the *Gaucho* had only just snagged from the lunar surface when it exploded—twelve hundred tons of freshly mined and refined lunar oxygen, the first full-sized shipment from our lunar factory.

QL: Well, while we're quibbling, what about the other end of the bolo, Senator? While the oxy was going up, our supplies were coming down! After *Gaucho* blew, we had no ice cream for six months! Had to live off algae paste, plankton-pond scum, and wishful thinking.

SM: Order! . . . Mr. Lewis, we are all aware of how you and your colleagues suffered before a new rotating elevator could be established to replace the *Gaucho* system. Making light of that struggle for survival does you credit. But although you starved with the rest, yours is a special case.

QL: Right. Sacrificial lamb. Scapegoat. Yum. Thanks for the honor.

SC: Now sir. Nobody's holding you responsible for the loss of the *Gaucho* or its cargo. It's what you did *afterward* that we're concerned about here. Seven days later, before full-scale investigations had even begun, you used the traffic-control apparatus at your base to send commands to the approaching space-craft *Eclipse*, did you not?

QL: That *was* my job, Senator. Giving trajectory instructions to approaching spacecraft is what a traffic coordinator is for.

SC: Indeed. And you ordered the computer pilot of the robot freighter *Eclipse* to change course.

QL: I did, Senator. *Eclipse* was entering cislunar space fast, using her solar sail to decelerate toward a matched orbit with the moon. Her cargo was one hundred and fifty tons of dirty ice, scraped off asteroid 1986 DB. But when I realized *Gaucho* would no longer be available to snag the stuff . . .

Hello, Akiro? It's me again. Maybe I'd better explain here, since at this point Lewis gets awfully technical. You see, *Eclipse* was something very new back then, a robot-controlled solar sail freighter. The first of its kind. It was hauling the first load of ice ever harvested from an aster-oid.

Today, of course, we take space ice for granted. We get it from Saturn, the moons of Jupiter. But try to put yourself in their shoes, back then.

They'd found no ice on the moon, none even at the lunar poles. Oh, the lunar soils had plenty of oxygen, bound up with silicon and aluminum and iron. Twentieth-century studies had shown that it would be possible to set up mines and factories on the moon, to extract and separate all those elements for industrial purposes. The oxygen, in particular, would be terribly important as propellant for rockets in cislunar space. In fact, a lunar oxidizer would, they thought, bring space resources *just* past the point of break-even—where the whole endeavor to live and work profitably in space would start to make sense.

Anyway, it was convincing enough to get people to invest in a prototype factory, manned by sixteen astronauts, to see if they could harvest oxygen and other elements economically. They had a break when it proved possible to construct a whirling bola-type space elevator in orbit. Skimming above the lunar mountains, the bolo tip just missed grazing the surface, enabling it to snag cargos from the base and throw them into high transfer orbit. At the same time, it would bring fresh base supplies down to an almost gentle touchdown.

(Amazing, no? Ingenious people, our grandparents. Oh, but if only they could imagine what we've got today!)

Alas, though, it still wasn't paying. There were delays, problems to solve, glitches to iron out. Took a while to get the oxygen plants running. Back then people were impatient, for some reason. Wanted quick profits. (Maybe it was because their lives were so short.)

Anyway, it was beginning to look as if the whole project would just miss break-even. Already there were powerful voices at work to get the entire space resources bid canceled. And if that happened, there would go all chance of building up large-scale space industry, factories, colonies . . . (Can you imagine? I might have been born on Earth! Brrrr!)

Things would have been a lot different, of course, if anyone had ever found ice on the moon. Water is just so damned *useful*. (You Earthers tend to forget that, actually swimming in it as you do.) Besides life support and farming, it's particularly useful in providing hydrogen *fuel*.

So the economics of living and working in space would change forever if there was only a source of water that didn't have to be hauled all the way out of Earth's steep, deep pit of a gravity well.

All right. No ice on the moon. Where's the nearest al-

ternate source? Well, it's obvious to you and me now, but
back then lots of people laughed.

The asteroids, of course. The carbonaceous types. The
dead comets and dark sludgeballs, some of them as easy
to get to, in energy terms, as the moon.

Anyway, back around the turn of the century, a few dar-
ing science types finally persuaded Congress to fund *one*
mission. Send out an automatic scraper to a likely
'roid. . . .

But let's get back to Lewis's testimony and he'll tell it
in his own words.

QL: . . . entirely different kind of mining operation. The
      little robot didn't have to fight gravity at that tiny
      asteroid, or even *refine* the ice at all. All it had to
      do was scrape all that lovely dirty snow into a bag,
      then spread that beautiful solar sail and carry the
      goods home to us. We'd do all the refining at our
      plant on the moon. That water would make our jobs
      easier in a thousand ways that—

SM: Yes, yes, Mr. Lewis, we are aware of how enthu-
      siastic many of you were about that part of the pro-
      gram, and how you'll inevitably feel when we cancel
      the space industry—

SC: That's *not* been decided, yet!

SM: My apologies, Senator. But it's a foregone conclu-
      sion, now that Mr. Lewis has taken all that won-
      derful ice he so lusted after and simply *dumped* it!
      Jettisoned it, like so much garbage! Why did you
      do it, Mr. Lewis? Why did you do such a stupid
      thing?

QL: Well, Senator . . . it seemed like a good idea at the
      time.

SM: Order! If the spectators continue with these outbursts I'll have the room cleared. That is enough levity, Mr. Lewis.

SC: Um, in all fairness to the witness, I think it should be noted that the question was tendentious. Mr. Lewis, I assume you dumped *Eclipse*'s cargo because of the *Gaucho* disaster?

QL: Thank you, Senator. That's right. We'd intended for *Eclipse* to adjust her solar, tacking on sunlight, to slowly spiral her cargo onto just the right trajectory. It would have been snagged by *Gaucho*'s bolo hook and gently lowered to Copernicus Base. Meanwhile, relieved of her burden, *Eclipse* herself would fly on, sailing back out toward another asteroid and another load.

SM: That second mission had not been authorized, yet.

QL: That's right, Senator. But it was essential. Just 150 tons of water wouldn't pay for the investment already made. But *Eclipse* could go back again and again, for more and more ice. And that ice would make all the difference between getting rich colonizing the solar system and struggling just to break even, or even retreating, as some cowards would have us do—

SM: I'd watch it, if I were you, Mr. Lewis. You're bordering on contempt. Already the Attorney General has contemplated filing charges of attempted murder—

QL: [Laughter] For what? Throwing snowballs?

SM: Order! That part of it is very serious, Mr. Lewis. Not only did you dump *Eclipse*'s cargo, but you sent

it on a trajectory that just missed a potentially catastrophic collision with Copernicus Base! You and
all your comrades might have died! Was that your
motivation? When you saw the *Gaucho* destroyed,
and with it all your hopes, did you try to end it all
in one grand murder-suicide that failed?

QL: Oh, I assure you, Senator, I'm a better shot than
that. If I had wanted to, I could have smacked Copernicus head-on. I hit were I aimed, all right.
Caused a moonquake, too. We felt it a hundred kilometers away.

SC: But—

QL: Senators, I had two reasons for what I did. First, I
had to dump the cargo. It was that or lose *Eclipse*.

SC: Explain, please.

QL: Surely. You see, at the time the solar sail freighter
was coming in, cislunar space was still filled with
debris from the *Gaucho* explosion. Shreds of tether
material were flying all over the place, as well as
chunks of our freeze-dried coffee and duck paté.
[Laughter] Anyway, while we we busy feeling sorry
for ourselves, it suddenly occurred to me just how
incredibly delicate a solar sail is.

SC: What . . . Oh, I see.

QL: I'll bet you do, Senator. *Eclipse* is a terrifically efficient machine, you see. Solar sails may be too slow
to be useful carrying human beings, but they're by
far the best way to send bulk cargo, the sort of cargo
where you don't care so much when it arrives, just
so long as it *gets* there. Handle them right, with
good programming and a smart robot pilot, and they

simply can't be beat. But there's only one problem with them. It's generally not a good idea to send a sun clipper tacking straight into a cloud of shrapnel! Does bad things to the sails, if you know what I mean.

SC: So your intention was to divert *Eclipse* before she entered an unstoppable collision course with the debris?

QL: That's right. After dumping the cargo, she was much more maneuverable. I tilted her sails and filled them with sunlight to lift her out of harm's way on a new course, toward a new asteroid site, a very promising one—

SM: That was not authorized! Besides, Mr. Lewis, weren't your priorities a little mixed up, there? Moonbase needed *Eclipse*'s first cargo—the first one—to prove the concept and rescue it from bankruptcy this year. If that had worked, we might have been willing to fund more solar sail freighters.

QL: Might. Maybe. After how long a delay? *Eclipse* was there, man. She was working! Odds were she'd be the only solar sail freighter available for a long, long time. We had to save her!

SM: Fine. So you dumped her first cargo and sent her out for a second. And that second won't arrive, even if all goes well, for two more years! Did it ever occur to you that there now probably won't *be* a moon factory to receive that new load, when *Eclipse* finally returns? It was the first cargo that mattered, Mr. Lewis. The *first*. You dumped that cargo—

QL: Ah. Let me see, now. I think I see the problem here. It's one of terminology. You see, Senator . . .

Hi, Akiro. Me again. Have you figured it out yet?

So much for the "inexorable forces of history" argument. Important, crucial decisions *are* sometimes made by great men and women. And figure this: hardly anybody even knows the name Lewis anymore. Everyone gives Cesarone the credit for fighting the Space Freighters Bill through, back in 2014. There are factories and streets and even a city named after him, out on Ceres, but hardly a back-asteroid lane named for Lewis.

Who can figure history?

QL: . . . any faster than that and it will hit with the force of a typical meteorite, resulting in flash vaporization, kicking most of the material back upward in a fine spray. Of course, anything striking the moon at speeds like those will be unrecognizable in microseconds.

SC: Ah . . . wait a minute. That's if the material hits at a speed greater than the speed of sound?

QL: The speed that sound travels in rock, Senator. A meteoroid striking faster than that . . . well, there's no place for the kinetic energy to go except into a big explosion. Certainly anything volatile, like water, is gone instantly.

SC: But if it lands *slower* . . . ?

QL: Very good, Senator, you used the word *land*.

SM: I don't see what difference it makes—

SC: All the difference in the world, George! Don't you see? We're used to the idea that anything falling from space has to hit with a bang. But that's because most meteoroids come in with—whatsit, hypergolic—

QL: *Hyperbolic* velocity, yes, that's if something arrives from deep space. But this stuff had already entered orbit! And the moon has a much shallower gravity well than Earth.

SC: How fast was the ice traveling when it hit the surface, Mr. Lewis?

QL: Oh, we were able to bring *Eclipse* close enough so its cargo landed at about eighty meters per second, give or take.

SC: That slowly?

SM: What's going on here? Will you explain what you're talking about?

SC: Let's see, that's about three hundred kilometers per hour . . . less than the speed of sou . . . Say. The ice wouldn't necessarily flash-vaporize, would it! There'd be some spraying, of course, and mixing with lunar soils, but—

QL: But it would stay pretty compact. That's right, sir. In effect, we've created a small *ore deposit*, just one hundred or so klicks from—

SC: [Laughing] So this is why you delayed giving us your testimony for so long, Lewis! All right, I see you clutching a space cablegram in your fist. Out with it. What have your buddies on the moon found?

QL: Well, sir, it took a while after the *Gaucho* disaster to get things back together, then a survey and assay party had to be sent out. Vehicles had to be modified. My people are actually rather upset with me for targetting the ore site so far away. Seems they resent my margin of safety . . . would rather I'd taken a chance of hitting them on the heads!

SC: Out with it, man!

QL: Well, along with a request for supplies to be sent up on the next shuttle, this cable contains confirmation of the complete purification of seventeen tons of pure-grade water—

SM: Seventeen tons!

QL: Yeah. Collins estimates they can probably refine another twenty or so before the lode runs out. I'm a bit disappointed, but the ice did come in pretty fast. A lot got turned into steam and drifted away. We'll do better next time.

SM: Order! Order! The spectators will remember that this is a closed session! Nothing about any of this will leave this room except as the committee decides. And . . . and . . . criminy, did you say seventeen *tons* of water?

QL: Yes, Senator. And now, about this new request for supplies. There's one item here . . . we'd appreciate it if someone would send up six pounds or so of elemental chlorine, which, I'm sure you are aware, is a very scarce element on the moon.

SC: [Laughter] No! You aren't going to say it's for your—

QL: And why not, Senator? While we're waiting to use it for fuel and farms and factories, to make everybody rich, while it's just sitting around, I see no reason why we shouldn't be allowed, in the meantime, to have a swimming pool.

Well, there you have it, Akiro. Our world of today, our wealthy community of the solar system—all resting on one moment's ingenuity. And you know something? They only stopped using the "dive-bomber" method to deliver ice ores to the moon just five years ago! By then, of course, it was so mundane and ordinary that nobody noticed. Finally had to quit because the Lunar Sierra Club objected to the way rainbows were starting to ruin the "stark vacuum beauty" of the moon!

Of course, by then the method was obsolete. The factories had moved to deeper space, along with a large chunk of humanity. But for decades it allowed the robot sail freighters to operate at maximum efficiency, allowing us to leverage a toehold into a living economy in space.

All this has made me think about *Eclipse*. I went to see her, last month, in the Museum of Transport. Crowds of sightseers hurried past, eager to look at *Orion* and *Gorshkov* and all the other famous manned exploration vessels. Who cares, after all, about just another little robot freighter, especially now that its once pretty sails are spalled and pitted and furled away for good?

We've grown used to the sight of them, the fleets of bright-winged freighters, cruising the solar system on winds of sunlight, patiently hauling the bulk cargoes while we humans go flitting about in our high-speed rockets. Frankly, I'd never even heard of *Eclipse,* the first one, until I began this research. But I was amazed when I looked up, yesterday, how many of her descendants are out there.

Four million, Akiro. Four million little spidery robot sunjammers, each with its own woven sail of gossamer, each patiently hauling ice from Saturn, iron from the inner belt, platinum from the Trojans. Making us all so rich we can turn your beloved Earth into a park . . . as if anyone with any sense would *want* to go trudging about in all that gravity.

Okay, I take that back.

But isn't it amazing? I'm not talking just about Quentin

Lewis, the first ice pilot, or even all the wonders we take for granted today. It goes beyond that, Akiro.

Right now I'm looking out my window and I can see another freighter passing by. Her sail is so immense she looks near enough to touch. And yet, she must be several thousand kilometers away, headed for Neptune, if I judge the trajectory right. Her cargo is probably terribly boring; still, she sparkles like a bright star.

Do you know they used to think of solar sails as *romantic*, Akiro? The idea of them inspired *poetry*, for heaven's sake! Do you think Lewis imagined we'd someday take them so for granted? Or think of them so little? As little as one today appreciates something as lovely but mundane as a diamond?

Or so beautifully ordinary as ice.

David Brin once swore he would never become a "professional" author, but that resolution became harder to keep after his second novel, *Startide Rising*, won the prestigious Hugo, Nebula and *Locus* awards for best novel of 1983. Another novel, *The Postman*, received the John W. Campbell Award and is scheduled to be made into a film from Warner Brothers. With *The Uplift War*, a 1987 best-seller and Hugo winner, what more is there to say?

David's latest novel, entitled *Earth*, deals with the danger and hope facing this island oasis world of ours over the decades ahead. It was delayed for a while, because he donated so much time to helping organize *Project Solar Sail*.

A Solar Privateer

by
Jonathan Eberhart

No racehorse ever champed the bit like a solar privateer.
To make flank speed on the sunlight's push is like
to take a year.
But when you're out with the stars set right, 'tis a
sight to make you cry.
No blast nor flames to rattle your brains—a seagull
in the sky.

On a *big* freight line you can make out fine, break-
ing orbit furled up tight.
With a hot box booster on your tail you can make
escape alright.
But the privateer knows the Deadman's Year on a
drift to vee subee,
With naught to do but sleep and stew till a sunbeam
sets you free.

It's when he's out on the dark and deep can the
solar sailor smile.
No cold LOX tanks or reactor banks—just Mylar
by the mile.
No stormy blast to rattle the mast—a sober wind
and true.
Just haul and tack and ball the jack like the water
lubbers do.

It's a long road out and a long road back, just drifting on the sun.

Your lover's hair will all grow long, a-pining for your fun,

Till looking upward from the ground, she'll know you've ceased to roam;

A golden spark in the endless dark—the light has brought you home.

Sunjammer

by
Poul Anderson

"Ol' Jonah was a transporteer, he was, he was.
Ol' Jonah was a transporteer, he was, he was.
   A storm at sea was getting mean,
   So he invented the submarine.
   Bravo, bravo, hurrah, for the transporteers!"

Lazing along a cometary orbit, a million-odd miles from
Earth, herdship *Merlin* resembled nothing so much as a
small bright spider which had decided to catch an elephant
and had spun its web accordingly. The comparison was
not too farfetched. Sometimes a crew on the Beltline found
they had gotten hold of a very large beast indeed.

Stars crowded the blackness in the control-cabin view-
ports, unwinking wintry points of brilliance; the Milky
Way cataracted around the sky, the Andromeda galaxy
shimmered mysteriously across a million and a half light-
years. The sunward port had automatically closed off, refusing so gross an overload. But Earth was visible in the
adjacent frame, a cabochon of clear and lovely blue, with
Luna a tarnished pearl beyond.

Sam Storrs, who was on watch, didn't sit daydreaming
over the scene as Edward West would probably have done.
He admitted there were few better sights in the system,
but he'd seen it before, and anyway that wasn't his planet
yonder. He was a third-generation asterite, a gaunt, crease-
cheeked, prematurely balding man who remembered too
well the brother he had lost in the Revolution.

Since there was no work for him to do at the moment,

69

he was trying to read Levinsohn's *Principles of Modern Political Economy.* It took concentration, and the whanging of a guitar from the saloon didn't help. He scowled as Andy Golescu's voice butchered the melody.

> *"King Solomon was a transporteer, he was, he was.*
> *King Solomon was a transporteer, he was, he was.*
>   *He shipped his wood on a boat for hire,*
>   *'Cuz a wheel's no good without a Tyre.*
>   *Bravo, bravo, hurrah for the transporteers!"*

"Ye gods," Storrs muttered, "how sophomoric is an adult allowed to get?"

He reached for the intercom switch, with the idea of asking Golescu to stop. But no, better not. It'd be a long time yet before their orbit brought them back to Pallas. Crew solidarity was as important to survival as the nuclear generator.

Andy's okay, Storrs argued to himself. *He just happens to be from Ceres. What do you expect of anyone growing up in that kind of hedonistic boom-town atmosphere? It was different for me, out on the Trojans. There puritanism still has survival value.*

No doubt the company psychomeds had known what they were doing when the picked Storrs, West, and Golescu to operate *Merlin.* You needed a balance of personality types. Still Storrs wondered about asking for a transfer when they returned to base.

> *"Ulysses was a transporteer, he was, he was . . ."*

The long-range radio receiver flashed. Storrs jerked. What the hell? That was no distress signal from a sunjammer, but a wide-beam call on the common band. He sucked in a breath and snapped the Accept switch.

> *". . . He stopped at Calypso's isle for beers,*
> *And didn't proceed for ten more years . . ."*

The loudspeaker seethed with cosmic static. "International Space Control calling Beltline Transportation main-

tenance ship eleven, computed to be in Sector Charlie
Adam. Come in, number eleven . . . International Space
Control—''

''Here we are.'' Storrs recollected his dignity. No
Earthling was going to say that a citizen of the Asteroid
Republic didn't know the rituals. ''Maintenance ship
eleven, *Merlin* out of Pallas, Engineer-Captain Storrs on
duty, acknowledging call from International Space Control. My precise position and orbit are . . .'' He read figures off the navigator screen. Storrs's skin began to prickle.
The messages that drew a herdship off her path were normally automatic: beeps from a sailship registering trouble.
Earth SCC seldom got involved directly.

The ship's transceiver web fixed on the incoming beam
and the maser swung about, causing *Merlin* to counterro-
tate a trifle.

> *''Columbus was a transporteer, he was, he was.*
> *Columbus was a transporteer, he was, he was.*
> *They put the royal crown in pawn*
> *To shut him up and move him on.*
> *Bravo . . .''*

Golescu must have noticed the motion. His singing cut
off abruptly. Storrs flipped the intercom open. ''Got a call
from Earth,'' he said concisely, to fill the others in.

His signal took half a dozen seconds to reach Earth.
The operator stopped chanting, heard Storrs out, and then
replied.

''Hello, maintenance ship eleven. Stand by please.
Switching you over to main office, groundside.'' A low
whistle drifted from the intercom. Golescu, posted at the
engine, had heard.

West entered, puffing from the climb up the companion-
way. He was a large man, his hair grizzled, face and stomach sagging a bit with middle age. But he was still highly
able, Storrs admitted, and decent for an Earthman. To be
sure, it helped that he was British. The Revolution had
been fought mainly against North Americans.

"Must be something big," West said. "Headquarters and all that." He settled into the navigator's chair.

"Hello, *Merlin,*" said a new voice on the radio. It was a baritone, clipped but heavy with authority. "Evan Bailey speaking, assistant director of ISCC's Bureau of Safety." This time it was West who whistled.

"A serious emergency has come up," Bailey went on. "There's no time to lose. Please calculate an interception curve for sailship number 128, that's one-two-eight. We'll assume that you start acceleration at maximum thrust in, well, fifteen minutes. As soon as possible, anyhow. Is there by any chance another craft like yours reasonably near? You'll want every bit of help you can get."

"No," Storrs answered. "Herdships are few and far between. You're lucky we happen to be this close right now."

That was not entirely coincidence. The orbits of the maintenance ships were planned to keep them never too distant from the great vessels of the Beltline. Some of the best mathematicians in the Republic had computed the optimization paths followed by sail and power craft: an intricate, forever changing dance across half the solar system.

West's fingers had been playing a tattoo on the keys before him. "One-two-eight," he murmured. "Yes, here we are. Cargo of . . . I say, this is an odd one. She's carrying eight hundred metric tons of isonitrate from the Sword's Jovian-orbit plant. Right now she's approaching Earth, only about half a million kilometers away, in fact. There were no indications of trouble during her latest data dump."

"Isonitrate what?" Golescu inquired over the intercom.

"An important industrial chemical," West explained. "Alkali complex of 2,4-benzoisopro—"

"Never mind," Golescu said. "I'm sorry I asked. Uh, everything's okay with our engines, if the gauges aren't liars."

Bailey had hesitated awhile at the other end. Storrs visualized the man, plump in a lounger behind several acres of mahogany desk, sweating that something might happen to interrupt his placid climb through the bureaucracy. His words, when they came, wavered slightly.

"The sun is going to flare."

"What?" Storrs jumped. An oath from Golescu bounced through the intercom. West paused at his work, hands frozen on the keys.

Bailey continued, unaware of the interruption. "The big flare cycles are predictable far in advance these days, but indications of small, short-lived ones are often not observable more than forty-eight hours ahead." His tone grew patronizing. " 'Clear weather season' only means a period in which there will be no major flares and the probability of minor ones is low. Still finite, however. You asterites don't have to worry about solar radiation, out where you are, so perhaps you forget these details. Around Earth, we're highly conscious of them."

You smug planet hugger! Storrs hung on to politeness with both hands. "I know the details well enough," he said stiffly. "I was only shocked. I can't believe isonitrate was shipped if there was any measurable chance of a flare while the vessel was inside the orbit of Mars."

The beam went forth. While they waited for reply, West said in a mild voice, "Call it an unmeasurable chance, then, Sam. The chap's right, you know. Solar meteorology is still not a completed science. It's either assume the hazard, knowing you'll lose an occasional ship, or else have no space traffic whatsoever. A coincidence like this one was bound to happen sooner or later."

"But for crying in the beer!" exclaimed Golescu from aft. "Why couldn't it have happened to a cargo of metal or ice?"

"It does, quite often," Storrs reminded him. "Metal and ice aren't hurt by radiation. Remember?" Sarcastically: "I've heard you gripe so often about how dull these cruises are most of the time. Well, here's your chance for some action."

Bailey had hung fire again. A rustle, penetrating the dry

star-whisper, suggested he had been searching through a
report prepared for him. "The flare is expected in about
twenty hours," he said. "Predicted duration is three hours.
Estimated peak in Earth's vicinity is four thousand roentgens per hour. As you know, that will cause isonitrate to
explode."

Storrs exploded himself. *"Twenty hours!* You bastards
musta known about it at least two days ago! Why didn't
you alert us then? It'll take us ten of those blithering hours
just to make rendezvous!"

"Take it easy there, Sam," West said *sotto voce.* "Some
of those high-caste officials are even touchier than that
isonitrate."

As if in confirmation, Bailey's words turned hard.
"Kindly watch your language, Captain. The delay is unfortunate, I admit, but no one is to blame. The prediction
was issued in the usual way, and records were checked as
per regulations. The nearness of 128 was noted. However,
it is an unmanned craft. You can't expect an ordinary clerk
to know the danger involved in this particular cargo. That
was only pointed out when the data reached my office for
routine double check. And then a policy decision had to
be reached. We haven't the lugger capacity to unload so
much material in time. It would have been simple for us
to send a crew out to bleed off the gas and thereby save
the sailship from being destroyed. But a staff physicist
showed this was impossible. I was informed of the dilemma the moment I came back from lunch, and immediately ordered contact be made with the nearest herdship.
What more do you want, man?"

Storrs unpinched his lips, sat down again, and said,
"Well, Mr. Bailey, you might as well order that crew of
yours to jettison. We can't do anything more than that ourselves. Or have you some other suggestion?"

Waiting out the transmission lag, he heard Golescu say,
"Whoof! Looks as if there's going to be more excitement
than I bargained for."

West chuckled. ''Weren't you caroling about the mad, merry life of a transporteer?''

''Shucks, Ed, I was only practicing my act. Those glamour boys from the scoopships and the prospector teams have been latching on to all the girls back home. Something's got to be done for our kind of spaceman.''

''That gas must positively not be released so close to our orbital facilities,'' Bailey stated. ''It would contaminate the entire inner region. If even a monolayer of vapor by-products were to coat the delicate optics we have up there—weather satellites, arms-control observatories—the cost would be astronomical!

''You may valve it out when you are no less than a million kilometers outbound from cislunar space. That's a direct order, by my authority under this jurisdiction and the Interplanetary Navigation Agreement. Are you recording? I repeat—''

''Judas priest!'' Golescu yelled. ''You expect us to haul away a bomb?''

A humming silence fell over the ship. Storrs became acutely aware of how the stars glistened, the power plant and ventilators murmured, the deck quivered slightly. He felt the roughness of his overalls on his skin, which had become damp and sharp-smelling. He stared at the meters on the pilot panel, and they stared back like troll eyes, and still the silence waxed.

Bailey broke it. ''Yes. Unless you have some other plan, we do expect you to remove that stuff to a safe distance, under terms of your company's franchise for terrestrial operations. What's the problem, anyway? According to your rated thrust, you should be able to get the sailship's cargo section far enough away in fourteen or fifteen hours.''

''The hell you say,'' Storrs barked. ''We can't use full power on such a load. Too much inertia. We'd rip our hull open. Anyway, we've got to uncouple the sail first, to get proper trim—at least two hours' work.'' Desperately: ''You're giving us no safety margin. If the flare happens sooner than you claim, the explosion will destroy us. And you'll still have space contamination. Plus a lot of ship fragments."

"Also people fragments," Golescu added. "We got a legal right to refuse an impossible job, don't we?"

"But not an improbable one," West said. His gaze went to Earth. "I did want to see Blighty again."

"You will," Storrs said. "We're not going to commit suicide for the benefit of a lot of Earthlings."

"Like me, Sam?" West asked softly.

Bailey came back on: "You are not expected to act without due precautions. You can safety tow at the end of a cable several miles long, can't you?"

"Know how much mass that adds?" Storrs snapped. "But never mind. The fact is, our class of ship isn't designed for cable tows. We hook on directly by geegee. A cable would tear us apart, just like hauling under max thrust."

After a moment, assuming briskness like a garment, Bailey said: "We'll do what we can. Alert the International Rescue Service. Commandeer whatever else we can find that may be of help. I can't make any promises, with so little time to go through channels. But I'll do whatever is humanly possible."

"Amoebically possible, you mean," Storrs said. He managed to keep it under his breath. Shaking himself, he answered aloud: "We'll get started now. When we've made rendezvous with 128, we'll call you on the short-range 'caster. Stand by for that. Over and out."

He didn't wait for a response, but snapped off transmission as if the switch were Evan Bailey's neck.

2

"Righto." West heaved his bulk out of the navigator's chair and started aft.

"What're you doing?" the Englishman asked when he returned with sandwiches.

"Trying to figure if we can't boil off some of the liquid as we tow, so gradually that it won't affect space too much, so fast that we'll shed noticeable mass. But hell and sulfur! I don't have the thrust parameter. Not knowing what sort of tugs we'll have available . . . How about hitching that Bailey character to the load and cracking a whip over him? A big wire whip hooked up to five hundred volts AC."

West achieved a smile. "What'd he push against?"

"Hmmm, yeah, that's right. Okay, we'll get extra reaction by cutting Bailey into small pieces—very, very small pieces—and pitching him aft."

West's look moved out to Earth. The half disk was becoming a crescent as *Merlin* approached the spaceward side, but it was also rapidly growing. He traced bands that were clouds, white in a summer sky, the mirror sheen of ocean and the blurred greenish-brown coast of Europe.

"There's England," West said.

Storrs's features softened a trifle. "Kind of tough, huh? Passing this close to your wife and not getting a chance to see her."

West picked up the tray. "I'll take Andy his lunch," he said.

Passing through the tiny saloon, West heard the plink of Golescu's guitar. Words bounced after:

"George Washington was a transporteer, he was,
he was.
George Washington was a transporteer, he was, he
was.
He paddled across the Delaware
To find the buck he'd shot-put there . . .

He entered the workshop just forward of the bulkhead that sealed off the nuclear generator. A man was always supposed to stand by here under acceleration, in case of trouble. But *Merlin* had yet to develop any collywobbles, and Golescu was sitting by. His chair was tilted back against the big lathe, his feet on the rungs and his instrument on his lap. He was a squat, dark young man with squirrel-bright eyes.

"Hi," he said. "Also yum."

West set the tray down and poured two cups of coffee. "By the bye," he said, "I'm not too well up on American folklore, but wasn't it the Potomac that Washington threw the dollar over?"

"Don't ask me. My parents came to Ceres direct from Craiova."

West shook his head. "D'you know, I can't help pitying children who've never felt wind or rain."

"Everything I heard about weather makes it sound more dismal," Golescu said through a mouthful. "Me, I feel sorry for kids that never get to ride a scooter with the whole universe shining around them."

He chewed for a while, then blurted, "Hey, what *is* this problem of ours, Ed? There's no hazard in jettisoning boil-off cargo, not to anybody except the insurance carrier. Is there? It's not like when 43's sail rotation went crazy. I still get nightmares about that one! Why can't we just valve off the isowhatsit, adjust the sail to whatever new track is right, and get back inside *Merlin*'s rad screen field long before the sun burps?"

"Space contamination," West said. "Weren't you listening?"

"Yeah, but I didn't get it. Eight hundred long tons of gas aren't going to make any dent in all that hard vacuum."

"The devil they aren't. You'd still need instruments to detect the difference, but—well, let's figure it out." West extracted paper, pencil, and a calculator from a workbench drawer. "At a distance of six thousand miles from sea level, Earth has an angular diameter of, um, call it forty-three and a half degrees. Adding in the surrounding volume of space that concerns us, we can say about fifty-seven and a half. If we jettison, nearly all the gas will arrive there; the molecules have an Earthward component of velocity. Between the upper atmosphere limit and, say, a fifteen-hundred mile radius from the surface, the concentration of matter will go from about ten molecules per cubic centimeter, if I remember the figure rightly, to . . . good Lord, I have trouble believing this myself! Over fifteen thousand per cc!''

''And so? That's not going to cause any friction worth mentioning.''

''We'd actually do better to let the ship blow up,'' West mumbled, still bent over his work. ''In that case the gas will scatter every which way, and maybe only two percent or so will come near Earth. That's still intolerable, though.''

''Hell, it'll dissipate again.''

''Not for a month, I'll bet. Remember the trapping effect of a planetary magnetic field. But even a few hours of that kind of contamination means the biggest economic disaster since the Nucleus failed.''

''How come?''

''The equipment in orbit, man! There're hundreds of assorted devices near Earth these days. Photocells, for instance, directly exposed to space. Monitoring instruments. How d'you think solar meteorologists get their data? One of the primary sources is a set of ultraclean metal surfaces with characteristic responses to various radiations—automatic spectrometers sending continuous information to the computers Earthside on the relative output of UV, X-rays, the whole band of solar emissions. Then there are fine optics. What do you imagine bombardment by so many metallic-complex molecules, and adsorption, are going to do to the work function of these metals? How about the weather satellites, or communications cybernets, or search-and-rescue? Arms control sats?''

Golescu put down his coffee cup with great care and jammed hands into pockets. A muscle jumped at the corner of his jaw. ''I get you,'' he said.

You know, it occurred to West, *the economic repercussions might even be such that my own government will have to put a surtax on everyone who has any money left, sim-*

ply to feed the unemployed. Mary could lose the house yet.
He discovered that his appetite was gone.

3

You don't scramble into a full suit of space armor, no matter what the hurry. You wriggle and grunt your way in. Helping Storrs secure a knee joint, Golescu remarked, "And to think, when I was a kid, I figured it would've been real romantic being one of King Arthur's knights."

"Shut up and keep going," Storrs answered.

Maybe I am, though, in a way, Golescu's mind continued. *Or at least it's a line to feed the ladies. That dragon outside is fixing to spew some mighty hot fire.*

The intercom speaker in the locker room resounded with West's voice from the bridge: "*Merlin* calling International Space Control. Come in, Control."

"Bailey here," said the speaker.

"West speaking, now in command," said the Englishman. "We're near rendezvous with 128. I haven't picked up anything else on the radar. You do have tugs here, don't you?"

This close to Earth, there was no longer much noticeable time lag. "I'm sorry, no," Bailey said. It was hard to tell whether his tone was curt or merely defensive. "Unfeasible."

"But three or four to help us—"

"How will you attach more than one hauler by geegee to a load so small? If we had a ship so big it could take the container aboard, there would be no problem. Its radiation screen would protect the cargo. But we don't."

Silence extended itself. Golescu could imagine West, alone before the pilot board, his sad eyes resting on the stars and unreachable Earth, methodically trying to think his way out of the trap.

"Build a frame around the gasbag, you Oedipal clotbrain!" Storrs snarled.

"Sam, please," West begged. To Bailey: "Forgive us. We are rather overwrought here, you understtand. Er . . . what about it, though? A skeleton of girders around the bag, giving a large effective surface to which several tugs could grapple."

"How long would it take to build?" the man on the ground countered. "You know how ticklish and special-ized a job construction in orbit is. The sun would flare hours before any such project could be finished." Some-thing like eagerness came into his speech. "The Rescue Service is prepared to take you aboard one of its own units. You need only detach the sail and other excess mass, hook onto the cargo section, and operate your ship by remote control from ours. Quite safe."

" 'Fraid not." West said. "Herdships don't include equipment for unforeseeable cases either. All we could do by remote control is turn the Emetts on and off. Which is insufficient. We'll need a pilot on deck." He sighed. "Bring your ship around, though. Only one of us has to be on board."

Bailey's tone was somber. "I agree."

Storrs swallowed something and clanged his faceplate shut.

"Very well, then," West said tiredly. "We'll proceed as best we can. Dispatch that ship of yours. Maintain con-tact. Let us know if you come up with any better ideas."

"Certainly. Good luck, *Merlin*. Out."

Golescu said "How long till rendezvous, Ed?"

"About ten minutes," West answered. "Better run off your suit checks fast."

"A checked suit . . . in space?" Golescu closed his own faceplate.

By the time he and Storrs had verified that everything was in order and had clumped their way to the air lock, deceleration was ended. They stood unspeaking while the chamber exhausted for them. The outer door opened, a cup that brimmed with stars.

4

Golescu touched the controls of his geegee unit and went forth. Suddenly he was no longer encased in clumsiness, he flitted free as an Earthdweller can only be in dreams. *Merlin* dwindled to a toy torpedo. Blackness surrounded him, lit by twelve thousand visible suns.

He did not look at his own sun. It could have struck him blind before it struck him dead. And Luna was occulted from here. But Earth lay enormous to one side, a dark ball with one dazzling thin edge and a rim of refracted light. There was not much poetry in his makeup, but he found it hard to pull his gaze from the planet.

Storrs's broadcast voice sounded in his receiver. "We're clear, Ed. Stay where you are till we finish."

"Righto," said West. "Your velocity relative to target is . . ." He reeled off the figures.

There was scant need. As Golescu swung about, the sailship which had been at his back, loomed like another Earth.

He had snapped down his glare filter. The stars vanished; he could now have stared Sol in the eye. The disk of the sail reflected with nearly the same brilliance. Protected, he saw it as a great white moon, growing as he sped across the few miles between. The suit radar controlled a series of beeps to inform him of vectors and distance. It made a dry, crickety music for his flight. Not exactly the Ride of the Valkyries, he thought—scarier. He found himself whistling soundlessly, the words running defiant through his head.

> *"Chuck Lindbergh was a transporteer, he was, he was,*
> *Chuck Lindbergh was a transporteer, he was, he was.*

His lonesome song was in the news:
The Spirit of St. Louis Blues.
Bravo, bravo, hurrah for the transporteers!''

"Hey, Ed," Storrs called.

"Yes?" West replied.

"I've been considering. The way this job has developed, it's most likely an impossible one."

"We must try."

"Sure, sure. But listen. It won't do us any good to watch telescopically for the commencement of that flare. The highest energy protons don't travel at much under the speed of light. And there's that whopping probable error in the time prediction. One hour in advance let's cast off, and to hell with those precious satellites."

"Sorry, old chap, no. *Merlin's* going to stay coupled and hauling till the end of the run . . . or her. I'll pilot. We can dispense with the engine watch. You and Andy wait aboard the rescue ship."

"Stow that," Golescu said. "What kind of guts do you think we have?"

"You're both young men," West said dully.

"And you're a married man. And I got a reputation to keep up."

"Ease off on the heroics, you two," Storrs said. "If it comes to that, maybe we can cut cards. Meanwhile, every mile we can drag that canned stink spaceward will help some, I suppose—so let's get on with it."

The sail now nearly bisected the sky, four and a half miles across. The foam-filled members that stiffened it were like Brobdingnagian spokes with its slow rotation. That disk massed close to two tons, and yet it was ghostly thin, a micron's breadth of aluminized polymer.

While the pressure of sunlight in Earth's neighborhood is only some eighty microdynes per square centimeter, this adds up unbelievably when dimensions stretch out into miles. The sunjammers were slow, their shortest passage measured in months, but that vast steady wind never ended

for them; it weakened as they drove starward, but so did
solar gravity, and in exact proportion. They cost money to
build, out in free space, yet far less than a powered ship;
for they required no engines, no crews, no fuel, simply a
metal coating sputtered onto a sheet of carbon compounds, a configuration of sensors and automata, and a
means to signal their whereabouts and their occasional
needs. Those needs rarely amounted to more than repair
of some mechanical malfunction. Otherwise little happened on the long blind voyages. Micrometeorites eroded
the sails, which must eventually be replaced; cosmic rays
sleeted through the carrier sections, unheeded by unalive
cargoes—

*So they weren't designed to prevent solar flares from
blowing them to hell and gone*, Golescu thought.

First time it's ever happened, he reminded himself.
*Probably the last time too. Unique event. I'm privileged to
be on hand for it. What'm I offered, ladies and gentlemen,
for my share of this privilege?*

He noticed, with a slight surprise, that he wasn't afraid.
Well, nothing very dreadful was going to take place for
several hours yet. Except a lot of hard work. Dreadful
enough. *I shoulda tried for scoopship pilot. Still, you got
to make your money somehow, and the pay here is good,
to compensate for having nothing to spend it on. A few
more cruises, and I'll have me that stake to go prospect-
ing. Now there's the life!*

Passing near the middle of the disk, he noticed the hub
in which the sunjammer kept its transmitter and its navigational sensors. Then he had slipped around behind. The
monstrous moon turned black for him. He raised his filter
and saw it become dim blue with reflected starlight.

Carefully, he moved with Storrs toward the opposite
hub. It was linked by a universal joint to a large, dully
gleaming cylinder which held the motors. Those drew their
power—they didn't need much—from solar batteries in the
sunward hub, and used it to control rotation and preces-
sion of the sail according to instructions from the pilot

computer. For the sunjammer must tack from orbit to orbit, across the ever-radial energy wind. Gravitation helped
only on a trip from the outer to the inner system; and even
then the reduction vector was a continuously changing
thing.

Golescu felt the slight jar as his boots made contact with
the precessor hull. They clung, and he rested weightless.
The motors beneath had been turned off on radio command from *Merlin*. He stood for a moment letting his eyes
complete their adjustment to the wan illumination.

Storrs landed beside him. "Come on," said the impatient voice. "Get the lead out of your rectifier. We'll need
every bit of two hours to unhitch the cargo section as is."

"Yes, sure." Golescu began unstrapping the collapsible
tool rack from his shoulders. He and his companion were
hung about with equipment like a robot family's Christmas
tree.

"I haven't worked on one of this type very often," he
admitted. "You'd better be straw boss." He grinned. "I'll
be the straw."

Storrs made a sour noise.

The gas carriers were a pretty special model at that.
Their cargoes must be shaded by the sail, lest temperature
go above critical, the liquefied material boil, and the containers rupture. The standard form of sunjammer used a
curved sail controlled by shroud lines, which pulled rather
than pushed the load. Such an arrangement permitted a
considerably larger light-catching area and proportionate
freight capacity. The drawback was that maintenance crews
on a standard vessel had to begin with erecting a shield
between them and the reflector . . . if they didn't want to
be fricasseed in their spacesuits.

West called: "Ed speaking. I had to drop behind. The
sail was screening me off from you. Everything in order?"

"Just fine," Golescu said. "Apart from having an itch
on my back that I can't scratch, and more work ahead of
me than I'd dare load on any machine, and a prospect of
getting blown to nanosmithereens, and no women in sight,

and hell's own need for beer, I can't complain. Or, rather, I can, but it wouldn't do much good.''

"Don't you ever stop chattering, Andy?" Storrs grumbled.

"Let him be, Sam," West advised. "We each need some outlet."

Storrs grumbled. "Doesn't the consignee want his stuff? This load is worth eight million dollars FOB."

"I just told you, Andy, the really important job is keeping those satellites functional." West's tone became thoughtful. "Y'know, if we do succeed, there ought to be rather a nice bonus for us."

Golescu snorted. "That's about as likely as the Milky Way curdling. Beltline ain't gonna be happy. Sure, they'll have gained goodwill Earthside. But they'll have lost a sunjammer and a shipment. Somebody'll have to make the loss good. If it's an insurance company, as I suppose . . . well, imagine what the premiums are going to go up to!"

Golescu's frame was now also in place. He flitted "up" to install a battery of floodlamps, "down" again to plug them in. Light glared, harsh and undiffused, on the spot where the work must be done.

That was the heavy U-joint connecting precessor with cargo section. The latter was also illuminated in part. Hitherto it had appeared only as a circle of blackness. Now, beyond the framework that held it in place, ponderously counterrotating, the translucent bag glimmered a deep, angry red.

It was not very large to contain so much hell . . . or so much money, Golescu reflected. Space-cold and liquefied under high pressure, the isonitrate occupied a sphere only some ten yards in diameter. Its substance, even the metal atoms, had been reaped from the atmosphere of Jupiter— a chill great brilliance shining in Gemini, two firefly moons visible beside it, treasure house and grave of more asterites than Golescu cared to think about. They were brave men, too, who manned the orbital station where the Jovian organic complexes were processed. An accident there would not be quite like a nuclear warhead going off, but the difference was academic.

Yet Earth needed those energy-crammed molecules, as the starting point for scores of chemical syntheses. It was wealth such as this that kept billions from starving. And Earth was willing to pay.

Golescu unclipped his tools and hung them near at hand. A sense came to him of his own muscles, but not merely in arms but in legs and belly and neck, constantly interplaying with centrifugal and Coriolis forces to hold him in balance on this free-falling shell. That led him to notice how the breath went in and out of his nostrils, tasting of recycler chemicals, and how his heart pumped the blood slowly around the intricate circuit of veins and arteries, and how that made an incessant tiny throb in his ears. He was getting hungry again, and had not lied about wanting a beer . . . ah, cool tickling over his tongue, yes, that was why the asterites must sell to Earth, they hadn't yet succeeded in brewing decent beer themselves.

"Wait a bit," West hailed them. *"Just got a signal from the Rescue Service ship. Want me to relay to you?"*

"Might as well," Golescu said. "For the laughs."

A new voice, accented English: " 'Allo, *Merlin.* International Space Control Commission Rescue Service cutter *Rajasthan,* commanding officer Villegas speaking. Come in, *Merlin.* " Golescu searched for the newcomer, but it must still be only a spark, lost among the stars.

"Acknowledging," said West shortly, and identified himself.

"We 'ave your position and path, *Merlin.* Do you plan to maintain same for t'e present? Yes? T'en we will adopt t'e same orbit, with thirty-kilometer lag. Unless we can do something to 'elp."

"Tell him to send over anybody he's got along who has sailship experience," Storrs said. "With an extra man or two, we'll finish sooner."

West passed the idea on. Villegas hemmed for a moment

before answering, "I am most sorry, but we 'ave no such persons with us. You should 'ave asked for t'em before."

"We assumed you weren't infinitely dunderheaded," Storrs bit off. "Our mistake."

"Don't blow your gaskets, Sam," Golescu counseled. "Sunjammers are oddball craft. Earth hasn't got any. How could they know?"

The byplay had not been relayed. Villegas was saying: "No use to send any of my engineers, yes? T'ey 'ave not t'e special skills. By t'e time t'e men you want could arrive yours will 'ave finished uncoupling and you will be under acceleration, I trust."

"Well, you'll take mine aboard first," West said. "We only need a pilot here for that maneuver."

"I never thought of Ed as the hero type," Golescu remarked. He squatted to fit a wrench around a bolthead. "Shall we oblige him?"

"What a dilemma," Storrs said acridly. "If I do, I'm a coward. If I don't, and we cut cards, I might end up risking my neck for Mother Earth."

"Come off that shtick, Sam. The war's over, or hadn't you heard? Besides, we may reach jettisoning distance before the flare pops. It's just as likely to be later than prediction as earlier. Or . . . you know, in armor, with a strong metal shield around him, a man might even survive the explosion. There's no air to carry blast. When *Merlin* breaks apart, he could be tossed into space in one piece."

"Sure. Into four thousand roentgens per hour. That means nine minutes for a lethal dose. The other ship isn't going to find him in any nine minutes, chum."

"Hmm . . . true. Damn! What we need is a pocket size rad screen generator. Or something very thick to hide behind—"

Golescu's words cut off. He stared before him, into the icy light of Jupiter, until its afterimage danced through his vision.

All the stars danced.

"What's eating you now?" Storrs growled. "Get to work."

Golescu's yell nearly shattered his own eardrums. Its echoes were still flying around in his helmet when West cried, "What is it? I say, what happened? I'm coming, be there in a few minutes, hang on, boys!"

"No . . . wait . . . hold everything," Golescu stammered. "Not so fast. We're okay. Better than okay."

Storrs closed gauntlet fingers on the other man's shoulderpieces and shook him. "What's the matter, you clown?"

"Don't you see?" Golescu howled. "We can save the whole shooting match!"

5

Words flew between sunjammer and herdship. The decision was quickly reached; a spaceman who could not make up his mind from a standing start was unlikely to clutter his profession very long. West called *Rajasthan*. ". . . Send us every hand you can possibly spare," he concluded. "I'll raise Bailey and have him rush us more crews from your service's fleet in orbit. But they can hardly arrive for a few hours yet, and we've got to make what progress we can meanwhile."

"Craziest thing I ever heard of," Storrs panted. "It *ought* to work, but—why didn't anybody think of it on Earth?"

"Same reason you and Ed didn't, I guess," Golescu said. "It's so crude and obvious, only a low-wattage brain like mine would see it. At least see it quick-like. I suppose somebody would've hit on it eventually."

"That would have been too late." Storrs' gaze traveled across the awesome blue plain that wheeled before him, curtaining off half the universe. "May be too late already. Hell's kettles, what a huge job!"

6

"Don't remind me. I got troubles of my own. Ready? Okay, let's stop rotation."

Storrs opened the shield over the manual controls, made several adjustments, replaced the cover, and used the handle of a small crescent wrench to push a deeply recessed button. At once he leaped back, off the cylinder. Golescu went simultaneously.

They were none too soon. Gears meshed, flywheels began to spin, the motor and cargo sections took up the angular momentum that was being removed from the sail. At the same time, the disk was precessed to face the sun directly.

So great a mass could not be stopped fast. Storrs and Golescu flitted clear, out into the fierce light. Their thermostatic units began to labor, converting heat into electricity and storing it in the suit capacitors. That energy would be needed; the men were going to be at work for quite a spell.

"You know," Storrs said, "you weren't right about saving everything. The sail will be lost."

"So?" Golescu returned. "The kit is what matters. A couple of million bucks' worth of caboodle is cheap for salvaging the rest."

West contacted them: "I'm having a bit of a tussle with Bailey. Let me cut you into the circuit."

"Ridiculous arrangement," Bailey's tinny voice said. "The whole concept is fantastic. Eight hours—less than that—to handle sixteen square miles of material?"

"One micron thick," West pointed out. "A hundred square yards masses only about a pound. It's not like building a frame for tugs to grapple. This job is elementary. Any spacehand with a geegee unit on his suit can do it."

"I forbid this lunacy. You're ordered to carry on with standard procedures."

An inarticulate sound vibrated in Storrs' throat. Golescu said bad words. West spoke with complete calm:

"You can't forbid it, or issue any order except for us to do our best. Please read the texts you've been citing to me. If Beltline is responsible for this operation, Beltline's agents have to have authority to decide how it will be carried out. And our decision is to go for broke. Without your cooperation, we are bound to fail. And what excuse will you offer then? I respectfully suggest, Mr. Bailey, that you get cracking."

Stillness hummed, except for the noise of the crowding, flashing stars. Earth rolled tremendous against an ultimate dark. The sail began to bend at the edges as centrifugal force waned. Had it not faced the sun head on, it could have buckled into a hopeless tangle. As matters stood, when rotation ended it would approximate a section of a sphere.

Bailey's gulp gurgled in earplugs. "You win."

7

The work had been brutal. They sat in the saloon with untasted mugs of coffee, staring emptily at the bulkheads, while West rode the controls.

Outside, Lucifer ran free. Coughed from the sun, ions with energies in the millions of electron volts flooded all space. Down on Earth, tourists in the Antarctic lodges crowded into the observation domes to watch the winter sky come alive with vast flapping curtains of aurora. Elsewhere, men who had heard the news huddled near their television screens, waiting for word. Reception was poor. The nuclear generators of ships beyond the atmosphere poured power into screen fields deflecting that murderous torrent from their hulls. The engineers' eyes never left the gauges.

Merlin throbbed. Now and then, as she moved to keep the load at the end of her grapnel on an even keel, her members groaned with stress. That was the only token granted the men in the saloon. They dared not interrupt the pilot with questions.

"It's got to work," Storrs said stupidly, for the dozenth time. He rubbed his chin. The bristles of beard made an audible scratching.

"Sure it will," Golescu said. "My idea, wasn't it?" The cockiness had left his voice.

"Well," Storrs said, "If it doesn't—if that cargo explodes—we'll never know." He laid his fist on the table and regarded the knobby knuckles. "I'd like to know, though. How I'd laugh at those fat Earthlings."

Golescu reached for his coffee. It had gone cold. "They aren't that bad. And if you've got to be such a hot-bottomed patriot, don't forget that trouble on Earth would affect the Republic. We need them, same as they need us."

After a pause, he asked, "Scared?"

Storrs spat in the ashcatcher. "No. Tired and angry. This means one thing to Ed. Economic breakdown on Earth would hurt him directly. But you and me—"

"Oh, fork all those fancy moral issues," Golescu said. "This is what we get paid for."

The sun's arrows rushed on through vacuum. Where they encountered *Merlin*'s screen, they swerved, with a spiteful gout of X-radiation that her internal shielding drank up. Where they struck at the cargo section—

They hit a barrier of plastic and aluminum: the sail, cut into fifteen-meter squares that were layered within a welded framework. The shielding factor came to about fifty grams per square centimeter. Light metals and hydrogen-rich carbon compounds are highly effective stoppers of stripped small atoms like the hydrogen and helium ions which make up nearly the whole of flare emission.

But the whole clumsy ensemble of shield, cargo section, and herdship must be kept facing directly into the blast. And gravitation kept trying to swing it into orbit, which brought gyroscopic forces into play. Control was exercised at the end of a long arm; the mass had considerable turning moment, difficult to control.

"If we ride this one out," Golescu said, "we really will get that bonus Ed was faunching for."

"Uh-huh." Storrs raised dark-rimmed eyes. "Andy, you're a good oscar and I hope we can ship out together again, but right now I've got some thinking to do. Keep quiet, huh?"

"Okay," Golescu said. "Though thinking's the last thing I want to do."

He prowled aft to have a look at the engine-room meters. Not that he could improve matters much if anything was going awry, in his present condition.

His bleared vision focused on the bank of indicators. Everything operating smoothly—good ship. Wait a second! The external radiation count—

"Yi-yi-yip!" he screamed. "She's going down! The flare's dying!" And he did a war dance around the workshop and up the length of the corridor beyond.

Slowly, slowly, the storm faded. Until at last West said from the intercom, "It's over with. We're alive, boys."

Storrs began to dance, too.

After a while West reported, "Earth called in. Congratulations and so forth. They'll send a tug at once for this cargo, and hold it in the moon's shadow while they unload. We're invited groundside for a celebration." Wistfulness tinged his voice. "D'you think the company would mind if we accepted?"

"They'd better not." Storrs said.

"We need a checkout anyway, after putting the ship to so much stress," Golescu added. "And they'll have to compute a new orbit for the rest of our mission. We're bound to have a few days' layover." Exhaustion dropped from him. "Fleshpots, here I come!"

He snatched up his guitar and bellowed forth:

"Ol' Einstein was a transporteer, he was, he was.
Ol' Einstein was a transporteer, he was, he was.

His racing car used too much gas;
It shrank the time but it raised the mass.
Bravo, bravo, hurrah for the transporteers!''

Now he had a story to embroider for the girls in Pallas
town.

Poul Anderson was born in 1926 in the U.S.
but of Scandinavian parents, hence the first name.
After being raised in various places and conditions of life, he received a bachelor's degree in
physics from the University of Minnesota, but
went into writing instead. Among his better-known
books are *Brain Wave, The Broken Sword, The
High Crusade, Tau Zero,* and *The Boat of a Million Years.* He has long lived in the San Francisco
Bay area with his wife, Karen, who also occasionally writes. Their daughter, Astrid, is married to
their colleague, the up and coming, award-
winning author, Greg Bear.
Speaking of awards, Poul has won nearly every
one to be had. He, too, hauled an old chestnut
out to donate it to this anthology. It's nice to see
that good old stories, like good old writers, live
on and on.

A Rebel Technology
Comes Alive

by
Chauncey Uphoff and Jonathan Post

Since the days of Sputnik, we have grown used to a notion that would have seemed bizarre to our ancestors—that you need big government to explore a new frontier. In fact, since *Homo erectus* left Africa, several million years ago, human beings have been inveterate explorers. And generally, whenever we sought out new territory, new opportunities, it was in small groups, unconstrained by bureaucracies and red tape.

To be sure, governments have taken part. Latin America was subdued under the flag of the kings of Spain. British troops expanded an empire. Even in the Wild West, with its spirit of rugged individualism, who could downplay the importance of the telegraph and railroads—both stimulated by federal support?

Still, it was individuals and families and small enterprises that did most of the work, creating wealth and new opportunities on a new frontier. Governments provided infrastructure and other help. But it was people, endeavoring to improve their circumstances, who actually dug the mines and built the homes and ran the factories.

The same must hold, eventually, for the newest frontier—the solar system. There's plenty for governments to do, such as establishing the means to haul heavy masses out of Earth's deep gravity into low orbit, and helping set rules so we treat the new territories well.[1] But there must also be room for individuals, small groups, entrepreneurs. And without tax dollars to count on, these people will have

to find a way to move about in space that's safe, effective
. . . and cheap!

Ideally you should be able to use local fuel available at
the frontier itself, as did the wood-burning steam locomotive that civilized the American West. When trains ran
out of fuel, operators had only to stop and cut more wood.
But an even more elegant example would be the sailing
ships of those days, which tapped another renewable resource, the wind.

Eventually, we will have to do this in space—we will
have to make use of what we find there, instead of relying
solely on what we bring along. In other words, our descendants will want to loosen the chains that bind them
too tightly to Old Earth.

Pioneers will need pioneer technology, like the Ken-
tucky rifle and the Conestoga wagon. Perhaps that's one
reason solar sails bother some bureaucrats so much. Like
the horse that could graze along the way, like trading
sloops and clipper ships, certain transportation systems just
inherently lend themselves to freedom of action, letting
people cut the apron strings and go forth on their own.

Not all space industry officials are scared by this, of
course. Indeed, many of them share the same dream. Just
as wind ships opened up the New World to commerce,
lightsails may someday make regular runs from Earth to
Mars or Venus, resupply a power-intensive industry near
the sun, or haul cargo back from the asteroid belt. The
need for fuel limits most other forms of deep-space transportation. In a very real sense, the development of the
solar sail is a fundamental investment in the future of civilization.

The concept of light pressure has been around for some
time. Kepler correctly suggested it as an explanation for
why comet tails point away from the sun. The dust particles from comets are terrific little solar sails themselves;
they are so small that they have a very large area to mass
ratio, which makes them very susceptible to light pressure.

Even so, it proved very difficult to measure the light

pressure in laboratories, because the gas molecules in the best vacuum chambers swamped the force of light. Its pressure wasn't unambiguously measured until 1897 by Lebedev, and independently in 1903 by Nichols and Hull.

As described elsewhere, it was two Russians, Tsander and Tsiolkovsky,[2] who thought up the first modern concept of solar sailing. But their notions went into hibernation until independent discovery of the concept by Carl A. Wiley in his article called "Clipper Ships of Space," published under the pseudonym Russell Saunders in the May 1951 issue of *Astounding Magazine*.

Later on, Richard Garwin, James Fletcher, and Jerome Wright oversaw the reawakening of solar sailing in the mid-1970s for possible use on a mission for Halley's comet. Dr. Louis Friedman's book *Starsailing: Solar Sails and Interstellar Travel* gives a firsthand account of the exciting times of the Halley Rendezvous Project. Although eventually canceled, that endeavor nevertheless spawned private efforts leading to the Engineering Development Mission of the World Space Foundation.

The Pasadena Project

In a freshly painted workroom in Pasadena sits what is probably the first solar sail fabricator, a strange-looking contraption with big rollers at each end of a long table. Strips of aluminized Mylar are wound around the rollers. Although well-designed and well-built, it isn't a bit fancy. Its objective is to seam and fold plastic film into large square sheets. The machine was developed and tested by staff of the World Space Foundation, headed by Robert L. Staehle, to construct the world's first solar sail.

For the past decade, the foundation has been committed to the development of an engineering test vehicle to demonstrate that solar sail spacecraft are deployable, controllable, feasible.

The Solar Sail Project was started originally as a NASA

enterprise by Jerome Wright, discoverer of a solar sail rendezvous trajectory with Halley's comet. Although NASA eventually canceled the proposed Halley mission in 1986, development continued through the private efforts of the foundation's Engineering Development Mission.

The EDM is a precursor of more ambitious endeavors. If the design is shown viable during a first launch, a more advanced and higher-performance vehicle may be constructed to rendezvous with an asteroid. As more experience is gained, a high-temperature sail may be constructed for close polar orbit of the sun. Either project would demonstrate the enormous potential of solar sails for accomplishing missions in the inner solar system.

The World Space Foundation is a nonpolitical foundation dedicated to supporting and conducting space research and development, funded by tax-deductible subscriptions and cooperative efforts with other organizations. At the end of this volume, readers will learn how they can find out more.

A Regatta Past the Moon?

An exciting suggestion has been proposed to the aerospace community, under the auspices of the American Institute of Aeronautics and Astronautics, for a solar sail race similar to the one in Arthur C. Clarke's story "The Wind from the Sun."

The race would take place in 1992, the quincentennial of Columbus's discovery of the new world, and entries from all countries are being sought. Many teams have filed an intent to respond to the AIAA request for proposals, even though the entries, race rules, and qualification requirements were unclear as this book went to press.

Races have traditionally stimulated performance improvements that often are reflected later in products offered for mass consumption. For instance, automobile racing has a long history of transferring technology first to sports cars and then to the general public. Competition also stimulates a kind of short-term excitement that allows onlookers to participate.

And there are esthetic reasons for racing. There is something of the hope that springs eternal in the realization of the effort, and people identify with the long hours and hard physical effort required to excel, the grueling hours of rigorous effort. When the race is on, almost everyone can identify with the driver.

But racing can also have dangerous consequences. The Stanley brothers thought that all the advertising their steamer needed was to win the race to Pike's Peak every year. For many years the Stanley steamer held the world's land speed record at 142 miles per hour. Then one year it flew off the ground and nearly killed the driver. Reliance on the race probably cost the Stanley brothers their business.

Many solar sail enthusiasts are also concerned that a race may perpetuate an attitude among some aerospace managers that solar sailing is an amateur or "playboy" technology. The effect would be especially damaging if the race got lots of publicity, then fizzled.

Robert Staehle voices some of the concerns. Imagine that in 1901, an international commission organized an airplane race. Suppose the prospect of international competition whipped up popular fervor and national pride. Reports of the short hops claimed by a couple of bicycle mechanics from Ohio would be considered amateur, and the commission would probably have said, "These short flights are not worthy of such a race. Let's fly across the Channel." The result could easily have been three or four piles of wood and canvas at the base of the white cliffs of Dover, which would have set back aviation many years.

But these concerns aside, a well-organized and carefully thought-out race might be effective if it does not place unrealistic strain on designs and participants. Publicity and excitement might attract real investment capital from the private sector. It is here that the solar sail will certainly flourish, not as racecars but as the magnificent and highly profitable ocean liners of the future. But if it takes a race to get things started, then, by all means hoist sails!

The Future of Lightships

All this is not to claim that solar sails will soon make rockets obsolete. No lightship we can envision could climb through Earth's atmosphere and surface gravity into space. Also, current-technology sails are probably too slow to be useful for transporting astronauts.

But high-tech sails of the future, like those suggested by Drexler, Forward and Dyson, could someday make the trip from Earth to Mars in a few months and would not be subject to the delays of ballistic trajectories, or waiting for the planets to line up for return to Earth. In the long run, people, too, may ride "sunjammers."

Even current-technology sails would be highly useful as cargo haulers. Foundation president Robert Staehle has described how lightship freighters might assist a manned mission to Mars. Sent four years ahead of the astronauts' takeoff, these cargo robot sloops would carry all the supplies for the astronauts' return trip (including bulky water and food and fuel) plus two Mars landing vehicles and a space station equipped for a long stay in Mars orbit. (The astronauts would have to live there for more than a year before the alignment of the planets allowed them to return.)

Furthermore, says Jerome Wright, "The sail freighter wouldn't be used up after one trip, but could provide that kind of service for twenty or thirty years. A single sail shuttle might cost $20 million and in a decade save billions."

As discussed in other essays and stories in this volume, some contend that lightships could open up the vast mineral wealth of the asteroids. At least seventy thousand of these rocky "minor planets" circling the sun are more than a mile in diameter, large enough to be interesting yet small enough not to foul a lightship's rigging with gravity or atmosphere. Some might provide badly needed water ice and carbon. And we already know that many other bodies contain rich accumulations of rare metals. The solar system might someday flow with great commercial shipping lanes, with lightships bringing ore back to Earth, or to manufacturing operations in Earth orbit.

In a tempting speculation, an asteroid or two "could fill the factories of Earth with raw materials," according to Eric Drexler of the Foresight Institute. "The metal on a typical midsized asteroid probably contains $1,000 per ton worth of platinum-group metals: platinum, iridium, osmium, and paladium. These are strategic metals needed by the West. Over ninety percent of the world's supply of platinum now comes from the Soviet Union and South Africa."

Drexler wants to develop sails that would have a "couple of dozen" times more acceleration than those currently envisioned. The trick (described in more detail elsewhere in this volume) is to make sails of thin aluminum film alone, without the heavy plastic backing planned for the EDM mission. The plastic is what allows the sails to be folded for transport off the Earth, so pure aluminum sails will have to be manufactured in space. Drexler contemplates sails as thin as a ten-millionth of an inch could be so produced out in weightless vacuum.

The lightship has one limitation yet unmentioned so far: that of the solar system itself. Lightships may be fine for visiting the sun and asteroids and inner planets, but by the time one passes Pluto, the sun starts looking like just another bright star. Lightship travel beyond that is out of the question—or is it?

There's always someone with a scheme, and this time it's Robert Forward, a retired senior scientist with Hughes Research Laboratories in Malibu, California, and also a successful science fiction author.

"Right after the laser was invented, I realized its beam

brightness was greater than that of the sun and that if you had a big enough one you could push sails to the stars,'' Forward says. So he conceived of a laser drawing its energy from the sun with the power of 65,000 of today's bigger nuclear power plants, floating in space near Mercury. By passing the beam through a lens made from rings of thin plastic sheeting, measuring six hundred miles across and located between Saturn and Uranus, the laser could maintain its focus tens of light-years away. The nearest star, Alpha Centauri, is only four light-years away, and so the laser could keep pushing all the way there, sending a one-ton sailing ship there in only forty years.

The scheme seems incredible. And indeed, Forward says he explored the idea originally as a means of transporting characters to a nearby star in one of his science fiction novels. But he also recently filled ten pages of a technical journal with equations proving the feasibility of his idea. And in his essay later in this volume, he makes a convincing case that we may yet see vast laser-driven sails, putting forth for the stars.

NOTES

1. Of course, today we've also seen, in dramatic terms, what can happen when individual self-interest goes too far. The ecological destruction going on around us testifies that there must be some socially accepted limit placed on human greed. Changes in public awareness and government action that reflects that awareness are both causing us to change some of our worst habits.

These new, more enlightened attitudes will have to follow us into space. For although the riches awaiting us out there are vast and seemingly inexhaustible, that was exactly how the forests of North America appeared to our ancestors only two centuries ago!

Of course, we know of no ''ecosystems'' in space—no life forms or food chains that might be disrupted by pollution. But that's no guarantee we can't do harm out there if we aren't careful. In fact, today NASA and other agencies are worried about debris from old rockets and satellites causing hazards in low Earth orbit.

Solar sails offer a special opportunity, then, to take good habits with us to a new frontier. As discussed in the article by Staehle and Friedman, they are inherently nonpolluting, relying on what may be an infinitely renewable resource—starlight.

They are also *delicate* things, which won't work if we fill space with too much garbage! In effect, investing in solar sails means we intend to tread lightly on the new frontier—even as we head out there to live and learn and get rich.

2. Although Tsiolkovsky and Tsander deserve primary credit, more information has recently become available from Ron Muir of San Jose, California, and Sergei Golotyuk of the U.S.S.R., who point out the 1881 science fiction story "Adventures Extraordinaires d'un Savante Russe" by Georges LeFavre and Henri de Graffigny contains the concept of solar sailing "though not in a quite clear form." Furthermore, a 1913 story "Upon the Ethereal Waves" by B. Krasnogorsky describes a viable solar sail. (There are even hints that solar pressure propulsion was mentioned by Jules Verne!)

Chauncey Uphoff has been involved in the space program since the early 1960s, when as a student at the University of New Hampshire, he worked on one of his professor's satellite tracking projects. (One of his duties was to adjust the receivers to measure the Doppler shift of the signal from Sputnik IV.) Born in 1940, he was fortunate enough to be in the right place at the right time to be among the first professional aerospace engineers. While at JPL, he won the NASA exceptional service medal for pioneering work on the gravity-assisted satellite tour portion of the Galileo mission and was instrumental in the decision to study the solar sail as a potential deep-space propulsion system.

Jonathan Post is a graduate of the California Institute of Technology. He has worked for JPL and is now with a prominent aerospace firm helping lay plans for the twenty-first century. He is a well-respected poet and a member of the Science Fiction Writers of America.

Argosies of Magic Sails— Excerpts from "Locksley Hall"

by
Alfred, Lord Tennyson

Many a night from yonder ivied casement, ere I
went to rest,
Did I look on great Orion sloping slowly to the
West.

Many a night I saw the Pleiads, rising thro' the
mellow shade,
Glitter like a swarm of fire-flies tangled in a silver
braid.

Here about the beach I wander'd, nourishing a
youth sublime
With the fairy tales of science, and the long result
of Time;

When the centuries behind me like a fruitful land
reposed;
When I clung to all the present for the promise that
it closed:

When I dipt into the future far as human eye could
see;
Saw the Vision of the world, and all the wonder
that would be;

*Saw the heavens fill with commerce, argosies of
magic sails,*

*Pilots of the purple twilight, dropping down with
    costly bales;*

Heard the heavens fill with shouting,
    and there rain'd a ghastly dew
From the nations' airy navies grappling in the cen-
    tral blue . . .

Ion Propulsion:
The Solar Sail's Competition for Access to the Solar System

by
Bryan Palaszewski

A solar sail has grace and potential simplicity to capture the imagination of engineer, scientist, and layman alike. But another type of propulsion technology has equal elegance. It is called ion propulsion, and this innovative technology may accomplish some things more cheaply and easily than any other way of moving about in space. In fact, some call ion technology the "friendly competitor" with solar sails.

Exploring the Solar System

Cost-effective exploration of the solar system requires two major breakthroughs. First, access to low Earth orbit must be made cheaper and easier. Getting off the planet's surface demands huge amounts of energy to be applied in a short time. For the near future, rockets remain the only way to provide that first push off the Earth.

But even if there are major advances in launch capabilities, that won't be the answer alone. A lot can be accomplished in low Earth orbit, but to really *use* space, we'll need a second breakthrough, getting much farther out to where the real riches wait.

Why Ion Propulsion?

With current space propulsion systems, the cost can be very high, and it will only get higher when we begin planning complex multipart endeavors, like sending people to Mars, or returning to the moon. Many flights of large boosters will be needed to lift vehicle components into orbit. But even more expensive will be the propellant (fuel and oxidizer) needed by space tugs and other vehicles out there.

Also, because so many launches may be needed, the length of time to assemble a space vehicle will be extended, adding to the cost and complexity of each mission.

Why is it so hard to get from place to place out there? To understand movement in space, the idea of Newton's Third Law must be understood. Simply stated, any action produces an equal and opposite reaction. As we throw mass (propellant) away from a spacecraft or any object, the object will move in the opposite direction. This is the case for solar sails, which "bounce" sunlight one way and recoil the other. It is also true for chemical *and* ion rockets, which carry their own propellant and achieve a change in orbit by flinging mass away from themselves.

The performance level of this process is called *specific impulse*. In most cases, the higher the specific impulse of a rocket engine, the lower the mass of propellant needed to accomplish a mission. The specific impulse of an ion engine can be four to twenty times higher than that of a chemical propulsion system, and that of a solar sail approaches infinity. (Since there is no propellant, one might say that a sail's "equivalent specific impulse" is determined by its mass and the total mission velocity it accumulates over a lifetime.

So it makes sense to compare these two revolutionary technologies, and explore how each of them might help us explore and develop space.

Flight Paths and Trajectories

"The easiest way to get from point A to point B is to go in a straight line." But this adage was developed before the advent of interplanetary travel. For more than a generation, space planners have gotten used to the limitations of orbital mechanics. You blast toward a distant planet with one huge rocket boost, drift in a long curving orbit, then match velocities at the other end with another rocket blast. With chemical rockets, the energy to leave orbit is spent quickly and the spacecraft coasts the rest of its way. Ion rockets, on the other hand, burn faintly but continuously, for a very long time.

To leave the orbit of a planet, the low thrust of an ion propulsion system limits acceleration, so the escape path is a long, spiraling one, taking as many as hundreds of days. But once the spacecraft is out orbiting the sun (in heliocentric space), ion propulsion can give a fast trip, especially to the outer planets. This is because the drive *can keep on pushing,* long after a chemical rocket would have burned out. Quicker voyages can make future human exploration a possibility rather than a gleam in the eye of space engineers.

How Ion Propulsion Works

With an ion drive, the mass we throw away from the spacecraft is in the form of ionized atoms, accelerated by electric fields in a machine called a thruster. These ions reach very high velocities: 20,000 to 100,000 meters per second, or more. For most missions within the solar system, 30,000 to 60,000 m/s provides the "best" (but not necessarily the shortest) trip times, or the lowest mass starting in low Earth orbit (LEO).

Several propellants can be used in ion thrusters. In the past, mercury and cesium (liquid metals) were used, but these brought unwanted problems. So inert gases are now the propellants of choice: xenon, krypton, and argon.

To give the gas its very high speed, its component atoms are each stripped of an electron—ionized—in the thruster. This diffuse plasma (charged gas) is the heart of an ion propulsion system. The ions are then accelerated down a lightweight cylinder with a set of magnets and electrical grids to control the ions' direction. The ions that depart the engine form a diffuse beam, much faster than the thermal output of a chemical rocket. The faster the propellant leaves, the less weight you have to carry along for a flight.

Benefits of Ion Propulsion

Two types of missions have been studied extensively by the NASA Office of Exploration for possible application of ion drives. These programs involve many flights to the moon and Mars over several years. Their ultimate goal is to help eventually construct permanent settlements from which humans can range and explore, seeking the knowledge of new worlds.

Consider a manned mission to Mars. NASA mission planners have suggested sending the food, science payloads, and propellants needed at the Red Planet by astronauts aboard cargo vehicles, sent well ahead of the vehicle carrying people. Since the manned craft would be lightened, a faster flight would be possible, which would minimize the crew's exposure to solar flares and other space hazards. Once both vehicles were in orbit around Mars, they would rendezvous and transfer the food and other items.

In one design, the cargo to be taken to Mars would be 180 metric tons. But with fuel added, the total mass of the Mars cargo vehicle, using oxygen and hydrogen propellants, would be 590 tons! With ion propulsion that total would only be 295 tons.

So a Mars mission using ion propulsion for the cargo

vehicles could weigh as little as half a comparable mission using oxygen and hydrogen propellants. Also, the Mars craft could be placed in Earth orbit more quickly because fewer flights would be needed to launch the vehicle components, especially propellant. (In this mission, solar sails would have a slight edge in efficiency, but might be slower. In any event both would be far cheaper than chemical rockets.)

Flights to lunar orbit could also significantly benefit from alternative propulsion, and here ion drives come out even ahead of sails.

The total mass that must be delivered for a lunar base is large: 300 to 1,000 tons for Phase One alone in one NASA scenario. Each piece could be transported from the ground to Earth orbit by conventional rocket, and then to lunar orbit by an ion propulsion vehicle at a mass savings of 50 percent over oxygen and hydrogen propulsion. Solar sails, on the other hand, would have little room to maneuver on the way to the moon. One thing that would strongly affect the sail is the Earth's atmosphere. Because of its large surface area, the sail would have to be deployed at a high altitude. If it were unfurled below 1,000–2,000 kilometers altitude (625–1,250 statute miles), the sail would begin to reenter the atmosphere. But an ion propulsion system could be deployed at 500 kilometers (313 statute miles). A lower starting orbit would mean either smaller launch vehicles to put the payload up or more payload launched by the same rocket from Earth. The sail's very large area also could make it difficult to maneuver close to Earth—and it would have to maneuver every orbit to keep the best angle to the sun.

Solar-powered ion propulsion at very high power levels (many tens of megawatts) has the same problems as a sail because of the large collectors required. However, the power level used for most missions would be modest. For these reasons, ion drives may edge out sails for use in Earth-lunar space.

Other missions proposed by the Jet Propulsion Laboratory include extensive exploration of all aspects of the solar system, from the tenuous dust trails surrounding comets to the multihued clouds wreathing the outer planets. Like solar sails, ion propulsion could provide great benefits to all of these explorations. But there is one extra advantage ion systems would bring to such missions: *added power* for science experiments. After the spacecraft arrived at its destination, the power source used to propel the ions wouldn't be needed for that purpose anymore. Whether it was solar or nuclear, the source could then provide electricity to advanced science instruments, such as powerful radars. These could probe the dense atmospheres of outer planets, determine the subsurface structure of Mars and the moon, and provide better communications with Earth. By using this power other than solely for propulsion, the entire spacecraft would become more capable and more cost-effective.

Power: The Other Big Piece of the System

While we're on the subject, power is a crucial part of any ion propulsion system. (This is one major distinction from solar sails, which get both their power and "fuel" from sunshine.) Both nuclear and solar power sources are possible. Any space power source must be efficient and lightweight.

Electronics must then take the power from the source and provide it at the right voltage and current to the engines. Together, the power source and electronics might make up more than 70 percent of the ion spacecraft's weight (without propellants).

If the ion system uses nuclear power, a long boom between the power source and the rest of the spacecraft would be required to keep high-level radiation away from the crew and instruments. Or an ion-drive spacecraft might use solar power, concentrating sunlight to provide thousands of kilowatts. The solar panels might have an area of 10,000 square meters, larger than two football fields, but smaller than a sail used to carry the same payload.

Rebel Technology?

It has been asserted that space development calls for "rebel" technologies, to allow wide access to spaceflight. These technologies would provide not just big governments but corporations and even citizens the freedom to get into and out of Earth orbit inexpensively. Propulsion and power will certainly be two of the most important technologies enabling this "rebellion," toward the settlement and industrialization of the planets. Making these widely available, and user-friendly, will be a great and exciting challenge.

This revolution will have to be a friendly one. The initial investment, proving the spaceworthiness of ion-propulsion spacecraft, must be financed by governments. But later, as with solar sails, the technology could be made available at significantly lower cost. Private users could then avail themselves of ion propulsion's benefits. As the short story by Charles Sheffield demonstrates, some of these benefits may be astounding and even fun.

The Bright Future

There are few ideas or experiences which match the wonder of spaceflight. Exploration of the solar system thus far has been among humanity's finest achievement. Future exploration will require new technologies, developed by NASA and other innovative organizations. Just as it has been unwise to ignore the potential of solar sails, it would seem silly not to explore the great possibilities offered by ion propulsion as well. This is an area in which a little friendly competition can only help us all.

Bryan Palaszewski has recently joined the NASA Lewis Research Center's Space Propulsion Technology Division. Prior to joining NASA, he was a member of the technical staff at the NASA Jet Propulsion Laboratory for six years. During that time, he led many diverse studies of advanced propulsion systems, including chemical propulsion and especially electric propulsion.

In our next story, Charles Sheffield illustrates some of the possibilities opened up by ion drives. And if the theme (a speed race in outer space) strikes you as familiar, well, aren't some ideas so good they deserve another look?

Grand Tour

by
Charles Sheffield

Tomas Lili had won the Stage, square if not fair, and now he was wearing the biggest, sweatiest grin you have ever seen. Tomorrow he would also wear the yellow jersey on the next-to-last Stage of the Tour.

Ernie Muldoon had come second. In one monstrous last effort of deceleration, I had almost squeaked in front of him at the docking, and hit the buffer right on the maximum allowable speed of five kilometers an hour. We had been given the same time, and now we were collapsed over our handlebars. I couldn't tell about Ernie, but I felt as though I were dying. For the last two hours I had been pedaling with a growing cramp in my left thigh, and for the final ten minutes it was as though I had been working the whole bike one-legged.

After five minutes' rest I had recovered enough to move and speak. I unbuckled my harness, cracked the seals, and climbed slowly out of my bike. As usual at the end of a Stage, my legs felt as though they had never been designed for walking. I did a couple of deep knee-bends in the half-g field, then straightened up and staggered over to Muldoon. He had also flipped back the top of his bike and was slowly levering himself free.

"Tomas was lucky," I said. "And he cheated!"

Muldoon looked at me with eyes sunk back in his head. He was even more dehydrated than I was. "Old Persian proverb," he said. "Luck is infatuated with the efficient."

"You don't think he cheated?"

"No. And he wasn't lucky, he was smart. He bent the

rules, but he can't get called on it. Therefore, he didn't cheat. He was just a bit smarter than the rest of us. Admit it, Trace, you'd have done it too if you'd thought of it.''

"Maybe."

"Maybe, schmaybe. Come on. I've been cramped in this bike for too long. Let's beat the crowd to the showers.''

He was right; the others were streaming in now, one every few seconds. As we left the docking area a whole bunch zoomed in together in practically a blanket finish. I saw five riders from Adidas, so close I was sure they'd been slipstreaming for a sixth member of their team. That *was* outside the rules, and they were bound to be caught. Five years ago, slipstreaming had been worth doing. Today, it was marginal. The teams did it anyway—because the man who benefited from the slipstreaming was not the one doing anything illegal. The rider who had given the momentum boost would be disqualified, but that would be some no-hoper in the team. Illogical? Sure. The Tour had a crazy set of rules in the first place, and as more and more riders became part of the big teams, the rules became harder to apply. Ernie Muldoon and I were two of the last independents racing the Grand Tour. Ernie, because he was famous before the team idea caught on; me, because I was stubborn enough to want to win on my own.

Tomas was already sitting in the cafeteria as we walked through it, surrounded by the microphones and cameras. He was enjoying himself. I felt angry for a moment, then decided that it was fair enough. We waved to the media and went on to the showers. Let Tomas have his day of glory. He was so far down in the overall ratings that there was no way he could be the outright Tour du Système winner, even if he won tomorrow's and the final Stages by big margins.

Ernie Muldoon thought that the overall Grand Tour winner was going to be old and wily Ernest Muldoon, who had already won the Tour du Système an unprecedented five times; and I thought it was going to be me, Tracy

Collins, already identified in the media coverage as the Young Challenger; or maybe, as Ernest put it, the Young Pretender. Which made *him,* as I pointed out, the Old Pretender.

I had modeled my whole approach to the Tour on Ernie Muldoon, and now it was paying off. This was only my third year, but unless I was disqualified I was certain to be in the top five. My cumulative time for all the Stages actually placed me in the top three, but I hate to count them little chickens too soon.

The shower facilities were as crummy as we've grown to expect. You've got one of the premier athletic events of the Solar System, with coverage Earth-wide and Moon-wide, and still the showers at the end of each Stage are primitive. No blown air, no suction, no spin. All you get is soap, not-warm-enough water, drying cloths. It must be because we don't attract top video coverage. People are interested in us, but what sort of TV program can you build out of an event where each Stage runs anything up to thirty-six hours, and the competitors are just seen as little dots for most of the time? Maybe what the media need are a few deaths to spice things up, but so far the Tour has been lucky (or unlucky) that way.

Muldoon slapped me on the back as we were coming out of the shower area. "Three quarts of beer, three quarts of milk, thirty ounces of rare beef, and half a dozen potatoes from the original Owld Sod, and you'll not even notice that leg of yours. Are you with me, lad?"

"I'm with you—but not this minute. Don't you want to get a weather report first, for tomorrow?"

"A quick look, now. But I doubt if we'll see anything special. The wind forecasts for tomorrow have all been quiet. It's my bet we'll see stronger winds for the final Stage. Maybe a big flare-up."

Muldoon was casual, but he didn't really fool me. He had told me, a dozen times, that the solar wind forecast was the most important piece of a rider's knowledge—more relevant than local gravity anomalies or superaccurate trajectory calculations. We went over to the weather center and looked at the forty-eight-hour forecast. It was pretty calm. Unless there was a sudden and dramatic change, all the riders could get away with minimal radiation shielding.

That wasn't always the case. Two years ago, the second half of the Tour had taken place when there was a massive solar flare. The solar wind of energetic charged particles had been up by a factor of a hundred, and every rider added another two hundred kilos of radiation shielding. If you think that doesn't make a man groan, when every ounce of shielding has to be carried around with you like a snail carrying its shell—well, then you've never ridden the Tour.

Of course, you don't *have* to carry the shielding. That's a rider's choice. Four years ago, on the eleventh Stage of the Tour, Crazylegs Gerhart had done his own calculation of flare activity, and decided that the radiation level would drop nearly to zero a few minutes after the Stage began. When everybody else crawled away from Stage-start loaded down with extra shielding, Crazylegs zoomed off with a minimal load. He won the Stage by over two hours, but he just about glowed in the dark. The wind level hadn't become low at all. He docked so hot with radiation that no one wanted to touch him, and he was penalized a hundred and fifty minutes for exceeding the permissible dosage per Stage by ninety-two rads. Worse than that, they dumped him in the hospital to flush him out. He missed the rest of the Tour.

Every rider had his own cookbook method for guessing the optimal shielding load, just as everyone had his own private trajectory program and his own preferred way of pacing the race. There were as many methods as there were riders in the Tour.

Muldoon and I made notes of the wind—we'd check again, last thing at night—and then went back to the cafeteria. A few of the media people were still there. Without looking as though we were avoiding them, we loaded our

trays and went off to a quiet corner. We didn't want the
Newsies tonight. The next-to-last Stage was coming up
tomorrow morning, and it was a toughie. We had to ride
nearly twenty-five thousand kilometers, dropping in from
synchronous station, where we had docked today, to the
big Sports Central station in six-hour orbit.

Some people complain because we call it the Tour du
Système when the only part of the solar system we travel
is Earth-Moon space. But they've never ridden the Tour.
When you have, the six-hundred-thousand-kilometer
course seems quite long enough. And the standards of
competition get tougher every year. All the original Stage
records have been broken, then broken again. In a few
years' time it will be a million-kilometer Tour, and then
we'll zip way out past the moon before we start the in-
bound Stages.

Muldoon and I stuffed ourselves with food and drink—
you can't overfeed a Tour rider, no matter what you give
him—then went off quietly to bed. Two more days, I told
myself; then I'll raise more hell than the devil's salvage
party.

Next morning my first worry was my left thigh. It felt
fine—as it ought to; I'd spent an hour last night rubbing a
foul green embrocation into the muscles. I dressed and
headed for breakfast, wanting to beat the rush again.

"Well, Tracy, me boyo." It was Muldoon, appearing
out of nowhere and walking by my side. "An' are you still
thinking ye have the divil's own chanst of beating me?"

He can speak English as well as I can, but when he
senses there are media people around he turns in   the
most dreadful blarney-waffling stage Irishman you could
find.

"Easily." I nudged him in the ribs. "You're a tough
man, Muldoon, but your time has come. The bells will be
pealing out this time for handsome young Tracy Collins,
overall winner of the Grand Tour du Système." (So maybe
I respond to the media, too; I sounded confident, but Mul-

doon couldn't see my fingers, crossed on the side away from him.)

"Not while there's breath in this breast, me boy," he said. "An' 'tis time we was over an' havin' a word here with the grand Machiavellian Stage winner himself."

Muldoon stopped by Tomas Lili's table, where a couple of press who must have missed the Stage winner the previous night were sitting and interviewing. "Nice work, Tomas, me boy," Muldoon said, patting the yellow jersey. "An' where'd you be getting the idea of doin' that what yer did?"

A couple of media people switched their recorders back on. Tomas shrugged. "From you, Ernesto, where we all get our ideas. You were the one who decided that it was easier—and legal—to switch the ion drive around on the bike at midpoint rather than fight all the angular momentum you'd already built up in your wheels if you tried to turn the bike through a hundred and eighty degrees. I just built from there."

"Fair enough. But your trick won't work more than once, Tomas. We'll be ready."

Tomas grinned. He had won a Stage, and that's more than his Arianespace sponsors had expected of him. "What trick ever did work more than once, Ernesto? Once is enough."

The media rats at the table looked puzzled, and now one of them turned to Ernest Muldoon. "I don't understand you. What 'trick' is this you're talking about?"

Muldoon stared at the woman, noted she was young and pretty, and gestured at her to sit down. He poured everyone a liter of orange juice. We competitors sweat away seven or eight kilos, pedaling a Stage, and we have to make sure we start out flush-full with liquids. Tomas took the opportunity to slide away while Muldoon was pouring. He'd had his juice, and some of the other competitors who were still straggling in might have a less enlightened attitude toward Tomas's innovation of the previous Stage.

"D'you understand how we change directions round in

Clipper ships helped open new frontiers. Enthusiasts regard light ships as the potential clippers of a new age. (Photos: U.S. Coast Guard and Robert L. Staehle)

Rockets have taken men to the moon and landed picture-snapping robots on Mars and Venus. They have tossed Voyager space probes (carrying recordings of Bach and Chuck Berry) beyond the solar system (for the amusement of whatever aliens should recover them). But rockets are expensive throwaway vehicles that burn thousands of pounds of fuel in a few seconds, and then fizzle out. This is fine for lifting material from Earth to near space. But once you are in orbit, rockets start to look terribly inefficient. (Photo courtesy NASA)

Konstantin Tsiolkovsky (left), a Russian schoolteacher and researcher, was probably the first person to fully describe the theoretical foundations and practical benefits of solar sailing. In the 1920s, Fridrikh Tsander (right), another Russian, formulated mathematical relations governing the operation of a solar sail in space. (Photos courtesy Frederick Ordway collection)

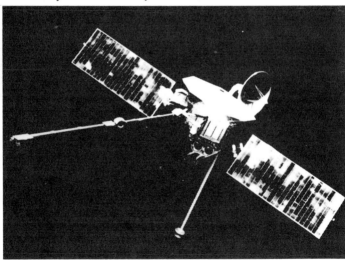

Mariner 10 was the first spacecraft to employ the pressure of light. Its large solar panels caught sunshine, and used its pressure to help maintain the vehicle's proper attitude. The onboard propellant thus saved was used to achieve a second flyby of Mercury. (Photo courtesy JPL)

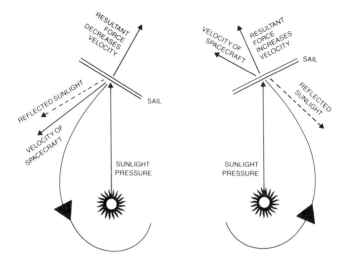

A solar sail is a mirror in space that reflects sunlight, and gets a tiny but very persistent push. In space there is no atmospheric drag, nothing to crumple a sail's delicate span, only sunlight to drive it faster and faster. Starting from a standstill and running directly away from the sun, a lightship with a sail a third of a mile on a side would accelerate to less than 10 miles an hour after one hour. After one day, however, it would be traveling at 200 miles an hour. After eighteen days the speed would be a mile a *second,* and the acceleration continues, free of charge. (Illustration courtesy The Planetary Society)

NASA began serious work on solar sailing in preparation for a possible mission to match orbits with Halley's Comet. (Photo by Eleanor Helin/JPL)

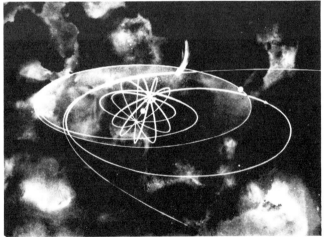

To rendezvous with the retrograde Halley's Comet, the sail would first travel inward toward the sun, where intense photon pressure coud be used to rotate its orbital plane. Following this, the sail travels outward, now in the proper direction to meet the comet. (Illustration courtesy JPL)

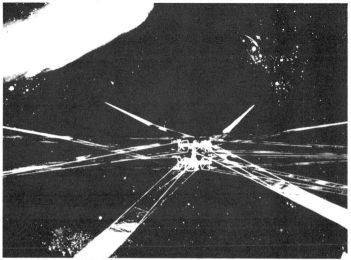

After considering several solar sail designs for the Halley's Comet rendezvous mission, NASA's preferred candidate was a sail type known as the heliogyro. Its performance was impressive, though its development risk was considered high. (Art courtesy JPL)

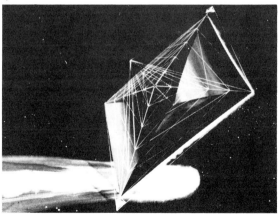

A more conservative design would involve a square sail. This variety will be used for the World Space Foundation's first test missions. (Art courtesy JPL)

The objective of the World Space Foundation Engineering Development Mission is to deploy and demonstrate the controllability of a 28-meter (93-foot) square solar sail. The sail will be deployed on diagonal crosspieces (spars) of welded lenticular beams which can be rolled up on a drum, but regain stiffness after being unrolled. Sail attitude will be controlled by two triangular vanes at the tips of one of the diagonals and by a movable boom that can be used to shift the vehicle's center of mass.

Fabrication of the first full-size prototype sail is complete. The photo on the right is of a half-scale engineering demonstration deployment in 1981. (Art: Jean-Luc Beghin. Photo: Richard Dowling)

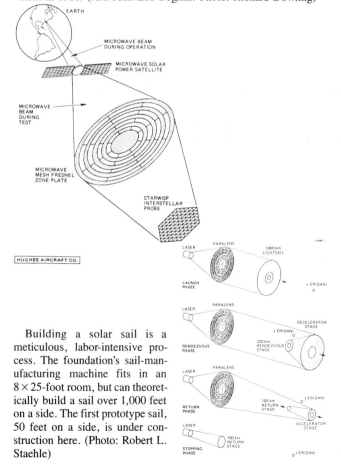

Building a solar sail is a meticulous, labor-intensive process. The foundation's sail-manufacturing machine fits in an 8 × 25-foot room, but can theoretically build a sail over 1,000 feet on a side. The first prototype sail, 50 feet on a side, is under construction here. (Photo: Robert L. Staehle)

Dr. Robert Forward's Starwisp concept is a sail pushed not by light but by microwaves, which are the same kind of energy as light, differing only in wave length. The microwaves are generated by a solar-powered maser in Earth orbit. Starwisp is 1 kilometer across but weighs only 20 grams, some of which is a tiny instrumented payload! It can reach Alpha Centauri in just 21 years. (Illustration courtesy Robert L. Forward and Hughes Research Laboratories)

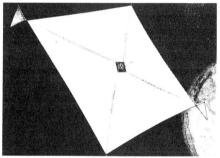

Another concept of Dr. Forward's is a three-stage concentric lightsail, which can send a manned crew on a round-trip mission to the star Epsilon Eridani, about 11 light-years away. A Gigantic solar-powered laser in the inner solar system provides the propulsive light pressure. This can be used to accelerate away from Earth, stop at the target, and accelerate back home again. The latter two feats are achieved by reflecting the laser light off the outer sail stage back toward the inner sail area. After 51 years the crew will return to Earth, having logged humanity's greatest adventure. (Illustration courtesy Robert L. Forward and Hughes Research Laboratories)

Carter Emmart Solar Sail Cargo Vessel (Mars base backup if the SSCV doesn't arrive in time) is expected to arrive on December 6, 1989.

On July 20, 1989, President George Bush chartered the manned exploration of the planet Mars as the long-term goal of the United States space program. Solar sails used for logistical supply can play a key role in the realization of this effort. (Art: Carter Emmart)

This book, and its creation to support the World Space Foundation's Solar Sail Project, was the brainchild of Robert J. Cesarone, a first-class trajectory designer and spacecraft navigator at the Jet Propulsion Laboratory. (Bob was one of the earliest volunteer staff members for the foundation.) *He worked as trajectory and maneuver analyst for the Voyager 2 flybys of Uranus and Neptune. Having run out of giant outer planets to explore, Mr. Cesarone has recently assumed new duties as the trajectory designer for the Mars Observer Mission.*

the middle of each Stage?'' Muldoon asked the reporter. One reason Ernie is so popular with the Press is that he's never too busy to talk to them and explain to them. I noticed that now he had her hooked he had dropped the stage-Irish accent.

"I guess so. But I don't understand *why*. You're out in empty space, between the Stage points, and you've pedaled hard to get the wheels rotating as fast as you can. And then you shift everything around!''

"Right. An' here's the why. Suppose the rider—say, Trace here, the likely lad—hasn't reached the halfway point yet, and let's for the moment ignore any fancy maneuvers at Stage turn points. So he's pedaling like a madman—the only way he knows—and the wheels are whizzing round, and he's built up a voltage of something respectable on the rotating Wimshurst disks—say, a couple of million volts. That voltage goes into accelerating the ion stream out of the back of the bike, eh? The faster he pedals, the higher the voltage, the better the exhaust velocity on the ion drive, and so the faster goes our lad Tracy. And he's *got* to get that exhaust velocity as high as he can, because he's only allowed fifty kilos of fuel per Stage, total. All right?''

"Oh, yes.'' The lady looked into Muldoon's slightly squinty eyes and seemed ready to swoon with admiration. He beamed at her fondly. I was never sure that Ernie Muldoon followed through with a woman while we were riding the Tour—but I'm damned sure if he *didn't* have them between Stages, he saved up credits and used them all when the Tour was over.

"All right.'' Muldoon ran his hand out along the table-top. "Here's Trace. He's been zooming along in a straight line, faster and faster. But now he gets to the halfway point of the Stage, an' now he's got to worry about how he'll get to the finish. See, it's no good arriving at the final docking and zooming right on through—you have to *stop*, or you're disqualified. So now Trace has a different problem. He has to worry about how he's going to *decelerate* for the rest of the run, and finish at a standstill, or close to it, when the bike gets to the docking point. The old-fashioned way—that means up to seven years ago—was pretty simple. Trace here would have turned the whole bike round, so that the ion drive was pointing the other way, toward the place he wanted to get to, and he'd keep on pedaling like the dickens. And if he'd planned well, or was just dumb lucky, he'd be slowed down by the drive just the right amount when he got the final docking, so he could hit slap against the buffers at the maximum permitted speed. Sounds good?''

She nodded. ''Fine.'' I didn't know if she was talking about the explanation, or Ernie-the-Lech Muldoon's hand resting lightly across hers. ''But what's wrong with that way of doing it?'' she went on. ''It sounds all right to me.''

Someday they're going to assign reporters to the Tour du Système who are more than twenty-two years old and who have some faint idea before they begin of the event they are supposed to be covering. It will ruin Muldoon's sex life, but it will stop me from feeling like an antique myself. All the young press people ask the same damned questions, and they all nod in the same half-witted way when they get the answers.

I wanted to see how Ernest handled the next bit. Somehow he was going to have to get across to Sweet Young Thing the concept of angular momentum.

''Problem is,'' he said, ''while the wheels are spinning fast the bike don't want to turn. Those wheels are heavy glassite disks, rubbing against each other, and they're like flywheels, and so the bike wants to stay lined up just the way it is. So in the old days, the biker would have to stop the wheels—or at least slow 'em down a whole lot—then turn the bike around, and start pedaling again to get the wheels going. All the time that was happening, there was no potential difference on the Wimshurst's, no ion drive, and no acceleration. Big waste of time, and also for the second half of the Stage you were flying ass-backwards. So I did the obvious thing. I mounted a *double* ion drive on my bike, one facing forward, one facing back—turned out that the rules don't *quite* say you can't have more than one drive. They only say you can't have more than one ion drive on your bike *in use at one time*. They don't say you can't have two, and switch 'em in the middle of the Stage. Which is what I did. And won, for about two Stages, until everybody else did the same thing."

"But what was it that Tomas Lili did? He seems to have come up with something new."

"He installed an ion drive that had more than just the two positions, fore and aft. His can be directed in pretty much any way he wants to. So, first thing that Tomas did on the last Stage, he went off far too fast—at a crazy speed, we all thought. And naturally he got ahead of all of us. *Then* what he did was to direct his ion beam at whoever was close behind him. The ions hit whoever he was pointing at—me, or Trace, or one of the others—and just about canceled out our own drives completely. We were throwing a couple of tenths of a gram of ion propellant out of the *back* of the bike at better than ten kilometers a second, but we were being hit on the front by the same amount, traveling at the same speed. Net result: no forward acceleration for us. It didn't *hurt* us, physically, 'cause we're all radiation-shielded. But it slowed us. By the time we realized why we were doing so badly, he was gone. Naturally, Tomas wasn't affected, except for the tiny bit he sacrificed because his exhaust jet wasn't pointing exactly aft." Muldoon shrugged. "Neat trick. Works once—next time we'll stay so far out of his wake he'll lose more forward acceleration turning off-axis to hit us than he'll gain."

"You explain everything so clearly!" Their hands were still touching.

"Always try to help. But we've got to get ready for the Stage now. Will you be there at the finish?"

"Of course! I wouldn't miss it for anything."

Muldoon patted her hand possessively. "Then why don't

we get together after it, and we can go over the action together? Next to last Stage, there ought to be fireworks.''

"Oh, yes! Please.''

As we left for the start dock, I shook my head at Muldoon. "I don't expect any particular fireworks today. No tricky course change, no solar flares—it should be the tamest leg of the Tour.''

He stared back at me, owl-eyed, "And did I say the action would be on the course, boyo?''

We walked side by side to the main staging area. In twenty minutes we would be on our way. I could feel the curious internal tension that told me it was Tour-time again—more than that, it was the final Stages of the Tour. Something in my belly was winding me up like an old-fashioned watch. That was fine. I wanted to hang there in that start space all ready to explode to action. I touched Muldoon lightly on the shoulder—*Good luck, Muldoon*, it meant; *but don't beat me*—then I went on to my station.

There was already a strange atmosphere in the preparation chamber. As the Tour progresses, that strangeness grows and grows. I had noticed it years ago and never understood it, until little Alberto Maimonides, who is probably the best sportswriter living (my assessment) or ever (his own assessment), sampled that changing atmosphere before the Stages, and explained it better than I ever could. Either one of Muldoon's tree-trunk thighs has far more muscle on it than Maimonides's whole body, but the little man understood the name of the game. "At the beginning of the Tour,'' he said to me one day, "there are favorites, but everyone may be said to have an equal chance of winning. As the Tour progresses, the cumulative time and penalties of each rider are slowly established. And so two groups emerge: those with the potential to win the whole thing, and those with no such potential. Those two different potentials polarize the groups more and more, building tension in one, releasing tension in the other. Like the Wimshurst disks that you drive as you turn the pedals, the competitors build up their own massive potential difference. Beyond the halfway mark in the Tour, I can tell you in which group a competitor lies—without speaking a word to him! If a rider has a chance of winning, it is seen in the tension in neck and shoulders, in the obsessive attention to weather data, in the faraway look in the man's eyes. I can tell you at once which group a rider is in.''

"And can you—'' I began.

"No,'' he interrupted me. "What I cannot do, Trace, to save my life, is tell you who will win. That will be, by definition, the best man.''

I wanted to be that best man, more than I had ever wanted anything. I was thinking of Alberto Maimonides as I lifted open the shell of my bike and began to inspect the radiation shielding. It was all fine, a thin layer in anticipation of a quiet day without much solar wind. The final Stage was another matter—the forecasts said we would see a lot more radiation; but that was another day, and until we finished today's effort the final Stage didn't matter at all.

The fuel tank came next. The competitors were not allowed to charge the fuel tank themselves, and the officials who did it always put in an exact fifty kilograms, correct to the microgram. But it didn't stop every competitor worrying over the tank, afraid that he had been shortchanged and would run out of fuel in the middle of the Stage. People occasionally used their fuel too fast, and ran out before the end of a Stage. Without ion-drive fuel they were helpless. They would drift miserably around near the docking area, until someone went out and fished them in. Then they would be the butt of all the other competitors, subject to the same old jokes: "What's the matter, Tish, got thirsty and been drinking the heavy water again?'' "You're four hours late, Sven, she gave your dance to someone else.'' "Jacques, my lad, we all warned you about premature ejaculation.''

I climbed into the shell and checked my trajectory. It was too late to change anything now, except how hard I would pedal at each time in the Stage. It would need something exceptional to change even that. I had planned this Stage long ago, how I would pace it, how much effort I would put in at each breakpoint. I slipped my feet into the pedal stirrups, gripped the handlebars hard, looked straight ahead, and waited. I was hyperventilating, drawing in the longest, deepest breaths I could.

The starting signal came as an electronic beep in my headset. While it was still sounding I was pedaling like mad, using low gears to get initial torques on the Wimshursts. After a few seconds, I reached critical voltage, the ion drive triggered on, and I was moving. Agonizingly slowly at first—a couple of thousandths of a g isn't much and it takes a while to build up any noticeable speed—but I was off.

All the way along the starting line, other bikers were doing exactly the same thing. There were various tricks to riding the Tour in the middle part of a Stage, but very little choice at the beginning. You rode as hard as your body would stand, and got the best speed as early as possible. Once you were moving fast you could relax a little bit, and let the bike coast. At the very end of the Stage, you made the same effort in reverse. Now you wanted to hold your speed as long as possible, to minimize your total time for the Stage. But if you had been too energetic at the beginning, or if your strength failed you at the end, you were in real trouble. Then you'd not be able to decelerate your bike enough. Either you'd shoot right through the docking area and whip out again into open space, or you'd demolish the buffers by hitting them at far more than the legal maximum. Both those carried disastrous penalties.

After half an hour of frantic pedaling I was feeling pretty pleased. My leg was giving me no trouble at all—touch wood, though there was none within thirty thousand miles. I could see the main competition, and it was where I wanted it to be. Muldoon was a couple of kilometers behind, Rafael Rodriguez of the NASA team was almost alongside him, and Tomas Lili was already far in the rear. I looked ahead, and settled down to the long grind.

This was a Stage with few tricky elements. During the Tour we started from low earth orbit, went all the way to L-4 in a series of thirty variable-length Stages, and then looped back in halfway to the moon before we began the drive to Earth. Some Stages were geometrically complex, as much in the calculations as the legs. This one was the sort of Stage that I was thoroughly comfortable with. The only real variables today were physical condition and natural stamina. I was in the best shape I had ever been, and I was convinced that if my legs and determination held out I had everyone beat.

Twenty-six hours later I was even more convinced. We had passed the crossover point long ago, and I had done it without any complication. I could still see Muldoon and Rodriguez in my viewfinder, but they had not closed the gap at all. If anything, I might have gained a few more seconds on them. No one else was even in sight. There was a terrible urge to ease off, but I could not do it. It was *cumulative* time that decided the Tour winner, and Muldoon and Rodriguez had both started this Stage nearly a minute ahead of me. I wanted to make up for that today, and more. The yellow jersey might be enough for Tomas Lili, but not for me. I wanted the whole pie.

I had taken my last liquid three hours ago, draining the juice bottle and then jettisoning it to save mass. Now my throat was dry and burning, and I'd have given anything for a quarter liter of water. I put those thoughts out of my head, and pedaled harder.

It turned out that I left my final sprint deceleration almost too late. Twenty-five kilometers out I realized that I was approaching the final docking area too fast. I would slam into the buffers at a speed over the legal limit. I put my head down, ignored the fact that my legs had been pumping for nearly twenty-seven hours straight, and rode until I thought my heart and lungs would burst. I didn't even see the docks or the final markers. I guess my eyes were closed. All I heard was the loud *ping* that told of an arrival at legal speed. And then I was hanging on the handlebars, wishing some kind person would shoot me and put me out of my misery.

My chest was on fire, my throat was too dry to breathe, my heart was racing up close to two hundred beats a minute, and my legs were spasming with cramps. I clung to the handlebars, and waited. Finally, when I heard a second *ping* through my helmet's radio, I knew the second man was in. I looked up at the big-board readout. It was Muldoon, following me in by one minute and seventeen seconds. He had started the day one minute and fourteen seconds ahead of me on the cumulative total. I had won the Stage—and I was now the overall Tour leader.

I groaned with pain, released my harness, and cracked open my bike. I forced a big grin onto my face for the media—more like a grimace of agony, but no one would know the difference—and managed to climb out onto the docking facility just as though I was feeling light and limber. Then I sauntered along to where Muldoon was slowly opening his bike. One cheery smile for the benefit of the cameras, and I was reaching in to lift him lightly clear of the bike.

He glared up at me. "You big ham, Trace. What was your margin?"

"One minute and seventeen seconds."

"Ah." It was more a groan of physical agony than mental as he tried to stand up on the dock. His thigh muscles, like mine, were still unknotting after over a day of continuous effort. "So you're ahead then. Three seconds ahead. And with a new Stage record. Damn it."

"Thanks. You're just a terrific loser, Muldoon."

"Right. And it takes one to know one, Trace." He did a couple of deep knee-bends. "What about the others? Where did they finish?"

"Schindell came in two minutes after you. He's about four minutes behind us, overall. Something must have happened to Rodriguez, because he's still not in."

"Leg cramps. We were riding side by side for a long

time, then he dropped way behind. I'm pretty sure he had to stop pedaling.''

"So he's out of the running."

We stared at each other. "So it's me an' thee," said Muldoon after a few moments. "Barring a miracle or a disaster, one of us will be *it.*"

It! Overall Tour Winner! I wanted that so much I could taste it.

Muldoon saw my face. "You're getting there, Trace," he said. "Muscle and heart and brains will only take you so far. You have to *want* it bad enough."

I saw *his* face, too. His eyes were bloodshot, and sunk so far back that they were little glowing sparks of blue at the end of dark tunnels. If I had reached a long way into myself to ride this Stage, how far down had Muldoon gone? Only he knew that. He *wanted it,* as much as I did.

"You're getting old, Ernie," I said. "Alberto Maimonides says that the Tour's a young man's game."

"And what does he know, that little Greek faggot!" Muldoon respected Maimonides as much as I did, but you'd never know it if you heard them talk about each other. "He's talking through his skinny brown neck. The Tour's a *man's* game, not a *young* man's game. Go an' get your yellow jersey, Trace, and show your fine profile to the media."

"What about you? They'll want to see you as well— we're neck and neck for overall Tour position. How long since nonteam riders have been one and two in Tour status?"

"Never happened before. But I've got work to do. Weather reports to look at, strategy to plan. You can handle the damned media, Trace—time you learned how. And I'll tell you what." He had been scowling at me, but now he smiled. "You look at all the pretty young reporters, and you pick out the one who'd be my favorite. An' you can give her one for me."

He stumped off along the dock. I looked after him before I went to collect the yellow jersey that I would wear for the final Stage, and pose with it for the waiting media-men. Ernie hadn't given up yet. There was brooding and scheming inside that close-cropped head. He was like a dormant volcano now, and there was one more Stage to go. Maybe he had one more eruption left in him. But what could it possibly be?

I was still asking that question when we lined up for the beginning of the final Stage. Yellow jersey or no yellow jersey, I hadn't slept well last night. I dreamed of the swoop toward the finishing line, with its massed cameras and waiting crowds. There would be hordes of space tugs, filled with spectators, and video crews from every station on Earth or moon. And who would they be homing in on, to carry off and interview until he could be interviewed no more?

In the middle of the night I had awakened and wandered off to where the rows of bikes were sitting under twenty-four-hour guard. The rules here were very simple. I could go to my bike, and do what I liked with it; but I could not touch, or even get too close to, the bike of another competitor. The history of the rule was something I could only guess at. It made psychological sense. No competitor wanted *anybody* else touching his beloved bike. We suffered the organizers to fill our fuel tanks, because we had no choice; but we hovered over and watched every move they made, to make sure they did not damage so much as a square millimeter of paint.

The bike shed was quiet when I got there. A couple of competitors were inside their bikes, fiddling with nozzles, or changing the position of juice bottles or viewfinders or computers. It was all just nerves coming to the fore. The changes they were making would not improve their time by a tenth of a second. Ernie Muldoon was inside his bike, too, also fiddling with bits and pieces. He stopped when he saw me, and nodded.

"Can't sleep either?"

I shrugged. "It's not easy. Plenty of time for sleep tomorrow night, when the Tour's over."

"Nobody wants to sleep when it's over. We'll all be partying, winners and losers."

"Wish it were tomorrow now."

He nodded. "I know that feeling. Good luck, Trace."

"Same to you, Ernie."

I meant it. And he meant it. But as I sat at the starting line, my feet already in the pedal stirrups, I knew what that well-wishing meant. Neither of us wanted anything bad to happen to the other; all we wanted was to *win*. That was the ache inside. I looked around my bike for the last time. The radiation shielding was all in position. As we had surmised the day before yesterday, the weather had changed. There was a big spike of solar activity sluicing through the inner system, and a slug of radiation was on its way. It would hit us close to the halfway point of the final Stage, then would diminish again when the Tour was over. The maximum radiation level was nowhere near as high as it had been in the Tour two years ago, but it was enough to make us all carry a hefty load of shielding. The prospect of hauling that along for twenty-six thousand kilometers was not one I was looking forward to.

The electronic beep sounded in my helmet. We were off. A hundred and six riders—we had lost thirty-four along the way to injuries and disqualification—began to pedal madly. After half a minute of frenzied, apparently unproductive activity, the line slowly moved away from the starting port. The airlock had been opened ten minutes before. We were heading out into hard vacuum, and the long, solitary ride to the finish. No one was allowed to send us any information during the Stage, or to respond to anything other than an emergency call from a competitor.

The optimal trajectory for this Stage had been talked about a good deal when the competitors held their evening bull sessions. There were two paths that had similar projected energy budgets. The choice between them depended on the type of race that a competitor wanted to ride. If he was very confident that he would have a strong final sprint deceleration, then trajectory one was optimal. It was slightly better overall. But if a rider was at all suspicious of his staying power at the end, trajectory two was safer.

The two trajectories diverged early in the Stage, and roughly two-thirds of the riders opted for the second and more conservative path. I and maybe thirty others, praying that our legs and lungs would stand it, went for the tougher and faster route.

Muldoon did neither of these things. I knew the carapace of his red-and-black bike as well as I knew my own, and I was baffled to see him diverging from everyone else, on another path entirely. I had looked at that trajectory myself—we all had. And we had ruled it out. It wasn't a disastrous choice, but it offered neither the speed of the one I was on nor the security of the path most riders had chosen.

Muldoon must know all that. So where was he going?

I had plenty of time to puzzle in the next twenty-four hours, and not much else to occupy my attention. Before we reached midpoint, where I reversed my drive's direction, all the other riders in my group had diminished to dots in my viewfinder. They were out of it, far behind. I had decided that after today's Stage I would take a year to rest and relax, but I wouldn't relax now. I pushed harder than I had ever pushed. As the hours wore on I became more aware of the radiation shielding, the stone that I was perpetually pushing uphill. A *necessary* stone. Outside my bike was a sleet of deadly solar particles.

Even though the group of competitors who had ridden my trajectory were just dots in the distance behind me, I didn't feel at all relaxed. On the Tour, you *never* relax until the final Stage is ridden, the medals have been awarded, *and* the overall winner has performed the first step-out at the Grand Dance.

At the twenty-third hour I looked off with my little telescope in another direction. If anyone in the slow, conser-

vative group had by some miracle managed to ride that
trajectory faster than anyone had ever ridden it, he ought
to be visible now in the region that I was scanning. I
looked and saw nothing, nothing but vacuum and hard,
unwinking stars.

The final docking area was at last in sight, a hundred
kilometers ahead of me. I could begin to pick up little dots
of ships, hovering close to the dock. And unless I was
very careful, I was going to shoot right through them and
past them. I had to shed velocity. That meant I had to
pedal harder than ever to slow my bike to the legal docking
speed.

I bent for one last effort. As I did so, I caught sight of
something in my rear viewfinder.

A solitary bike. Red and black—Muldoon. But going far
too fast. He was certainly going to overtake me, but he
was equally certainly going to be unable to stop by the
time he reached the dock. He would smash on through,
and either be disqualified or given such a whopping time
penalty he would drop to third or fourth place.

I felt sorry for him. He had done the almost impossible,
and ridden that inefficient alternate trajectory to within a
few seconds of catching me. But it was all wasted if he
couldn't dock; and at the speed he was going, that would
be just impossible.

Then I had to stop thinking of him, and start thinking
of myself. I put my head down and drove the cranks
around, gradually increasing the rate. The change in deceleration was too small for me to feel, but I knew it was
there. The ions were pushing me back, easing my speed.
I was vaguely aware of Muldoon's bike moving silently
past mine—still going at an impossible pace.

And so was I. It was the mass of all the shielding, like
a millstone around my bike. The inertia of that hundred
extra kilos of shielding material wanted to keep going,
dragging me and the bike with it. *I had to slow down.*

I pedaled harder. Harder. The docking area was ahead.
Harder! I was still too fast. I directed the bike to the line

instinctively, all my mind and will focused on my pumping legs.

Stage line. Docking guide. Docking. Docked!

I heard the *ping!* in my helmet that told of a docking within the legal speed limit. I felt a moment of tremendous satisfaction. *All over. I've won the Tour!* Then I rested my head on my handlebars and sat for a minute, waiting for my heart to stop smashing out of my rib cage.

Finally I lifted my head. I found I was looking at Muldoon's red-and-black racing bike, sitting quietly in a docking berth next to mine. He was slumped over the handlebars, not moving. He looked dead. The marker above his bike showed he had made a legal docking. Impossible!

His bike looked different, but I was not sure how. I unlocked my harness, cracked the bike seals, and forced myself outside onto the dock. As usual my legs were jello. I wobbled my way along to Muldoon's bike. I knocked urgently on the outside.

"Muldoon! Are you all right?" I was croaking, dry-throated. I didn't seem to have enough moisture left in my body for one spit.

I hammered again. For a few seconds there was no response at all. Then the cropped head slowly lifted, and I was staring down into a puffy pair of eyes. Muldoon didn't seem to recognize me. Finally he nodded, and reached to unlock his harness. When the bike opened, I helped him out. He was too far gone to stand.

"I'm all right, Trace," he said. "I'm all right." He sounded terrible, anything but all right.

I took another look at his bike. Now I knew why it looked different. "Muldoon, you've lost your shielding. We have to get you to a doctor."

He shook his head. "You don't need to. I didn't get an overdose. I didn't *lose* that shielding. I shed it on purpose."

"But the radiation levels—"

"Are down. You saw the forecasts for yourself—the

storm was supposed to peak during the Stage and then run way down. I spent most of last night fixing the bike so I could get rid of the shielding when the solar flux died away enough. That happened six hours ago."

I suddenly realized how he had managed that tremendous deceleration at the end of the race. Without an extra hundred kilos of shielding dragging him along, it was easy. I could have done the same thing.

And then I felt sick. Any one of us could have done what Muldoon had done—if we'd just been smart enough. The rules let you jettison anything you didn't want; empty juice bottles, or radiation shielding. The only requirement is that you don't interfere with any other rider. Muldoon had thrown a lot of stuff away, but by choosing a trajectory where no one else was riding, he had made sure he could not be disqualified for interference.

"You did it again," I said. "How far ahead of me were you when you docked?"

He shrugged. "Two seconds, three seconds. I'm not sure. I may not have done it, Trace. I needed three seconds. You may still have won it."

But I was looking at his face. There was a look of deep, secret joy there that not even old stoneface Muldoon could hide. He had won. And I had lost. Again.

I knew. He knew. And he knew I knew.

"It's my last time, Trace," he said quietly. "This one means more than you can imagine to me. I'll not win any more. Maimonides is quite right, the Tour's a young man's game. But you've got lots of time, years and years."

I had been wrong about the moisture in my body. There was plenty, enough for it to trickle down my cheeks. "Damn it, I don't *want* it in years and years, Ernie, I want it *now*."

"I know you do. And that's why I'm sure you'll get it *then*." He sighed. "It took me eight tries before I won, Trace. Eight tries! I thought I'd never do it! You're still only on your third Tour." Ernie Muldoon reached out his arm and draped it around my shoulders. "Come on now, lad. Win or lose, the Tour's over for this year. Give a poor old man a hand, and let's the two of us go and talk to them damned media types together.''

I was going to say no, because I couldn't possibly face the cameras with tears in my eyes. But then I looked at his face, and knew I was wrong. I could face them crying. Ernie Muldoon was still my model. Anything he could do, I could do.

Charles Sheffield is Chief Scientist of Earth Satellite Corporation and serves on its Board of Directors. He is past-President of the American Astronautical Society, past-President of the Science Fiction Writers of America, a Fellow of the American Astronautical Society, a Fellow of the British Interplanetary Society, and a Distinguished Lecturer of the American Institute of Aeronautics and Astronautics.

In addition to ninety papers on orbit computation, earth resources, large-scale computer systems, and general relativity, Dr. Sheffield's published works include the best-selling volumes on space remote sensing, *Earthwatch* and *Man on Earth*, the reference volume *Space Careers*, nine science fiction novels, seventy short stories, and four story collections.

I might add that one of Charles's novels, *The Web Between the Worlds*, dealt with a wonderful and dramatic idea that was also conveyed, in the same year, in a little book called *Fountains of Paradise* by yours truly. The idea, of course, was the "skyhook" space elevator, which might work very well indeed with solar sails.

Lightsail

by
Scott E. Green

Sails unfold,
into space,
continent wide
       wings of
high tech lace.
Spun so fine
to snare
the pulse of light
hold the photon
       a nanosecond pause
fling it back
    into the sun.
Moving a spacecraft
      softly
      gracefully
above the wells of gravity.

Scott E. Green has been active as a poet in the science fiction, fantasy, and horror genres. His work has appeared in leading commercial and small press magazines. Recently Greenwood Press/Praeger Books published his reference work on genre poetry, *Science Fiction Fantasy and Horror Poetry. A Resource Guide*. He also wrote the essay on poetry for the *New Encyclopedia of Science Fiction*, edited by Professor James Gunn.

Rescue at L-5

by
Kevin J. Anderson and Doug Beason

Encased in the vast organic solar-sail creature, Ramis watched through the monitors, studying his course. Earth seemed like an oil painting below him, reaching out to swallow him in its oceans.

But the sail creature's orbit approached no closer than two Earth radii at its nearest point, then swooped back out again toward L-5. Leaving the planet behind, they climbed toward the *Orbitech 1* colony.

Ramis shifted his position in the cramped cyst as the sail creature tacked the solar wind. He had no room to move, no place to stretch. After sitting for a week, it began to frustrate him to tears. He took paranoid care not to bump or damage the seven sail-creature embryos at his feet.

The boy snapped open the faceplate of his spacesuit and filled his lungs with humid air. Ramis didn't want to leave the helmet open long; hard radiation still penetrated even the sail creature's tough exoskeleton—but the fresh oxygen in the cavity drove back the claustrophobic dankness for a while. The air smelled wet from the thick wall kelp growing unchecked inside the cyst. On the rescue mission he had brought several kelp nodules, enough to start a forest growing along the walls of *Orbitech 1,* and it gave him food to eat for the journey.

Ramis groped around the spongy cyst until he found the joystick controls for the external video camera. Swiveling the camera, he focused on the bright pinpoint of the L-5 colony waxing closer and closer. A week ago the starving colony had been invisible against the stars. Now under high magnification he could just make out the two counterrotating wheels of *Orbitech 1*. Also at L-5, the Soviet station revolved slowly into view on the fringe of the gravity well.

After the war, time was growing short for them—for him, for everybody.

"Calling *Orbitech 1!*" Ramis squinted at the screen in front of him. Why weren't they answering? "*Orbitech 1*, come in please."

Ramis muttered under his breath. He had been talking to himself too much in the past few days. "How am I supposed to rescue you if you won't answer?" He snapped the helmet shut.

Maybe his radio's gain was too weak. Maybe he had used the batteries too much over the past few days, discussing his orbit with people on the Filipino colony, the *Aguinaldo*—his home—just to quell his loneliness and isolation. As he swung close to Earth, he had scanned the radio bands. Briefly he caught a burst of political rhetoric, but it faded into static before he could make sense of it.

To keep himself occupied, he squinted at the cross hairs on the video screen. The camera angle constantly changed to account for the *Orbitech* colony's motion. By centering the image in the cross hairs, the sail creature would tack ahead and arrive at the right position to intercept the colony in its orbit. He was off course by only a fraction of a radian, but with thousands of kilometers left to travel, he would miss *Orbitech 1* with room to spare.

Time to steer again. Ramis withdrew a small knife, then looked at the cross hairs, judging the angle from inside the cyst. With the point of the blade he poked the creature's sensitive internal membrane.

The cyst tightened. Ramis felt a tension, a ripple, as the sail's reflexes turned it away from the knife's prick. The lumbering movement seemed to take years, but the L-5 colony finally drifted to the center of the cross hairs again.

Once more, he tried counting stars, then making up

rhymes, reciting the Biblical passages he had had to memorize during catechism years before. Anything to make him forget about the boredom for a while, or to forget about his incredibly slim chances of ever returning to the *Aguinaldo*. If he could only stretch his legs.

Ramis remembered coming by accident upon the *Aguinaldo*'s president, Yoli Magsaysay, four months before. The leader stood staring out a greenhouse window, mesmerized by the image of Earth—from here the planet shone blue and beautiful, looking unscarred from its last war. In the harsh shadows, Magsaysay appeared thin, with mottled brown skin and flecks of gray and white peppering his bushy hair. He moved painfully on joints calcified from years in low gravity.

Unaware of Ramis, Magsaysay muttered to himself. "We've always been able to find plenty of reasons for war, no matter how many problems we eliminate. A terrorist explodes an atomic weapon, and the fingerpointing escalates—"

Ramis startled the leader. "But they just can't leave us here to starve! How are we supposed to survive without the supply ships?"

Magsaysay turned back to Earth. "They have no choice. The war did not destroy them, but it caused enough damage that they cannot possibly send any more ships up here. It will be ten or more years before they can rebuild. They must conquer their own problems before they can come back for us.

"We people on the Lagrange colonies are just more casualties in another war. Our numbers are already written in their books. We are on our own."

Ramis had a frightening, claustrophobic realization of just how *isolated* they were on the colonies, stranded with no ships even to get to each other or back to Earth. The last shuttle transport had been hijacked by a gang of desperate people from *Orbitech 1* and had crash-landed near Clavius Base on the moon. The Lagrange colonies' few feeble attempts at self-sustenance—their symbolic but tiny hydroponic fields of wheat, corn, and rice—would not be enough to last them very long.

But the Filipino bioengineering mavericks kept the people on the *Aguinaldo* alive, just barely, with a strain of experimental wall kelp and the sail creatures developed years before.

The wall kelp tasted bland, but it was better than no food. Ramis and all the others had been eating nothing else for four months now, ever since the supplies from Earth had dwindled away. Cut off and isolated at L-4, the *Aguinaldo* had listened to the transmissions from *Orbitech 1*. The pitiful pleas for help growing gradually more desperate; the grim news of starvation, rioting, and even hints of cannibalism. The Soviets in their colony had fallen silent soon after the war. The Filipino colonists could do nothing but listen—they had no ship to send, no help to offer.

Until now.

Inside the sail creature, looking at *Orbitech 1*, Ramis felt as if he were falling, falling down toward the station. Space gave him no reference, no horizon, no gravity. The direction ''down'' was where things fell when you dropped them . . . but out in space, everywhere was ''down.''

Ramis groped out to touch the walls of the cyst, searching for stability, trying to fight off the sickening vertigo. He would be falling forever because there was no place to land.

He squeezed shut his eyes. Sleep came, and with it, tumultuous memories. . . .

Being at Jumpoff, at one end cap of the *Aguinaldo*'s cylinder, was like standing at the bottom of a gargantuan well. The lightaxis stretched above as Ramis floated at one end of the zero-G core. He squinted to see the other end, ten kilometers away. The column of fiberoptic threads making up the lightaxis glowed with raw sunlight. Clusters of children played in the core, punctuated by sail creatures darting in and out, keeping the youngsters away from the

lightaxis. Adults circumnavigated the rim, leaping from
bouncer to bouncer in an ever-accelerating race around the
circumpond.

Living areas curled up around the cylindrical colony's
side, snaking across the fields, the rice paddies, stadiums,
streams, and the circumferential Sibyuan Sea. Fields of
taro and abaca dotted the living areas. Experimental sec-
tors of wall kelp covered the remainder of the *Aguinaldo,*
allowing little of the colony's metallic structure to show.

Revolving around the long lightaxis, Ramis's whole
world seemed as though it might collapse and fall to the
center. The sight always made him dizzy.

Pushing off, Ramis closed his eyes. As a child, he could
always escape here, be alone. His thoughts drifted to the
Council of Twenty. After all the talk, all the rhetoric, they
finally had decided to try to help the L-5 colonies.

Dr. Sandovaal had bullied them to try a desperate attempt, exploiting the sail creatures. The creatures had both
mitochondria and chloroplasts within their cell walls: They
were both plant and animal, a one-in-a-million accidental
success from the bioengineering labs. Somehow everything had worked exactly right; everything fit together, everything functioned as it should.

And when exposed to vacuum, Sandovaal argued, the
creatures would still metabolize, using the hard solar radiation for direct photosynthesis. It would be the sail creature's last gasp for survival—its fins would elongate in a
feeble attempt to maximize its light-collecting area for
photosynthesis. The sail creatures would metamorphose
and take on their plant attributes, becoming a largely im-
mobile receptor of solar radiation.

Working in vacuum, the bioengineers had attempted to
accelerate the growth of three of the creatures. As the
Aguinaldo's chief scientist, Dr. Sandovaal directed the
ejection of the first anesthetized creature. It had exploded
from its own internal pressure, unable to compensate for
the vacuum fast enough.

On the next attempt, they did not drug the second creature into complete dormancy—and it successfully expanded in the cold vacuum. But its metamorphosis had been too fast, too violent, for the restraining hooks connecting it to the *Aguinaldo*. The sail creature had torn free and drifted away.

Ramis was there peering out the window plates as two engineers wearing manned-maneuvering units jetted after the still-growing sail, but they could not recapture the creature and turn it around without damaging the thin membrane. The two engineers looked like tiny dolls as they floated back to the docking bay, side by side.

But the third creature had survived the accelerated metamorphosis. The bioengineers oriented the sail creature's proto-sails edge-on to the sun to prevent the solar photons from accelerating the sail before the process was complete. Day by day the creature's fins spread out, becoming vast cell-thin sails, immense and opaque, hundreds of kilometers to a side, as the creature desperately tried to soak up light. The main bodily core became rigid and exceedingly tough, like an organic "hull."

Ramis would have to ride inside, go to the L-5 colony.

President Magsaysay, Ramis's mentor, had gone out of his way to be with the boy, trying to talk to him. But Ramis wanted to be alone, to think. After all, Ramis had been picked for the mission—he deserved some time alone.

Now he ached for any company at all.

"What we want to do is this, so pay attention, boy." Dr. Sandovaal rapped on the surface of the stereotank with his old-fashioned pointer stick. The image in the tank jiggled, then focused again into a diagram of the Earth-moon system.

"When we release you from the *Aguinaldo,* you will turn the sail so that it faces the sun, taking the full momentum of the solar photons. You will then be moving 'backward' in orbit, relative to L-4. In about three hours, this will provide enough braking to slow you from our normal orbital velocity down to three kilometers per second. You must then turn your sail edgewise. You will drop like a stone toward Earth, skim past it at a distance of about an extra Earth radius, and then head back up to where you started.''

On the stereotank a blue dashed line appeared, tracing Ramis's planned trajectory. ''But while you've been going down and coming back up, the moon, L-4, and L-5 have been continuing their own orbits. By the time you return to the starting point, L-5 will be there instead of L-4.''

Ramis studied the diagram. ''So I am just killing time by going down to Earth? Waiting for the other points to change position?''

President Magsaysay watched Ramis, looking troubled, but Ramis ignored him, keeping a brave, calm expression on his face. Sandovaal rapped his fingers on the polished tabletop. ''Correct! Think of it as being on a merry-go-round. You are on one horse, which is the *Aguinaldo*. You hop off the merry-go-round, wait for the next horse to pass by—which is the moon—and then hop back on when the third horse comes into position. That is *Orbitech 1.*''

''But how long is this going to take?'' Magsaysay stared at the dashed blue line, as if counting time.

''Nine or ten days, depending on how large we can grow the sail and how accurately the boy can maneuver with it. We cannot leave him out there any longer than absolutely necessary. His suit and the sail creature's exoskeleton will provide little protection from the cosmic radiation . . . and we want to reach *Orbitech* as soon as possible.''

Ramis remained silent for a moment, looking around the empty chamber. The room was large, dominated by a long meeting table surrounded by unoccupied chairs. Overhead, shadows of passing pedal kites and playing children crossed over the skylights of the chamber. Ramis set his mouth. ''The sail creature—it will die, now that the metamorphosis has taken place?''

''Eventually.'' Sandovaal blinked his eyes at Ramis, as if wondering at the relevance of the boy's comment.

Ramis swallowed. ''How long do I have?''

"We cannot implant you too soon—the creature's physical structure is still hardening, you see. Still forming a rigid sheath to keep the new sails in place. But the timing will be close. After we encyst you, the trip should take ten days."

"You told me that. I want to know how long the sail creature will live."

Sandovaal switched off the stereotank, letting the images fade back into the murk. As the lights came up, Ramis watched Magsaysay nod to Sandovaal. Sandovaal pursed his lips. "It will die within two weeks, or possibly less. We have too few data to be confident. However, we will provide you with hormone injections to induce nerve reactions—you should still be able to move its sails. If the sail creature ceases to respond before you reach *Orbitech 1*, you will not be able to steer. And then you will be trapped."

Magsaysay's shoulders sagged and he started to speak up, but Sandovaal cut him off. "But it is still possible. I am confident."

The president did not look greatly consoled. He turned again to Ramis, as if pleading with him to change his mind. Ramis stood, his face expressionless as he pushed away from the meeting table. "Thank you, Dr. Sandovaal." He strode from the room and headed for Jumpoff to drift alone in the core.

Ramis was cramped, hot. The air in the cyst stifled him. The pain in his joints ached without relief. He felt dizzy most of the time now, sick to his stomach. Dr. Sandovaal had warned him that the suit might not protect him enough from the hard radiation—and he would have no chance if a large solar flare occurred. He envisioned a long time recovering from this journey . . . if he survived at all.

The sail creature hardly responded to Ramis's course-adjusting maneuvers anymore. Reluctant, Ramis had to resort to deep, vicious jabs with the knife to get the creature to turn even a little.

But the L-5 colony filled up most of the viewscreen, like a rotating dumbbell with two wheels spinning on a central axle.

Ramis reached out and stroked the cyst's inner membrane through the thick jungle of wall kelp growing unchecked inside the cavity. He didn't know if the creature could feel him, or respond, but he continued to caress. It kept his hands occupied.

Ramis conserved the batteries in his transceiver, using it only occasionally to send a signal to the L-5 colony; he had long ago passed out of range of the *Aguinaldo*. Magsaysay had promised that they would continue to transmit to *Orbitech 1*, telling them what to expect, how they could receive the life-saving supplies Ramis was bringing them. But the boy had no way of knowing if those messages had been acknowledged, or even received. Was anybody alive on the *Orbitech* colony?

The wheels' metallic surfaces glinted in the sunlight, causing bright flares and smears on the video screen. The colony's observation windows glimmered with light from the inside, naked and devoid of wall kelp. It looked strange to Ramis, but he could not focus the video camera enough to see inside.

What if he found no one at all? How would he ever get back? He would never even get inside the colony unless someone opened the airlock and took him in. And the sail creature was almost dead—that left Ramis with no way back home.

"*Orbitech 1,* I am almost to you."

A loud meaningless crackle returned, but Ramis kept trying. They had to know he was coming. No one could mistake the sight of the vast organic solar sail drifting closer every day. He almost missed it when a weak voice came from the speaker. He knew his transceiver battery was almost dead.

". . . tech here. . . . Ready . . . receive you."

As Ramis caressed the inner membrane of the sail creature, he silently willed the behemoth to remain alive just a short while longer.

They rapidly closed on the L-5 colony. To slow him down enough so that impact with the colony would not kill him, Ramis had to collapse the sail creature's broad and beautiful sails, draw them in to cushion him from the crash.

Orbitech 1 gleamed on the monitor. He knew which end would have the docking bay, where the people would be waiting for him. He watched the wheels turning, one clockwise, the other counterclockwise. With each rotation of the colony, the creature drifted nearer. Ramis swallowed. The picture on the monitor screen blurred from his tears.

Moving slowly, Ramis withdrew the pressurized vial from its cellophane pack, along with the tiny explosive-driven carrier pellets.

He had to judge when the time was right. He had to know, and he could not hesitate. If he botched this up, then he would have done all this for nothing and made a martyr of himself as well.

And more important, he would have extinguished the last hope of survival for those inside the L-5 colony.

He could see the details of the airlock now, the Orbitechnologies corporate logo, the viewing windows on either side of it. The colony swelled to fill the entire video screen.

Ramis felt the sweat of his fingers inside the gloves, holding the vial of pressurized trigger hormone, slick against the Mylar of his suit. He rammed the hypodermic cartridge inside the sail creature's membrane and ejected its contents.

Reacting with incredible slowness, the sails collapsed. They drew in toward the cyst, lumbering together as a butterfly might bring in its wings. The cell-thin sails stretched scores of kilometers out in front of the cyst. With the sudden movement wispy fragments tore away, rippling like the shrouds of a ghost.

The sail creature's crumpled body struck the L-5 colony, pushing against the tattered ends of its sails. Ramis felt the impact ripple through the creature's flesh, but the boy was padded by the curtains of wall kelp and kilometers of sail. The minute-long collision dragged on; it seemed to take hours.

He felt himself drifting back again, rebounding. Suddenly, panic burned through him. If he drifted out of the colony's grasp, then he would be stranded again, without even the sails for maneuvering.

The video monitor was dark; outside, the cameras had been covered up by folds of the collapsed sails. Ramis sealed his helmet, made certain that the sail creature embryos were protected in their airtight canisters, then took out his knife.

He had to get out; he had to do something before it was too late. Ramis shouted again into the transmitter. Nothing. He saw that he had left it on—the battery was dead.

He hesitated only a moment, then plunged the knife into the tough membrane, trying to cut his way out of the cyst. When the blade broke through to the outside, decompression almost ripped the knife out of his hand. The outrushing air tore the gash open wider, but acting as a jet to push him back toward the colony. Ramis continued to saw with the knife edge. Crystals sparkled as the humidity inside the cyst flash-froze, layering everything with a thin coating of ice. One of the wall-kelp bladders burst and froze in the same second.

Ramis could see partly through the opening in the cyst, and then he felt a tug on the carcass of the sail creature. He peered out and saw several figures in spacesuits near him, attaching a tether to keep him from drifting with the recoil from impact.

The boy felt drained with relief, but he could not yet relax. He kept hacking with his knife, trying to make the opening wide enough for him to emerge. One of the suited figures swam up in front of him, face to face, nodding.

Ramis was startled to see behind the faceplate a thin,

fearful expression; but the face bore a look of hope and wonderment that cut through weeks of despair.

The boy emerged from the hulk of the dead sail creature, feeling like a newborn coming out of a womb. He turned back to see the creature's shriveled remains. The once-magnificent sails now looked as if someone had crumpled up a gigantic wad of paper and tossed it aside.

Sharp needles of pain struck him in his joints, and uneasy tremors raced through his muscles. But it felt wonderful just to move again, to stretch, to be free. He stared down and saw only an infinity of stars, not the curved wall of the *Aguinaldo* as he was accustomed to seeing. If he started to fall, he would keep falling forever and ever. . . .

Dizzy, he looked up at the large observation windows on either side of the airlock. Pressed against them he saw scattered faces with large gaps between them—pitifully few faces. They looked as gaunt and anxious as the one he had seen inside the suit.

One of the men wrestled the knife from his hand. Ramis was too weary to struggle, so he released it and kicked toward the airlock. He tried to make motions to show them what they needed to get from the cyst. He saw them taking out the sail creature embryos; they also needed to remove the wall-kelp nodules. The wall kelp would survive for some time in the vacuum, but they needed to bring it inside as soon as possible.

As he drifted through the maw of the towering docking-bay doors, another spacesuited figure took his arm and directed him to one of the doors at the wall. He supposed it was an elevator shaft. His legs continued to tremble, and he felt ready to dissolve inside his suit.

Behind him, he saw the suited figures cutting at the dead creature's crumpled sails, getting at its body core. The severed tissue-thin sails drifted away as the L-5 colony continued in its orbit.

Though he felt incredibly weary and dizzy from his journey, Ramis waited by the elevator shaft and watched the other colonists bring in the wall kelp and embryos.

The frozen kelp strands were still edible, and the central nodules would survive. His escort seemed impatient and urged him to enter the elevator.

As the spokeshaft elevator descended, the chamber filled with air. Ramis could feel his weight increase as they traveled out to the rim of the wheel where the artificial gravity was strongest.

His escort cracked open his helmet and indicated for Ramis to do the same. Ramis took a deep breath of the warm, stale air of the industrial colony. A potpourri of odors wafted past, very different from the humid stifling air of the cramped cyst. The smell was metallic, scrubbed clean—more artificial than the *Aguinaldo*'s.

A buzz of people surrounded the elevator. Arms reached out to embrace him, and he almost collapsed in their grasp. He looked frantically around. The men with the embryos must have gone to one of the other elevators into another part of the wheel. Ramis stood on his tiptoes and called out, wondering what he should do. "Wait—the sail creatures! They are my only way back! I need to tell you about the wall kelp—"

One man stepped up to him, pushing his way through the crowd. "Curtis Brahms, acting director of *Orbitech 1.*" He seemed to be out of breath. He shook Ramis's gloved hand. "Welcome to our colony. I hope you brought a miracle with you. We had only . . . unpleasant options left."

Ramis studied the man, trying to quell the urgency he felt. "The wall kelp is a chance for you to survive."

"It's been taken to a safe place. You can speak to our scientists after we've shown you your quarters. You're in the same boat with the rest of us, I'm afraid. You'll be here awhile."

The boy tried not to think of the *Aguinaldo*, of the many years he would have to live here before the other sail-creature embryos reached maturity.

But a ripple of optimism ran through the crowd. Though

he knew the bad times weren't over, somehow he felt the birth of a new spirit of hope.

Kevin J. Anderson has sold eight novels and more than a hundred short stories. His first novel, *Resurrection, Inc.,* is a cross between hard science fiction and Gothic horror; it was a final nominee for the Bram Stoker Award. His second and third novels, *Gamearth* and *Gameplay,* are the first two books in a fantasy trilogy with Jules Verne and Dr. Frankenstein as main characters. Three of his upcoming novels are collaborations with Beason; all concern scientific issues and their effects on society.

Doug Beason is the author of several non-sci-fi techno-thriller novels, including *Honor, Assault on Alpha Base,* and *Strike Eagle.* Doug holds a Ph.D. in physics and was an assistant professor of physics at the U.S. Air Force Academy before his current job, heading up a high-energy plasma physics laboratory in Albuquerque.

So far we have kept to the solar system while talking about the future of lightsails. But some are never satisfied with the simple, or the obvious . . . or with playing in the backyard. Might we someday set sail to the stars themselves? Robert Forward and Joel Davis think it's very likely indeed.

Lightsails to the Stars

by
Robert L. Forward
and Joel Davis

It may not be tails of fusion fire or faintly glowing trails of *Star Trek* antimatter propulsion that propel humanity's initial interstellar probes to other stars. Our robot pathfinders to Proxima Centauri may well travel as Columbus did to the New World: by sail. The first space probe to another star may be a payload attached to a gossamer-thin aluminum sail some 4 kilometers wide and weighing a ton. Or it may be a kilometer-wide, semi-intelligent aluminum mesh weighing all of 20 grams.

Such spacecraft may sound more like fantasy than hard fact. But they may end up being more practical than Buck Rogers–type rockets. Interstellar travel is not a trivial endeavor. We really have no conception of how much *empty space* exists between the stars. We measure distances and travel times on a human scale: the distance from home to the office, the time it takes to travel from London to Paris. And talking with relatives in Perth is practically instantaneous, even though they are nearly halfway around the world.

The universe is *big*. Many of Earth's billions have never traveled more than 40 kilometers from their place of birth. Only twenty-seven men have traveled as far as the moon, 10,000 times farther or nearly 400,000 kilometers away.

The Voyager 2 spacecraft recently sped past the planet Neptune, currently the most distant planet in the solar system, 10,000 times farther than the moon or more than 4 billion kilometers away. But the nearest star to our solar system, Proxima Centauri, is 10,000 times more distant still at 40 *trillion* kilometers distant, some 4.3 light-years. Voyager 2 will leave the solar system at a speed of 58,000 kilometers per hour and will take over 80,000 years to cover 4.3 light-years. A flight system capable of traversing interstellar distances during a human lifetime must therefore be several orders of magnitude better than even our best present interplanetary flight systems.

This epic enterprise may still lie several decades in the future—or it could, with considerable effort, be only around the corner of the millennium. In fact, the United States of America is currently engaged in a multibillion-dollar research effort to produce one of the major components of an interstellar propulsion system—a high-power laser. The U.S. Department of Defense considers it part of the Strategic Defense Initiative (SDI), the so-called Star Wars project. But any science fiction aficionado will recognize that a superpowerful laser is a dandy tool to literally blow an interstellar probe out of our solar system and out to the stars.

In the last twenty-five years, humanity has begun developing the technology for interstellar travel. And it *does* exist, for at least one interstellar propulsion scheme called nuclear pulse propulsion. This is really just a fancy name for throwing hydrogen bombs out the back of your spaceship and letting the explosions push you to Sirius (or wherever) and back. The earliest work on nuclear pulse propulsion was done at the U.S. government's Los Alamos National Laboratory in the late 1950s. The researchers wanted to devise a way of getting to Mars and back by 1968. The proposed spaceship was called *Orion*. It would have been powered by hundreds of tiny hydrogen bombs ejected out the back of the ship. As each bomb exploded, its debris would hit a huge "pusher plate" at the rear of the ship. The impulse from the explosion would be transferred via giant shock absorbers to the rest of the vehicle. *Orion* would thus be "kicked" across space to its Martian destination.

No nuclear-pulsed spaceship ever reached Mars in 1968;

Orion remained on the drawing boards. In that very year, however, the visionary British-American physicist Freeman Dyson modified the *Orion* proposal and turned it into a manned interstellar space probe. Dyson's version of *Orion* would weigh some 400,000 metric tons and carry 300,000 1-ton fusion bombs. The interstellar *Orion* could also be built as a two-stage ship, so it could slow down as it neared its target star. The first stage of such a ship, Dyson calculated, would have to weigh 1.6 million metric tons. The 20,000-ton payload would include hundreds of men and women, along with everything necessary to maintain them and their descendants.

For Dyson's interstellar *Orion* would not be a fast boat to Alpha Centauri. The fusion devices would explode behind the ship at a rate of one every three seconds, accelerating the ship at a constant 1 gravity to 1/30 the speed of light in just ten days. At that speed (10,000 kilometers per second, or 36 million kilometers per hour) it would take 130 years to reach the nearest star. None of the original crew would live to reach their destination, since relativistic time-dilating effects are negligible at 1/30 c.

Orion is the only form of true interstellar transport which could have been built and sent on its way in the last decade. The reasons *Orion* was not built and launched were (1) the Nuclear Test Ban Treaty, which prohibits the explosion of nuclear devices in outer space, and (2) a monumental lack of interest on the part of the political, engineering, and scientific communities. The latter reason is the more important of the two. If there were sufficient interest in building *Orion*, mutually agreeable and acceptable ways could be found to sidestep or modify the Test Ban Treaty.

The technology to send (reasonably) fast space probes to other stars will soon be within our reach. These interstellar probes will be powered by photon pressure—from a microwave laser (i.e., a maser) in one case, and a visible-light laser in the other.

The idea of using a maser to propel an interstellar probe

originated with Freeman Dyson. In 1984 one of us
(R.L.F.) coupled that concept with the use of advanced
computer technology. The result is called *Starwisp*. A wire
hexagonal mesh sail 1 kilometer in diameter weighing only
20 grams would make up the entire spacecraft. At each of
the 10 trillion wire intersections of the mesh would be a
tiny microcircuit. These semi-intelligent chips not only
would work as a computer element in a 10-trillion-
component parallel-processing supercomputer, but would
be light-sensitive, and function as tiny pinhole cameras.

The propulsion system for *Starwisp* would not be on
board the space probe, but would stay "at home." It would
consist of a 20-gigawatt (20-billion-watts) microwave beam
from an Earth-orbiting solar-power satellite. *Starwisp*, because it would be so delicate, would be fabricated in space
at a point beyond the orbit of Mars. There it would unfold
like a delicate rose in deep space. The microwave beam
would be turned on and focused on the sail by a special
kind of lens called a Fresnel zone lens.

The lens would be huge, 50,000 kilometers wide or four
times the diameter of Earth. It would be a complex of wire
mesh rings alternating with empty rings. The radii of the
rings would be adjusted so that all the pathlengths of the
microwaves passing through the empty rings would be in
phase at the focal point of the Fresnel zone lens.

The focused microwave beam would accelerate *Starwisp*
by photon pressure, somewhat like terrestrial wind pushing a sailing ship. The 10 trillion microcircuits, like electronic halyards, would adjust the conductivity of the wires
in the mesh to maximize reflected photon power. Accelerating at 115 times Earth gravity, *Starwisp* would reach
one-fifth light speed (60,000 kilometers per second or 216
million kilometers per hour) in just one week.

Seventeen years later, *Starwisp* would be three-quarters
of the way to Proxima Centauri. The next part of the mission would begin as Mission Control turned the microwave
beam on again. A powerful pulse of energy would be sent
streaming through the target star system, arriving (at the

speed of light) as *Starwisp* arrived (at 0.2 c) four years later. The beam, though spread out, would still be strong enough to "turn on" *Starwisp*'s 10 trillion microcircuits. The circuits would use the wires of the mesh sail as microwave antennas to collect the energy of the beam. Each circuit would adjust its built-in internal clock to the phase of the microwave beam. Then, acting as the photoreceptors in the retina of this artificial "eye," the 10 trillion semi-intelligent chips would analyze the infrared, visible, and ultraviolet light they would sense coming from objects in the Proxima Centauri system.

At a velocity of 60,000 kilometers per second, *Starwisp* would make the fastest flyby in history. It took Voyager 2 about one week to pass through the system of Saturn's major moons and rings, a distance of about 8 million kilometers. *Starwisp* would race through the inner Proxima Centauri system (say 9 billion kilometers, or the distance across the orbit of Neptune) in *just forty hours*. During that time the energized superchips of *Starwisp* would produce twenty-five high-resolution images per second, close to frame rates for television. Using the timing information from the microwave beam from Earth, the mesh would configure itself as a directional antenna and beam the data back to Earth.

Four years after the flyby, *Starwisp* would be almost a light-year beyond Proxima Centauri. But its data stream would just be arriving at Earth, where computers would turn the numbers into photos to dazzle a waiting world just a quarter-century after *Starwisp*'s launch.

If some interesting planets were seen by *Starwisp*, the next step would be to send a more massive probe with a much better optical imaging system and an array of other sophisticated instruments. This would require a more powerful system, a *laser*-pushed lightsail. We call it *Starlite*.

The idea for a *Starlite*-type probe is somewhat older than that for *Starwisp*. Konstantin Tsiolkovsky talked about something like it as early as 1921. Detailed technical studies appeared in 1958 and 1959 (about the time Los Alamos researchers were designing the *Orion* H-bomb ship). However, the assumption in these studies was that the photon pressure would come from sunlight, not a laser. The first laser was "turned on" in 1960 at the Hughes Research Laboratories, where one of us (R.L.F.) was working. He realized that lasers could be used to propel a lightsail over interstellar distances, and he published his first paper on the subject in 1962. Several other papers have appeared since then, and the idea has been considerably refined.

Like *Starwisp*, *Starlite* would be quite large. For a one-way flyby of Proxima Centauri, a *Starlite* probe would have a sail 3.6 kilometers in diameter, made of aluminum film about 16 nanometers (or 160 angstroms) thick. An aluminum film with this thickness would reflect about 82 percent of the light hitting it, allow about 4.5 percent of the light to pass through, and absorb the remaining 13.5 percent. The sail plus attached probe would mass about 1,000 kilograms or a metric ton.

Propulsion would come from the photon pressure of a 65-gigawatt laser. The laser could be in Earth orbit, like the power system for the *Starwisp* probe, or in close orbit around the sun, where the solar flux is higher. Examples of power systems for such a laser include carbon dioxide electric discharge lasers at 10.6 micrometers wavelength, or solar-pumped iodine lasers at 1.315 micrometers wavelength. Building such a laser would not be easy; but work leading to such a device is already being done by contractors for the American SDI project. A Fresnel zone "lens" 1,000 kilometers wide, located at a "station-keeping" point 15 a.u. (between the orbits of Saturn and Uranus), would focus the laser beam onto the *Starlite* sail.

A 65-gigawatt laser would accelerate *Starlite* at 0.36 meters per second squared, or 4 percent of Earth's gravity. Three years of continuous acceleration would give *Starlite* a velocity of 11 percent of light speed. The probe would be 0.17 light-years from the sun at that point. The spot size of the laser would be 3.8 kilometers, only 200 meters wider than the sail itself, when it was finally turned off. *Starlite* would reach Proxima Centauri forty years after launch, taking twice as long to get there as *Starwisp*. This is despite the fact that *Starlite* would use a laser three times as powerful. The difference, of course, is in the mass of the probe itself—20 grams versus 1,000 kilograms. The more heavily instrumented *Starlite* probe, however, could do a much better job of finding planets that humans could visit in person. And larger versions of *Starlite* could take them there.

Consider, for example, the following scenario for a round-trip journey via laser-pushed lightsail craft to the star Epsilon Eridani, 10.8 light-years from Earth. For this mission we will use a super-*Starlite* vehicle: the *Starlite Special*. The sail will be 1,000 kilometers wide, the same as the Fresnel transmitting lens. The vehicle will mass about 75,800 metric tons. If we want to get the crew to Epsilon Eridani and back before they die of old age, they'll have to move at relativistic velocities. That will allow the Einstein time-dilation effect to kick in, as well as get them to their destination relatively quickly. A laser or cluster of lasers outputting a beam of 43,000 terawatts (TW) will accelerate the *Starlite Special* at one-third Earth gravity. In 1.6 years the vehicle will travel about 0.4 light-years, and will reach a cruise velocity of 150,000 meters per second—50 percent of the speed of light. It will thus take the *Starlite Special* just twenty years to get to Epsilon Eridani.

Now we mustn't forget Einstein. This velocity will cause a 13 percent increase in the mass of the lightsail craft and a concomitant time-dilation effect for the crew! It will also have a Doppler-shift effect on the laser beam's frequency and energy. To provide a constant one-third-g acceleration, therefore, the laser power will have to increase to a formidable 75,000 TW by the end of the acceleration phase. No one said it would be easy or cheap to get human beings to the stars! About 10.4 years before the craft arrives at its destination the laser banks will again be turned on, sending a "slug" of light energy racing through space to Epsilon Eridani.

The lightsail for the *Starlite Special* is itself special. It will be made in three concentric segments: an outer "decelerator stage" the full 1,000 kilometers wide; an inner "rendezvous stage" 320 kilometers wide; and an innermost "return stage" 100 kilometers wide. When the *Starlite Special* is 0.4 light-years from Epsilon Eridani, the outer decelerator stage sail will be cut loose from the other two sail stages that compose the rendezvous sail. The latter will be turned around so its reflective surface will be facing the now-detached deceleratory ring sail. The slug of laser light will hit the decelerator ring sail and bounce back to strike the rendezvous sail. The result, as far as the interstellar craft and its crew are concerned, will be the same as if it were being *slowed down* by a multi-terawatt laser beamed from Epsilon Eridani!

Deceleration time will be the same as acceleration time, 1.6 years. Thus the travel time to Epsilon Eridani will be 23.2 years by Earth clocks, and 20.5 years by shipboard clocks.

After our intrepid crew has spent a few years (let's say five) exploring the Epsilon Eridani system, it will be time to head back home. Now the return-stage sail, the innermost 100-kilometer-diameter part of the rendezvous sail, will be detached. The outer 320-kilometer-diameter ring sail will be flipped around so its reflective surface now faces Sol system. A third 1.6-light-year-long slug of laser light, fired from the sun-orbiting laser 10.8 years earlier, now pours through the Epsilon Eridani system and strikes the reflective surface of the detached ring sail. The light bounces back and hits the reflective surface of the return sail. Both sails are accelerated out of the Epsilon Eridani system, but the return sail and its attached crew module head back home toward Earth at one-third-g acceleration.

Of course it might be possible for the crew to make their *own* laser for the return voyage. But for the sake of argument, we assume here that they'll rely on power from home all the way.

Twenty years later the *Starlite Special* will approach the solar system at 50 percent light speed. It will be brought to a halt with a final burst of laser energy. The crew will have been away from earth for about fifty-one years. They will have aged about forty-six years.

This may sound like an awful long time, but who knows what the future may hold? Hibernation and extended life-spans are just two possibilities. If they, or as yet unknown technologies, become available, we do know this—it is physically possible to go to a distant star and return!

Interstellar travel via laser- or maser-pushed lightsails is not yet feasible. But it violates no laws of physics, and can be achieved with reasonable engineering extrapolations of current technologies in thin films and laser power generation and transmission. And it has a great advantage over more "conventional" interstellar propulsion system proposals. The engine stays at home, in the solar system, where it can be easily maintained, repaired, and upgraded as necessary, and the ship need carry no fuel.

There are formidable engineering problems, of course. Building superlarge lightweight structures; developing the necessary pointing and tracking capabilities; figuring out how to use a ring-shaped lightsail as a focusing lens; and, of course, building lasers and masers that can generate multi-gigawatt and terawatt power levels for weeks, months, or even years at a time; all are tasks that will be very difficult to accomplish.

But they can be done. Other interstellar propulsion technologies may ultimately be developed that are faster, less massive, less power-consumptive, and less risky. But the fact remains that although interstellar travel may be difficult, it is not impossible. Laser-pushed lightsails can one day take us to the stars and back in a human lifetime. Indeed, someday we may sail the starlanes on wings of light.

Dr. Robert L. Forward is a writer and aerospace consultant. For his Ph.D. thesis he built and operated the world's first bar antenna for the detection of gravitational radiation. The antenna is now on display in the Smithsonian museum. For thirty-one years, from 1956 until 1987, when he left in order to spend more time writing, Dr. Forward worked at the Hughes Aircraft Company Research Laboratories in Malibu, California, in positions of increasing responsibility, culminating with the position of Senior Scientist. From 1983 to the present, Dr. Forward has had a series of contracts from the Air Force Astronautics Laboratory to explore the forefront of physics and engineering in order to find new energy sources that will produce breakthroughs in space power and propulsion. His most recent published works are two science fact books, *Future Magic* and *Mirror Matter: Pioneering Antimatter Physics* (with Joel Davis). He has three published science fiction novels, *Dragon's Egg, The Flight of the Dragonfly,* and *Starquake,* and has just finished a fourth novel, *Martian Rainbow*.

Joel Davis is the author of numerous works, both fiction and popular science.

The notions Davis and Forward present are very interesting. Several authors have used them recently in novels. But to find a writer who could condense so much (and more) into a short story, we turn to Larry Niven.

The Fourth Profession

by
Larry Niven

The doorbell rang around noon on Wednesday.

I sat up in bed and—it was the oddest of hangovers. My head *didn't* spin. My sense of balance was quiveringly alert. At the same time my mind was clogged with the things I knew: facts that wouldn't relate, churning in my head.

It was like walking the high wire while simultaneously trying to solve an Agatha Christie mystery. Yet I was doing neither. I was just sitting up in bed, blinking.

I remembered the Monk, and the pills. How many pills?

The bell rang again.

Walking to the door was an eerie sensation. Most people pay no attention to their somesthetic senses. Mine were clamoring for attention, begging to be tested—by a backflip, for instance. I resisted. I don't have the muscles for doing backflips.

I couldn't remember taking any acrobatics pills.

The man outside my door was big and blond and blocky. He was holding an unfamiliar badge up to the lens of my spy-eye, in a wide hand with short, thick fingers. He had candid blue eyes, a square, honest face—a face I recognized. He'd been in the Long Spoon last night, at a single table in a corner.

Last night he had looked morose, introspective, like a man whose girl had left him for Mr. Wrong. A face guaranteed to get him left alone. I'd noticed him only because he wasn't drinking enough to match the face.

Today he looked patient, endlessly patient, with the patience of a dead man.

And he had a badge. I let him in.

"William Morris," he said, identifying himself. "Secret Service. Are you Edward Harley Frazer, owner of the Long Spoon Bar?"

"Part owner."

"Yes, that's right. Sorry to bother you, Mr. Frazer. I see you keep bartender's hours." He was looking at the wrinkled pair of underpants I had on.

"Sit down," I said, waving at the chair. I badly needed to sit down myself. Standing, I couldn't think about anything but standing. My balance was all-conscious. My heels would not rest solidly on the floor. They barely touched. My weight was all on my toes; my body insisted on standing that way.

So I dropped onto the edge of the bed, but it felt like I was giving a trampoline performance. The poise, the grace, the polished easel Hell. "What do you want from me, Mr. Morris? Doesn't the Secret Service guard the President?"

His answer sounded like rote memory. "Among other concerns, such as counterfeiting, we do guard the President and his immediate family and the President-elect, and the Vice President if he asks us to." He paused. "We used to guard foreign dignitaries too."

That connected. "You're here about the Monk."

"Right." Morris looked down at his hands. He should have had an air of professional self-assurance to go with the badge. It wasn't there. "This is an odd case, Frazer. We took it because it used to be our job to protect foreign visitors, and because nobody else would touch it."

"So last night you were in the Long Spoon guarding a visitor from outer space."

"Just so."

"Where were you night before last?"

"Was that when he first appeared?"

"Yah," I said, remembering. "Monday night . . ."

* * *

He came in an hour after opening time. He seemed to glide, with the hem of his robe just brushing the floor. By his gait he might have been moving on wheels. His shape was wrong, in a way that made your eyes want to twist around to straighten it out.

There is something queer about the garment that gives a Monk his name. The hood is open in front, as if eyes might hide within its shadow, and the front of the robe is open too. But the loose cloth hides more than it ought to. There is too much shadow.

Once I thought the robe parted as he walked toward me. But there seemed to be nothing inside.

In the Long Spoon was utter silence. Every eye was on the Monk as he took a stool at one end of the bar, and ordered.

He looked alien, and was. But he *seemed* supernatural.

He used the oddest of drinking systems. I keep my house brands on three long shelves, more or less in order of type. The Monk moved down the top row of bottles, right to left, ordering a shot from each bottle. He took his liquor straight, at room temperature. He drank quietly, steadily, and with what seemed to be total concentration.

He spoke only to order.

He showed nothing of himself but one hand. That hand looked like a chicken's foot, but bigger, with lumpy-looking, very flexible joints, and with five toes instead of four.

At closing time the Monk was four bottles from the end of the row. He paid me in one-dollar bills, and left, moving steadily, the hem of his robe just brushing the floor. I testify as an expert: he was sober. The alcohol had not affected him at all.

"Monday night," I said. "He shocked the hell out of us. Morris, what was a Monk doing in a bar in Hollywood? I thought all the Monks were in New York."

"So did we."

"Oh?"

"We didn't know he was on the West Coast until it hit the newspapers yesterday morning. That's why you didn't see more reporters yesterday. We kept them off your back. I came in last night to question you, Frazer. I changed my mind when I saw that the Monk was already here."

"Question *me*? Why? All I did was serve him drinks."

"Okay, let's start there. Weren't you afraid the alcohol might kill a Monk?"

"It occurred to me."

"Well?"

"I served him what he asked for. It's the Monks' own doing that nobody knows anything about Monks. We don't even know what shape they are, let alone how they're put together. If liquor does things to a Monk, it's his own lookout. Let him check the chemistry."

"Sounds reasonable."

"Thanks."

"It's also the reason I'm here," said Morris. "We know too little about the Monks. We didn't even know they existed until something over two years ago."

"Oh?" I'd only started reading about them a month ago.

"It wouldn't be that long, except that all the astronomers were looking in that direction already, studying a recent nova in Sagittarius. So they caught the Monk starship a little sooner; but it was already inside Pluto's orbit.

"They've been communicating with us for over a year. Two weeks ago they took up orbit around the moon. There's only one Monk starship, and only one ground-to-orbit craft, as far as we know. The ground-to-orbit craft has been sitting in the ocean off Manhattan Island, convenient to the United Nations Building, for those same two weeks. Its crew are supposed to be all the Monks there are in the world.

"Mr. Frazer, we don't even know how your Monk got out here to the West Coast! Almost anything you could tell us would help. Did you notice anything odd about him, these last two nights?"

"Odd?" I grinned. "About a Monk?"

It took him a moment to get it, and then his answering smile was wan. "Odd for a Monk."

"Yah," I said, and tried to concentrate. It was the wrong move. Bits of fact buzzed about my skull, trying to fit themselves together.

Morris was saying, "Just talk, if you will. The Monk came back Tuesday night. About what time?"

"About four-thirty. He had a case of—pills—RNA . . ."

It was no use. I knew too many things, all at once, all unrelated. I knew the name of the Garment to Wear Among Strangers, its principle and its purpose. I knew about Monks and alcohol. I knew the names of the five primary colors, so that for a moment I was blind with the memory of the colors themselves, colors no man would ever see.

Morris was standing over me, looking worried. "What is it? What's wrong?"

"Ask me anything." My voice was high and strange and breathless with giddy laughter. "Monks have four limbs, all hands, each with a callus heel behind the fingers. I know their names, Morris. Each hand, each finger. I know how many eyes a Monk has. One. And the whole skull is an ear. There's no word for ear, but medical terms for each of the—resonating cavities—between the lobes of the brain—"

"You look dizzy. You don't sample your own wares, do you, Frazer?"

"I'm the opposite of dizzy. There's a compass in my head. I've got absolute direction. Morris, it must have been the pills."

"Pills?" Morris had small, squarish ears that couldn't possibly have come to point. But I got that impression.

"He had a sample case full of—education pills—"

"Easy now." He put a steadying hand on my shoulder. "Take it easy. Just start at the beginning, and talk. I'll make some coffee."

"Good." Coffee sounded wonderful, suddenly. "Pot's ready. Just plug it in. I fix it before I go to sleep."

Morris disappeared around the partition that marks off the kitchen alcove from the bedroom/living room in my small apartment. His voice floated back. "Start at the beginning. He came back Tuesday night."

"He came back Tuesday night," I repeated.

"Hey, your coffee's already perked. You must have plugged it in in your sleep. Keep talking."

"He started his drinking where he'd left off, four bottles from the end of the top row. I'd have sworn he was cold sober. His voice didn't give him away. . . ."

His voice didn't give him away because it was only a whisper, too low to make out. His translator spoke like a computer, putting single words together from a man's recorded voice. It spoke slowly and with care. Why not? It was speaking an alien tongue.

The Monk had had five tonight. That put him through the ryes and the bourbons and the Irish whiskeys, and several of the liqueurs. Now he was tasting the vodkas.

At that point I worked up the courage to ask him what he was doing.

He explained at length. The Monk starship was a commercial venture, a trading mission following a daisy chain of stars. He was a sampler for the group. He was mightily pleased with some of the wares he had sampled here. Probably he would order great quantities of them, to be freeze-dried for easy storage. And alcohol and water to reconstitute.

"Then you won't be wanting to test all the vodkas," I told him. "Vodka isn't much more than water and alcohol."

He thanked me.

"The same goes for most gins, except for flavorings." I lined up four gins in front of him. One was Tanqueray. One was a Dutch gin you have to keep chilled like some liqueurs. The others were fairly ordinary products. I left him with these while I served customers.

I had expected a mob tonight. Word should have spread.

Have a drink in the Long Spoon, you'll see a Thing from Outer Space. But the place was half empty. Louise was handling them nicely.

I was proud of Louise. As with last night, tonight she behaved as if nothing out of the ordinary was happening. The mood was contagious. I could almost hear the customers thinking: *We like our privacy when we drink. A Thing from Outer Space is entitled to the same consideration.*

It was strange to compare her present insouciance with the way her eyes had bugged at her first sight of a Monk.

The Monk finished tasting the gins. "I am concerned for the volatile fractions," he said. "Some of your liquors will lose taste from condensation."

I told him he was probably right. And I asked, "How do you pay for your cargos?"

"With knowledge."

"That's fair. What kind of knowledge?"

The Monk reached under his robe and produced a flat sample case. He opened it. It was full of pills. There was a large glass bottle full of a couple of hundred identical pills; and these were small and pink and triangular. But most of the sample case was given over to big, round pills of all colors, individually wrapped and individually labeled in the wandering Monk script.

No two labels were alike. Some of the notations looked hellishly complex.

"These are knowledge," said the Monk.

"Ah," I said, and wondered if I was being put on. An alien can have a sense of humor, can't he? And there's no way to tell if he's lying.

"A certain complex organic molecule has much to do with memory," said the Monk. "Ribonucleic acid. It is present and active in the nervous systems of most organic beings. Wish you to learn my language?"

I nodded.

He pulled a pill loose and stripped it of its wrapping, which fluttered to the bar like a shred of cellophane. The Monk put the pill in my hand and said, "You must swallow it now, before the air ruins it, now that it is out of its wrapping.''

The pill was marked like a target in red and green circles. It was big and bulky going down.

"You must be crazy," Bill Morris said wonderingly.

"It looks that way to me, too, now. But think about it. This was a Monk, an alien, an ambassador to the whole human race. He wouldn't have fed me anything dangerous, not without carefully considering all the possible consequences.''

"He wouldn't, would he?"

"That's the way it seemed." I remembered about Monks and alcohol. It was a pill memory, surfacing as if I had known it all my life. It came too late . . .

"A language says things about the person who speaks it, about the way he thinks and the way he lives. Morris, the Monk language says a lot about Monks.''

"Call me Bill," he said irritably.

"Okay. Take Monks and alcohol. Alcohol works on a Monk the way it works on a man, by starving his brain cells a little. But in a Monk it gets absorbed more slowly. A Monk can stay high for a week on a night's dedicated drinking.

"I knew he was sober when he left Monday night. By Tuesday night he must have been pretty high."

I sipped my coffee. Today it tasted different, and better, as if memories of some Monk staple foods had worked their way as overtones into my taste buds.

Morris said, "And you didn't know it."

"Know it? I was counting on his sense of responsibility!"

Morris shook his head in pity, except that he seemed to be grinning inside.

"We talked some more after that . . . and I took some more pills.''

"Why?"

"I was high on the first one."

"It made you drunk?"

"Not drunk, but I couldn't think straight. My head was full of Monk words all trying to fit themselves to meanings. I was dizzy with nonhuman images and words I couldn't pronounce."

"Just how many pills did you take?"

"I don't remember."

"Swell."

An image surfaced. "I do remember saying. 'But how about something unusual? *Really* unusual.' "

Morris was no longer amused. "You're lucky you can still talk. The chances you took, you should be a drooling idiot this morning!"

"It seemed reasonable at the time."

"You don't remember how many pills you took?"

I shook my head. Maybe the motion jarred something loose. "That bottle of little triangular pills. I know what they were. Memory erasers."

"Good God! You didn't—"

"No, no, Morris. They don't erase your whole memory. They erase pill memories. The RNA in a Monk memory pill is tagged somehow, so that the eraser pill can pick it out and break it down."

Morris gaped. Presently he said, "That's incredible. The education pills are wild enough, but that—You see what they must do, don't you? They hang a radical on each and every RNA molecule in each and every education pill. The active principle in the eraser pill is an enzyme for just that radical."

He saw my expression and said, "Never mind, just take my word for it. They must have had the education pills for a hundred years before they worked out the eraser principle."

"Probably. The pills must be very old."

He pounced. "How do you know that?"

"The name for the pill has only one syllable, like *fork*. There are dozens of words for kinds of pill reflexes, for swallowing the wrong pill, for side effects depending on what species is taking the pill. There's a special word for an animal training pill, and another one for a slave training pill. Morris, I think my memory is beginning to settle down."

"Good!"

"Anyway, the Monks must have been peddling pills to aliens for thousands of years. I'd guess tens of thousands."

"Just how many kinds of pill were in that case?"

I tried to remember. My head felt congested.

"I don't know if there was more than one of each kind of pill. There were four stiff flaps like the leaves of a book, and each flap had rows of little pouches with a pill in each one. The flaps were maybe sixteen pouches long by eight across. Maybe. Morris, we ought to call Louise. She probably remembers better than I do, even if she noticed less at the time."

"You mean Louise Schu, the barmaid? She might at that. Or she might jar something loose in your memory."

"Right."

"Call her. Tell her we'll meet her. Where's she live, Santa Monica?"

He'd done his homework, all right.

Her phone was still ringing when Morris said, "Wait a minute. Tell her we'll meet her at the Long Spoon. And tell her we'll pay her amply for her trouble."

Then Louise answered and told me I'd jarred her out of a sound sleep, and I told her she'd be paid amply for her trouble, and she said what the hell kind of a crack was that?

After I hung up I asked, "Why the Long Spoon?"

"I've thought of something. I was one of the last customers out last night. I don't think you cleaned up."

"I was feeling peculiar. We cleaned up a little, I think."

"Did you empty the wastebaskets?"

"We don't usually. There's a guy who comes in in the morning and mops the floor and empties the wastebaskets and so forth. The trouble is, he's been home with flu the last couple of days. Louise and I have been going early."

"Good. Get dressed, Frazer. We'll go down to the Long Spoon and count the pieces of Monk cellophane in the wastebaskets. They shouldn't be too hard to identify. They'll tell us how many pills you took."

I noticed it while I was dressing. Morris's attitude had changed subtly. He had become proprietary. He tended to stand closer to me, as if someone might try to steal me, or as if I might try to steal away.

Imagination, maybe. But I began to wish I didn't know so much about Monks.

I stopped to empty the percolator before leaving. Habit. Every afternoon I put the percolator in the dishwasher before I leave. When I come home at three A.M. it's ready to load.

I poured out the dead coffee, took the machine apart, and stared.

The grounds in the top were fresh coffee, barely damp from steam. They hadn't been used yet.

There was another Secret Service man outside my door, a tall Midwesterner with a toothy grin. His name was George Littleton. He spoke not a word after Bill Morris introduced us, probably because I looked like I'd bite him.

I would have. My balance nagged me like a sore tooth. I couldn't forget it for an instant.

Going down in the elevator, I could feel the universe shifting around me. There seemed to be a four-dimensional map in my head, with me in the center and the rest of the universe traveling around me at various changing velocities.

The car we used was a Lincoln Continental. George drove. My map became three times as active, recording every touch of brake and accelerator.

"We're putting you on salary," said Morris, "if that's agreeable. You know more about Monks than any living man. We'll class you as a consultant and pay you a thousand dollars a day to put down all you remember about Monks.''

"I'd want the right to quit whenever I think I'm mined out."

"That seems all right," said Morris. He was lying. They would keep me just as long as they felt like it. But there wasn't a thing I could do about it at the moment.

I didn't even know what made me so sure.

So I asked, "What about Louise?"

"She spent most of her time waiting on tables, as I remember. She won't know much. We'll pay her a thousand a day for a couple of days. Anyway, for today, whether she knows anything or not."

"Okay," I said, and tried to settle back.

"You're the valuable one, Frazer. You've been fantastically lucky. That Monk language pill is going to give us a terrific advantage whenever we deal with Monks. They'll have to learn about us. We'll know about them already. Frazer, what does a Monk look like under the cowl and robe?''

"Not human," I said. "They only stand upright to make us feel at ease. And there's a swelling along one side that looks like equipment under the robe, but it isn't. It's part of the digestive system. And the head is as big as a basketball, but it's half hollow."

"They're natural quadrupeds?"

"Yah. Four-footed, but climbers. The animal they evolved from lives in forests of plants that look like giant dandelions. They can throw rocks with any foot. They're still around on Center; that's the home planet. You're not writing this down."

"There's a tape recorder going."

"Really?" I'd been kidding.

"You'd better believe it. We can use anything you happen to remember. We still don't even know how your Monk got out here to California."

My Monk, forsooth.

"They briefed me pretty quickly yesterday. Did I tell

you? I was visiting my parents in Carmel when my supervisor called me yesterday morning. Ten hours later I knew just about everything anyone knows about Monks. Except you, Frazer.

"Up until yesterday we thought that every Monk on Earth was either in the United Nations Building or aboard the Monk ground-to-orbit ship.

"We've been in that ship, Frazer. Several men have been through it, all trained astronauts wearing lunar exploration suits. Six Monks landed on Earth—unless more were hiding somewhere aboard the ground-to-orbit ship. Can you think of any reason why they should do that?"

"No."

"Neither can anyone else. And there are six Monks accounted for this morning. All in New York. Your Monk went home last night."

That jarred me. "How?"

"We don't know. We're checking plane flights, silly as that sounds. Wouldn't you think a stewardess would notice a Monk on her flight? Wouldn't you think she'd go to the newspapers?"

"Sure."

"We're also checking flying saucer sightings."

I laughed. But by now that sounded logical.

"If that doesn't pan out, we'll be seriously considering teleportation. Would you—"

"That's it," I said without surprise. It had come the way a memory comes, from the back of my mind, as if it had always been there. "He gave me a teleportation pill. That's why I've got absolute direction. To teleport I've got to know where in the universe I am."

Morris got bug-eyed. "You can teleport?"

"Not from a speeding car," I said with reflexive fear. "That's death. I'd keep the velocity."

"Oh." He was edging away as if I had sprouted horns.

More memory floated up, and I said, "Humans can't teleport anyway. That pill was for another market."

Morris relaxed. "You might have said that right away."

"I only just remembered."

"Why did you take it, if it's for aliens?"

"Probably for the location talent. I don't remember. I used to get lost pretty easily. I never will again. Morris, I'd be safer on a high wire than you'd be crossing a street with the Walk sign."

"Could that have been your 'something unusual'?"

"Maybe," I said. At the same time I was somehow sure that it wasn't.

Louise was in the dirt parking lot next to the Long Spoon. She was getting out of her Mustang when we pulled up. She waved an arm like a semaphore and walked briskly toward us, already talking. "Alien creatures in the Long Spoon, forsooth!" I'd taught her that word. "Ed, I keep telling you the customers aren't human. Hello, are you Mr. Morris? I remember you. You were in last night. You had four drinks. All night."

Morris smiled. "Yes, but I tipped big. Call me Bill, okay?"

Louise Schu was a cheerful blonde, by choice, not birth. She'd been working in the Long Spoon for five years now. A few of my regulars knew my name; but they all knew hers.

Louise's deadliest enemy was the extra twenty pounds she carried as padding. She had been dieting for some decades. Two years back she had gotten serious about it and stopped cheating. She was *mean* for the next several months. But, clawing and scratching and half-starved every second, she had worked her way down to 125 pounds. She threw a terrific celebration that night and—to hear her tell it afterward—ate her way back to 145 in a single night.

Padding or not, she'd have made someone a wonderful wife. I'd thought of marrying her myself. But my marriage had been too little fun, and was too recent, and the divorce had hurt too much. And the alimony. The alimony was why I was living in a cracker box, and also the reason I couldn't afford to get married again.

While Louise was opening up, Morris bought a paper from the coin rack.

The Long Spoon was a mess. Louise and I had cleaned off the tables and collected the dirty glasses and emptied the ashtrays into waste bins. But the collected glasses were still dirty and the waste bins were still full.

Morris began spreading newspaper over an area of floor.

And I stopped with my hand in my pocket.

Littleton came out from behind the bar, hefting both of the waste bins. He spilled one out onto the newspaper, then the other. He and Morris began spreading the trash apart.

My fingertips were brushing a scrap of Monk cellophane.

I'd worn these pants last night, under the apron.

Some impulse kept me from yelling out. I brought my hand out of my pocket, empty. Louise had gone to help the others sift the trash with their fingers. I joined them.

Presently Morris said, "Four. I hope that's all. We'll search the bar too."

And I thought: Five.

And I thought: I learned five new professions last night. What are the odds that I'll want to hide at least one of them?

If my judgment was bad enough to make me take a teleport pill intended for something with too many eyes, what else might I have swallowed last night?

I might be an advertising man, or a superbly trained thief, or a palace executioner skilled in the ways of torture. Or I might have asked for something really unpleasant, like the profession followed by Hitler or Alexander the Great.

"Nothing here," Morris said from behind the bar. Louise shrugged agreement. Morris handed the four scraps to Littleton and said, "Run these out to Douglas. Call us from there."

"We'll put them through chemical analysis," he said to Louise and me. "One of them may be real cellophane off a piece of candy. Or we might have missed one or two. For the moment let's assume there were four."

"All right," I said.

"Does it sound right, Frazer? Should it be three, or five?"

"I don't know." As far as memory went, I really didn't.

"Four, then. We've identified two. One was a course in teleportation for aliens. The other was a language course. Right?"

"It looks that way."

"What else did he give you?"

I could feel the memories floating back there, but all scrambled together. I shook my head.

Morris looked frustrated.

"Excuse me," said Louise. "Do you drink on duty?"

"Yes." Morris said without hesitation.

And Louise and I weren't on duty. Louise mixed us three gin and tonics and I brought them to us at one of the padded booths. Morris had opened a flattish briefcase that turned out to be part tape recorder. He said, "We won't lose anything now. Louise, let's talk about last night."

"I hope I can help."

"Just what happened in here after Ed took his first pill?"

"Mmm." Louise looked at me askance. "I don't know when he took that first pill. About one I noticed that he was acting strange. He was slow on orders. He got drinks wrong.

"I remembered that he had done that for a while last fall, when he got his divorce—"

I felt my face go stiff. That was unexpected pain, that memory. I am far from being my own best customer; but there had been a long lost weekend about a year ago. Louise had talked me out of trying to drink and bartend too. So I had gone drinking. When it was out of my system I had gone back to tending bar.

She was saying, "Last night I thought it might be the same problem. I covered for him, said the orders twice when I had to, watched him make the drinks so he'd get them right.

"He was spending most of his time talking to the Monk. But Ed was talking English, and the Monk was making whispery noises in his throat. Remember last week, when they put the Monk speech on television? It sounded like that.

"I saw Ed take a pill from the Monk and swallow it with a glass of water."

She turned to me, touched my arm. "I thought you were crazy. I tried to stop you."

"I don't remember."

"The place was practically empty by then. Well, you laughed at me and said that the pill would teach you not to get lost! I didn't believe it. But the Monk turned on his translator gadget and said the same thing."

"I wish you'd stopped me," I said.

She looked disturbed. "I wish you hadn't said that. I took a pill myself."

I started choking. She'd caught me with a mouthful of gin and tonic.

Louise pounded my back and saved my life, maybe. She said, "You don't remember that?"

"I don't remember much of anything coherent after I took the first pill."

"Really? You didn't seem loaded. Not after I'd watched you awhile."

Morris cut in. "Louise, the pill you took. What did the Monk say it would do?"

"He never did. We were talking about me." She stopped to think. Then, baffled and amused at herself, she said, "I don't know how it happened. All of a sudden I was telling the story of my young life. To a Monk. I had the idea he was sympathetic."

"The *Monk?*"

"Yes, the Monk. And at some point he picked out a pill

and gave it to me. He said it would help me. I believed him. I don't know why, but I believed him, and I took it.''

"Any symptoms? Have you learned anything new this morning?''

She shook her head, baffled and a little truculent now. Taking that pill must have seemed sheer insanity in the cold gray light of afternoon.

"All right," said Morris. "Frazer, you took three pills. We know what two of them were. Louise, you took one, and we have no idea what it taught you." He closed his eyes a moment, then looked at me. "Frazer, if you can't remember what you took, can you remember rejecting anything? Did the Monk offer you anything—" He saw my face and cut it off.

Because that had jarred something. . . .

The Monk had been speaking his own language, in that alien whisper that doesn't need to be more than a whisper because of the basic sounds of the Monk language are so unambiguous, so easily distinguished, even to a human ear. *This teaches proper swimming technique. A—— can reach speeds of sixteen to twenty-four——per—— using these strokes. The course also teaches proper exercises . . .*

I said, "I turned down a swimming course for intelligent fish.''

Louise giggled. Morris said, "You're kidding."

"I'm not. And there was something else." That swamped-in-data effect wasn't as bad as it had been at noon. Bits of data must be reaching cubbyholes in my head, linking up, finding their places.

"I was asking about the shapes of aliens. Not about Monks, because that's bad manners, especially from a race that hasn't yet proved its sentiency. I wanted to know about other aliens. So the Monk offered me three courses in unarmed combat techniques. Each one involved extensive knowledge of basic anatomy.''

"You didn't take them?''

"No. What for? Like, one was a pill to tell me how to

kill an armed intelligent worm, but only if I was an un-armed intelligent worm. I wasn't *that* confused."

"Frazer, there are men who would give an arm and a leg for any of those pills you turned down."

"Sure. A couple of hours ago you were telling me I was crazy to swallow an alien's education pill."

"Sorry," said Morris.

"You were the one who said they should have driven me out of my mind. Maybe they did," I said, because my hypersensitive sense of balance was still bothering the hell out of me.

But Morris's reaction bothered me worse. *Frazer could start gibbering any minute. Better pump him for all he's worth while I've got the chance.*

No, his face showed none of that. Was I going paranoid?

"Tell me more about the pills," Morris said. "It sounds like there's a lot of delayed reaction involved. How long do we have to wait before we know we've got it all?"

"He did say something . . ." I groped for it, and presently it came.

It works like a memory, the Monk had said. He'd turned off his translator and was speaking his own language, now that I could understand him. The sound of his translator had been bothering him. That was why he'd given me the pill.

But the whisper of his voice was low, and the language was new, and I'd had to listen carefully to get it all. I remembered it clearly.

The information in the pills will become part of your memory. You will not know all that you have learned until you need it. Then it will surface. Memory works by association, he'd said.

And: *There are things that cannot be taught by teachers. Always there is the difference between knowledge from school and knowledge from doing the work itself.*

"Theory and practice," I told Morris. "I know just what he meant. There's not a bartending course in the country that will teach you to leave the sugar out of an Old-Fashioned during rush hour.''

''*What* did you say?''

''It depends on the bar, of course. No posh bar would let itself get that crowded. But in an ordinary bar, anyone who orders a complicated drink during rush hour deserves what he gets. He's slowing the bartender down when it's crucial, when every second is money. So you leave the sugar out of an Old-Fashioned. It's too much money.''

''The guy won't come back.''

''So what? He's not one of your regulars. He'd have better sense if he were.''

I had to grin. Morris was shocked and horrified. I'd shown him a brand-new sin. I said, ''It's something every bartender ought to know about. Mind you, a bartending school is a trade school. They're teaching you to survive as a bartender. But the recipe calls for sugar, so at school you put in the sugar or you get ticked off.''

Morris shook his head, tight-lipped. He said, ''Then the Monk was warning you that you were getting theory, not practice.''

''Just the opposite. Look at it this way, Morris—''

''Bill.''

''Listen, Bill. The teleport pill can't make a human nervous system capable of teleportation. Even my incredible balance, and it *is* incredible, won't give me the muscles to do ten quick backflips. But I do know what it *feels* like to teleport. That's what the Monk was warning me about. The pills give field training. What you have to watch out for are the reflexes. Because the pills don't change you physically.''

''I hope you haven't become a trained assassin.''

One must be wary of newly learned reflexes, the Monk had said.

Morris said, ''Louise, we still don't know what kind of an education you got last night. Any ideas?''

''Maybe I repair time machines.'' She sipped her drink, eyed Morris demurely over the rim of the glass.

Morris smiled back. "I wouldn't be surprised."

The idiot. He meant it.

"If you really want to know what was in the pill," said Louise, "why not ask the Monk?" She gave Morris time to look startled, but no time to interrupt. "All we have to do is open up and wait. He didn't even get through the second shelf last night, did he, Ed?"

"No, by God, he didn't."

Louise swept an arm about her. "The place is a mess, of course. We'd never get it clean in time. Not without help. How about it, Bill? You're a government man. Could you get a team to work here in time to get this place cleaned up by five o'clock?"

"You know not what you ask. It's three-fifteen now!"

Truly, the Long Spoon was a disaster area. Bars are not meant to be seen by daylight anyway. Just because our worlds had been turned upside down, and just because the Long Spoon was clearly unfit for human habitation, we had been thinking in terms of staying closed tonight. Now it was too late.

"Tip Top Cleaners," I remembered."They send out a four-man team with its own mops. Fifteen bucks an hour. But we'd never get them here in time."

Morris stood up abruptly. "Are they in the phone book?"

"Sure."

Morris moved.

I waited until he was in the phone booth before I asked, "Any new thoughts on what you ate last night?"

Louise looked at me closely. "You mean the pill? Why so solemn?"

"We've got to find out before Morris does."

"Why?"

"If Morris has his way," I said, "they'll classify my head Top Secret. I know too much. I'm likely to be a political prisoner the rest of my life; and so are you, if you learned the wrong things last night."

What Louise did then I found both flattering and comforting. She turned upon the phone booth where Morris was making his call a look of such poisonous hatred that it should have withered the man where he stood.

She believed me. She needed no kind of proof, and was utterly on my side.

Why was I so sure? I had spent too much of today guessing at other people's thoughts. Maybe it had something to do with my third and fourth professions. . . .

I said, "We've got to find out what kind of pill you took. Otherwise Morris and the Secret Service will spend the rest of their lives following you around, just on the off chance that you know something useful. Like me. Only they *know* I know something useful. They'll be picking my brain until hell freezes over."

Morris yelled from the phone booth. "They're coming! Forty bucks an hour, paid in advance when they get here!"

"Great!" I yelled.

"I want to call in. New York." He closed the folding door.

Louise leaned across the table. "Ed, what are we going to do?"

It was the way she said it. We were in it together, and there was a way out, and she was sure I'd find it—and she said it all in the sound of her voice, the way she leaned toward me, the pressure of her hand around my wrist. *We.* I felt the power and confidence rising in me; and at the same time I thought: *She couldn't do that yesterday.*

I said, "We clean this place up so we can open for business. Meanwhile you try to remember what you learned last night. Maybe it was something harmless, like how to catch trilchies with a magnetic web."

"Tril—?"

"Space butterflies, kind of."

"Oh. But suppose he taught me how to build a faster-than-light motor?"

"We'd bloody have to keep Morris from finding out. But you didn't. The English words for going faster than light— hyperdrive, space warp—they don't have Monk translations except in math. You can't even say 'faster than light' in Monk.''

"Oh.''

Morris came back grinning like an idiot. "You'll never guess what the Monks want from us now.''

He looked from me to Louise to me, grinning, letting the suspense grow intolerable. He said, "A giant laser cannon.''

Louise gasped, "What?'' and I asked, "You mean a launching laser?''

"Yes, a launching laser. They want us to build it on the moon. They'd feed our engineers pills to give them the specs and to teach them how to build it. They'd pay off in more pills.''

I needed to remember something about launching lasers. And how had I known what to call it?

"They put the proposition to the United Nations,'' Morris was saying. "In fact, they'll be doing all of their business through the UN, to avoid charges of favoritism, they say, and to spread the knowledge as far as possible.''

"But there are countries that don't belong to the UN,'' Louise objected.

"The Monks know that. They asked if any of those nations had space travel. None of them do, of course. And the Monks lost interest in them.''

"Of course,'' I said, remembering. "A species that can't develop spaceflight is no better than animals.''

"*Huh?*''

"According to a Monk.''

Louise said, "But what *for?* Why would the Monks want a laser cannon? And on our moon!''

"That's a little complicated,'' said Morris. "Do you both remember when the Monk ship first appeared, two years ago?''

"No,'' we answered more or less together.

Morris was shaken. "You didn't notice? It was in all the papers. Noted Astronomer Says Alien Spacecraft Approaching Earth. No?''

"No."

"For Christ's sake! I was jumping up and down. It was like when the radio astronomers discovered pulsars, remember? I was just getting out of high school."

"Pulsars?"

"Excuse me," Morris said overpolitely. "My mistake. I tend to think that everybody I meet is a science fiction fan. Pulsars are stars that give off rhythmic pulses of radio energy. The radio astronomers thought at first that they were getting signals from outer space."

Louise said, "You're a science fiction fan?"

"Absolutely. My first gun was a GyroJet rocket pistol. I bought it because I read Buck Rogers."

I said, "Buck who?" But then I couldn't keep a straight face. Morris raised his eyes to heaven. No doubt it was there that he found the strength to go on.

"The noted astronomer was Jerome Finney. Of course he hadn't said anything about Earth. Newspapers always get that kind of thing garbled. He'd said that an object of artificial, extraterrestrial origin had entered the solar system.

"What had happened was that several months earlier, Jodrell Bank had found a new star in Sagittarius. That's the direction of the galactic core. Yes, Frazer?"

We were back to last names because I wasn't a science fiction fan. I said, "That's right. The Monks came from the galactic hub." I remembered the blazing night sky of Center. My Monk customer couldn't possibly have seen it in his lifetime. He must have been shown the vision through an education pill, for patriotic reasons, like kids are taught what the Star Spangled Banner looks like.

"All right. The astronomers were studying a nearby nova, so they caught the intruder a little sooner. It showed a strange spectrum, radically different from a nova and much more constant. It got even stranger. The light was growing brighter at the same time the spectral lines were shifting toward the red.

"It was months before anyone identified the spectrum.

"Then one Jerome Finney finally caught wise. He showed that the spectrum was the light of our own sun, drastically blue-shifted. Some kind of mirror was coming at us, moving at a hell of a clip, but slowing as it came."

"Oh!" I got it then. "That would mean a lightsail!"

"Why the big deal, Frazer? I thought you already knew."

"No. This is the first I've heard of it. I don't read the Sunday supplements."

Morris was exasperated. "But you knew enough to call the laser cannon a launching laser!"

"I just now realized why it's called that."

Morris stared at me for several seconds. Then he said, "I forgot. You got it out of the Monk language course."

"I guess so."

He got back to business. "The newspapers gave poor Finney a terrible time. You didn't see the political cartoons either? Too bad. But when the Monk ship got closer it started sending signals. It was an interstellar sailing ship, riding the sunlight on a reflecting sail, and it was coming here."

"Signals. With dots and dashes? You could to that just by tacking the sail."

"You *must* have read about it."

"Why? It's so obvious."

Morris looked unaccountably ruffled. Whatever his reasons, he let it pass. "The sail is a few molecules thick and nearly five hundred miles across when it's extended. On light pressure alone they can build up to interstellar velocities, but it takes them a long time. The acceleration isn't high.

"It took them two years to slow down to solar system velocities. They must have done a lot of braking before our telescopes found them, but even so they were going far too fast when they passed Earth's orbit. They had to go inside Mercury's orbit and come up the other side of the sun's gravity well, backing all the way, before they could get near Earth."

I said, "Sure. Interstellar speeds have to be above half the speed of light, or you can't trade competitively."

"What?"

"There are ways to get the extra edge. You don't have to depend on sunlight, not if you're launching from a civilized system. Every civilized system has a moon-based launching laser. By the time the sun is too far away to give the ship a decent push, the beam from the laser cannon is spreading just enough to give the sail a hefty acceleration without vaporizing anything."

"Naturally," said Morris, but he seemed confused.

"So that if you're heading for a strange system, you'd naturally spend most of the trip decelerating. You can't count on a strange system having a launching laser. If you know your destination is civilized, that's a different matter."

Morris nodded.

"The lovely thing about the laser cannon is that if anything goes wrong with it, there's a civilized world right there to fix it. You go sailing out to the stars with trade goods, but you leave your launching motor safely at home. Why is everybody looking at me funny?"

"Don't take it wrong," said Morris. "But how does a paunchy bartender come to know so much about flying an interstellar trading ship?"

"What?" I didn't understand him.

"Why did the Monk ship have to dive so deep into the solar system?"

"Oh, that. That's the solar wind. You get the same problem around any yellow sun. With a lightsail you can get push from the solar wind as well as from light pressure. The trouble is, the solar wind is just stripped hydrogen atoms. Light bounces from a lightsail, but the solar wind just hits the sail and sticks."

Morris nodded thoughtfully. Louise was blinking as if she had double vision.

"You can't tack against it. Tilting the sail does from

nothing. To use the solar wind for braking you have to bore straight in, straight toward the sun,'' I explained.

Morris nodded. I saw that his eyes were as glassy as Louise's eyes.

"Oh," I said. "Damn, I must be stupid today. Morris, that was the third pill."

"Right," said Morris, still nodding, still glassy-eyed. "That must have been the unusual, *really* unusual profession you wanted. Crewman on an interstellar liner. Jesus."

And he should have sounded disgusted, but he sounded envious.

His elbows were on the table, his chin rested on his fists. It is a position that distorts the mouth, making one's expression readable. But I didn't like what I could read in Morris's eyes.

There was nothing left of the square and honest man I had let into my apartment at noon. Morris was a patriot now, and an altruist, and a fanatic. He must have the stars for his nation and for all mankind. Nothing must stand in his way. Least of all, me.

Reading minds again, Frazer? Maybe being captain of an interstellar liner involves having to read the minds of the crew, to be able to put down a mutiny before some idiot can take a heat point to the *mpff glip habbabub,* or however a Monk would say it; it has something to do with straining the breathing air.

My urge to acrobatics had probably come out of the same pill. Free-fall training. There was a lot in that pill.

This was the profession I should have hidden. Not the palace torturer, who was useless to a government grown too subtle to need such techniques; but the captain of an interstellar liner, a prize too valuable to men who have not yet reached beyond the moon.

And I had been the last to know it. Too late, Frazer.

"Captain," I said. "Not crew."

"Pity. A crewman would know more about how to put

a ship together. Frazer, how big a crew are you equipped to rule?''

''Eight and five.''

''Thirteen?''

''Yes.''

''Then why did you say eight and five?''

The question caught me off balance. Hadn't I . . . ? Oh. ''That's the Monk numbering system. Base eight. Actually, base two, but they group the digits in threes to get base eight.''

''Base two. Computer numbers.''

''Are they?''

''Yes. Frazer, they must have been using computers for a long time. Eons.''

''All right.'' I noticed for the first time that Louise had collected our glasses and gone to make fresh drinks. Good, I could use one. She'd left her own, which was half full. Knowing she wouldn't mind, I took a swallow.

It was soda water.

With a lime in it. It had looked just like our gin and tonics. She must be back on the diet. Except that when Louise resumed a diet, she generally announced it to all and sundry. . . .

Morris was still on the subject. ''You use a crew of thirteen. Are they Monk or human or something else?''

''Monk,'' I said without having to think.

''Too bad. Are there humans in space?''

''No. A lot of two feet, but none of them are like any of the others, and none of them are quite like us.''

Louise came back with our drinks, gave them to us, and sat down without a word.

''You said earlier that a species that can't develop space-flight is no better than animals.''

''According to the Monks,'' I reminded him.

''Right. It seems a little extreme even to me, but let it pass. What about a race that develops spaceflight and then loses it?''

''It happens. There are lots of ways a spacegoing species can revert to animal. Atomic war. Or they just can't live with the complexity. Or they breed themselves out of food, and the world famine wrecks everything. Or waste products from the new machinery ruin the ecology.''

'' 'Revert to animal.' All right. What about nations? Suppose you have two nations next door, same species, but one has space flight—''

"Right. Good point, too. Morris, there are just two countries on Earth that can deal with the Monks without dealing through the United Nations. Us, and Russia. If Rhodesia or Brazil or France tried it, they'd be publicly humiliated.''

"That could cause an international incident.'' Morris's jaw tightened heroically. "We've got ways of passing the warning along so that it won't happen.''

Louise said, "There are some countries I wouldn't mind seeing it happen to.''

Morris got a thoughtful look . . . and I wondered if everybody would get the warning.

The cleaning team arrived then. We'd used Tip Top Cleaners before, but these four dark women were not our usual team. We had to explain in detail just what we wanted done. Not their fault. They usually clean private homes, not bars.

Morris spent some time calling New York. He must have been using a credit card; he couldn't have that much change.

"That may have stopped a minor war,'' he said when he got back. And we returned to the padded booth. But Louise stayed to direct the cleaning team.

The four dark women moved about us with pails and spray bottles and dry rags, chattering in Spanish, leaving shiny surfaces wherever they went. And Morris resumed his inquisition.

"What powers the ground-to-orbit ship?''

"A slow H-bomb going off in a magnetic bottle.''

"Fusion?''

"Yah. The attitude jets on the main starship use fusion power too. They all link to one magnetic bottle. I don't know just how it works. You get fuel from water or ice."

"Fusion. But don't you have to separate out the deuterium and tritium?"

"What for? You melt the ice, run a current through the water, and you've got hydrogen."

"Wow," Morris said softly. "Wow."

"The launching laser works the same way," I remembered. What else did I need to remember about launching lasers? Something dreadfully important.

"Wow. Frazer, if we could build the Monks their launching laser, we could use the same techniques to build other fusion plants. Couldn't we?"

"Sure." I was in dread. My mouth was dry, my heart was pounding. I almost knew why. "What do you mean, *if?*"

"And they'd pay us to do it! It's a damn shame. We just don't have the hardware."

"What do you mean? We've *got* to build the launching laser!"

Morris gaped. "Frazer, what's wrong with you?"

The terror had a name now. "My God! What have you told the Monks? Morris, listen to me. You've got to see to it that the Security Council promises to build the Monks' launching laser."

"Who do you think I am, the Secretary General? We can't build it anyway, not with just Saturn launching configurations." Morris thought I'd gone mad at last. He wanted to back away through the wall of the booth.

"They'll do it when you tell them what's at stake. And we can build a launching laser, if the whole world goes in on it. Morris, look at the good it can do! Free power from seawater! And lightsails work *fine* within a system."

"Sure, it's a lovely picture. We could sail out to the moons of Jupiter and Saturn. We could smelt the asteroids for their metal ores, using laser power. . . ." His eyes had momentarily taken on a vague, dreamy look. Now they snapped back to what Morris thought of as reality. "It's the kind of thing I daydreamed about when I was a kid. Someday we'll do it. Today—we just aren't ready."

"There are two sides to a coin," I said. "Now, I know how this is going to sound. Just remember there are reasons. Good reasons."

"Reasons? Reasons for what?"

"When a trading ship travels," I said, "It travels only from one civilized system to another. There are ways to tell whether a system has a civilization that can build a launching laser. Radio is one. Earth puts out as much radio flux as a small star.

"When the Monks find that much radio energy coming from a nearby star, they send a trade ship. By the time the ship gets there, the planet that's putting out all the energy is generally civilized. But not so civilized that it can't use the knowledge a Monk trades for.

"Do you see that they *need* the launching laser? That ship out there came from a Monk colony. This far from the axis of the galaxy, the stars are too far apart. Ships launch by starlight and laser, but they brake by starlight alone, because they can't count on the target star having a launching laser. If they had to launch by starlight too, they probably wouldn't make it. A plant-and-animal cycle as small as the life-support system on a Monk starship can last only so long."

"You said yourself that the Monks can't always count on the target star staying civilized."

"No, of course not. Sometimes a civilization hits the level at which it can build a launching laser, stays there just long enough to send out a mass of radio waves, then reverts to animal. That's the point. If we tell them we can't build the laser, we'll be animals to the Monks."

"Suppose we just refuse? Not *can't* but *won't.*"

"That would be stupid. There are too many advantages. Controlled fusion—"

"Frazer, think about the cost." Morris looked grim. He wanted the laser. He didn't think he could get it.

"Think about politicians thinking about the cost," he said. "Think about politicians thinking about explaining the cost to the taxpayers."

"Stupid," I repeated, "and inhospitable. Hospitality counts high with the Monks. You see, we're cooked either way. Either we're dumb animals, or we're guilty of a criminal breach of hospitality. And the Monk ship *still* needs more light for its lightsail than the sun can put out."

"So?"

"So the captain uses a gadget that makes the sun explode."

"The," said Morris, and "Sun," and "Explode?" He didn't know what to do. Then suddenly he burst out in great loud cheery guffaws, so that the women cleaning the Long Spoon turned with answering smiles. He'd decided not to believe me.

I reached across and gently pushed his drink into his lap.

It was two-thirds empty, but it cut his laughter off in an instant. Before he could start swearing, I said, "I am not playing games. The Monks will make our sun explode if we don't build them a launching laser. Now go call your boss and tell him so."

The women were staring at us in horror. Louise started toward us, then stopped, uncertain.

Morris sounded almost calm. "Why the drink in my lap?"

"Shock treatment. And I wanted your full attention. Are you going to call New York?"

"Not yet." Morris swallowed. He looked down once at the spreading stain on his pants, then somehow put it out of his mind. "Remember, I'd have to convince him. I don't believe it myself. Nobody and nothing would blow up a sun for a breach of hospitality!"

"No, no, Morris. They have to blow up the sun to get to the next system. It's a serious thing, refusing to build the launching laser! It could wreck the *ship!*"

"Screw the ship! What about a whole planet?"

"You're just not looking at it right—"

"Hold it. Your ship is a trading ship, isn't it? What kind of idiots would the Monks be, to exterminate one market just to get on to the next?"

"If we can't build a launching laser, we aren't a market."

"But we might be a market on the next circuit!"

"What next circuit? You don't seem to grasp the *size* of the Monks' marketplace. The communications gap between Center and the nearest Monk colony is about—" I stopped to transpose—"sixty-four thousand years! By the time a ship finishes one circuit, most of the worlds she's visited have already forgotten her. And then what? The colony world that built her may have failed, or refitted the spaceport to service a different style of ship, or reverted to animal; even Monks do that. She'd have to go on to the next system for refitting.

"When you trade among the stars, *there is no repeat business.*"

"Oh," said Morris.

Louise had gotten the women back to work. With a corner of my mind I heard their giggling discussion as to whether Morris would fight, whether he could whip me, etc.

Morris asked, "How does it work? How do you make a sun go nova?"

"There's a gadget the size of a locomotive fixed to the . . . main supporting strut, I guess you'd call it. It points straight astern, and it can swing sixteen degrees or so in any direction. You turn it on when you make departure orbit. The math man works out the intensity. You beam the sun for the first year or so, and when it blows, you're just far enough away to use the push without getting burned."

"But how does it work?"

"You just turn it on. The power comes from the fusion tube that feeds the attitude jet system. —Oh, you want to

know why does it make a sun explode. I don't know that.
Why should I?''

"Big as a locomotive. And it makes suns explode."
Morris sounded slightly hysterical. Poor bastard, he was
beginning to believe me. The shock had hardly touched
me, because truly I had known it since last night.

He said, "When we first saw the Monk lightsail, it was
just to one side of a recent nova in Sagittarius. By any
wild chance, was that star a market that didn't work out?"

"I haven't the vaguest idea."

That convinced him. If I'd been making it up, I'd have
said yes. Morris stood up and walked away without a word.
He stopped to pick up a bar towel on his way to the phone
booth.

I went behind the bar to make a fresh drink. Cutty over
ice, splash of soda; I wanted to taste the burning power of
it.

Through the glass door I saw Louise getting out of her
car with her arms full of packages. I poured soda over ice,
squeezed a lime in it, and had it ready when she walked
in.

She dumped the load on the bar top. "Irish-coffee makings," she said. I held the glass out to her and she said,
"No thanks, Ed. One's enough."

"Taste it."

She gave me a funny look, but she tasted what I handed
her. "Soda water. Well, you caught me."

"Back on the diet?"

"Yes."

"You never said *yes* to that question in your life. Don't
you want to tell me all the details?"

She sipped at her drink. "Details of someone else's diet
are boring. I should have known that a long time ago. To
work! You'll notice we've only got twenty minutes."

I opened one of her paper bags and fed the refrigerator
with cartons of whipping cream. Another bag held fresh-
ground coffee. The flat, square package had to be a pizza.

"Pizza. Some diet," I said.

She was setting out the glass coffeemakers. "That's for you and Bill."

I tore open the paper and bit into a pie-shaped slice. It was a deluxe, covered with everything from anchovies to salami. It was crisp and hot, and I was starving.

I snatched bites as I worked.

There aren't many bars that will keep the makings for Irish coffee handy. It's too much trouble. You need massive quantities of whipping cream and ground coffee, a refrigerator, a blender, a supply of those glass figure-eight-shaped coffeemakers, a line of hot plates, and—most expensive of all—room behind the bar for all of that. You learn to keep a line of glasses ready, which means putting the sugar in them at spare moments to save time later. Those spare moments are your smoking time, so you give that up. You learn not to wave your arms around because there are hot things that can burn you. You learn to half-whip the cream, a mere spin of the blender, because you have to do it over and over again, and if you overdo it the cream turns to butter.

There aren't many bars that will go to all that trouble. That's why it pays off. Your average Irish-coffee addict will drive an extra twenty minutes to reach the Long Spoon. He'll also down the drink in about five minutes, because otherwise it gets cold. He'd have spent half an hour over a Scotch and soda.

While we were getting the coffee ready, I found time to ask, "Have you remembered anything?"

"Yes," she said.

"Tell me."

"I don't mean I know what was in the pill. Just . . . I can do things I couldn't do before. I think my way of thinking has changed. Ed, I'm worried."

"Worried?"

She got the words out in a rush. "It feels like I've been falling in love with you for a very long time. But I haven't. Why should I feel that way so suddenly?"

The bottom dropped out of my stomach. I'd had thoughts like this . . . and put them out of my mind, and when they came back I did it again. I couldn't afford to fall in love. It would cost too much. It would hurt too much.

"It's been like this all day. It scares me, Ed. Suppose I feel like this about every man? What if the Monk thought I'd make a good call girl?"

I laughed much harder than I should have. Louise was getting really angry before I was able to stop.

"Wait a minute," I said. "Are you in love with Bill Morris too?"

"No, of course not!"

"Then forget the call-girl bit. He's got more money than I do. A call girl would love him more, if she loved anyone, which she wouldn't, because call girls are generally frigid."

"How do you know?" she demanded.

"I read it in a magazine."

Louise began to relax. I began to see how tense she really had been. "All right," she said, "but that means I really am in love with you."

I pushed the crisis away from us. "Why didn't you ever get married?"

"Oh . . ." She was going to pass it off, but she changed her mind. "Every man I dated wanted to sleep with me. I thought that was wrong, so—"

She looked puzzled. "Why did I think that was wrong?"

"Way you were brought up."

"Yes, but . . ." She trailed off.

"How do you feel about it now?"

"Well, I wouldn't sleep with *anyone*, but if a man was worth dating he might be worth marrying, and if he was worth marrying he'd certainly be worth sleeping with, wouldn't he? And I'd be crazy to marry someone I hadn't slept with, wouldn't I?"

"I did."

"And look how that turned out! Oh, Ed, I'm sorry. But you did bring it up."

"Yah," I said, breathing shallow.

"But I used to feel that way too. Something's changed."

We hadn't been talking fast. There had been pauses, gaps, and we had worked through them. I had had time to eat three slices of pizza. Louise had had time to wrestle with her conscience, lose, and eat one.

Only she hadn't done it. There was the pizza, staring at her, and she hadn't given it a look or a smell. For Louise, that was unusual.

Half-joking, I said, "Try this as a theory. Years ago you must have sublimated your sex urge into an urge for food. Either that or the rest of us sublimated our appetites into a sex urge, and you didn't."

"Then the pill unsublimated me, hmm?" She looked thoughtfully at the pizza. Clearly its lure was gone. "That's what I mean. I didn't used to be able to outstare a pizza."

"Those olive eyes."

"Hypnotic, they were."

"A good call girl should be able to keep herself in shape." Immediately I regretted saying it. It wasn't funny. "Sorry," I said.

"It's all right." She picked up a tray of candles in red glass vases and moved away, depositing the candles on the small square tables. She moved with grace and beauty through the twilight of the Long Spoon, her hips swaying just enough to avoid the sharp corners of tables.

I'd hurt her. But she'd known me long enough; she must know I had foot-in-mouth disease. . . .

I had seen Louise before and known that she was beautiful. But it seemed to me that she had never been beautiful with so little excuse.

She moved back by the same route, lighting the candles as she went. Finally she put the tray down, leaned across the bar, and said, "I'm sorry. I can't joke about it when I don't *know.*"

"Stop worrying, will you? Whatever the Monk fed you, he was trying to help you."

"I love you."

"What?"

"I love you."

"Okay. I love you too." I use those words so seldom that they clog in my throat, as if I'm lying, even when it's the truth. "Listen, I want to marry you. Don't shake your head. I want to marry you."

Our voices had dropped to whispers. In a tormented whisper, then, she said, "Not until I find out what I *do*, what was in the *pill*. Ed, I can't trust myself until then!"

"Me too," I said with great reluctance. "But we can't wait. You don't have time."

"What?"

"That's right, you weren't in earshot. Sometime between three and ten years from now, the Monks may blow up our sun."

Louise said nothing. Her forehead winkled:

"It depends on how much time they spend trading. If we can't build them the launching laser, we can still con them into waiting for a while. Monk expeditions have waited as long as—"

"Good Lord. You mean it. Is that what you and Bill were fighting over?"

"Yah."

Louise shuddered. Even in the dimness I saw how pale she had become. And she said a strange thing.

She said, "All right, I'll marry you."

"Good," I said. But I was suddenly shaking. Married. Again. Me. Louise stepped up and put her hands on my shoulders, and I kissed her.

I'd been wanting to do that for . . . five years? She fitted wonderfully into my arms. Her hands closed hard on the muscles of my shoulders, massaging. The tension went out of me, drained away somewhere. Married. Us. At least we could have three to ten years.

"Morris," I said.

She drew back a little. "He can't hold you. You haven't done anything. Oh, I *wish* I knew what was in that pill I took! Suppose I'm the trained assassin?"

"Suppose I am? We'll have to be careful of each other."

"Oh, we know all about you. You're a starship commander, an alien teleport, and a translator for Monks."

"And one thing more. There was a fourth profession. I took four pills last night, not three."

"Oh? Why didn't you tell Bill?"

"Are you kidding? Dizzy as I was last night, I probably took a course in how to lead a successful revolution. God help me if Morris found *that* out."

She smiled. "Do you really think that was what it was?"

"No, of course not."

"Why did we do it? Why did we swallow those pills? We should have known better."

"Maybe the Monk took a pill himself. Maybe there's a pill that teaches a Monk how to look trustworthy to a generalized alien."

"I did trust him," said Louise. "I remember. He seemed so sympathetic. Would he really blow up our sun?"

"He really would."

"That fourth pill. Maybe it taught you a way to stop him."

"Let's see. We know I took a linguistics course, a course in teleportation for martians, and a course in how to fly a lightsail ship. On that basis . . . I probably changed my mind and took a karate course for worms."

"It wouldn't hurt you, at least. Relax. . . . Ed, if you remember taking the pills, why don't you remember what was in them?"

"But I don't. I don't remember anything."

"How do you know you took four, then?"

"Here." I reached in my pocket and pulled out the scrap of Monk cellophane. And knew immediately that there was something in it. Something hard and round.

We were staring at it when Morris came back.

"I must have cleverly put it in my pocket," I told them. "Sometime last night, when I was feeling sneaky enough to steal from a Monk."

Morris turned the pill like a precious jewel in his fingers. Pale blue it was, marked on one side with a burnt orange triangle. "I don't know whether to get it analyzed or take it myself, now. We need a miracle. Maybe this will tell us—"

"Forget it. I wasn't clever enough to remember how fast a Monk pill deteriorates. The wrapping's torn. That pill has been bad for at least twelve hours."

Morris said a dirty thing.

"Analyze it," I said. "You'll find RNA, and you may even be able to tell what the Monks use as a matrix. Most of the memories are probably intact. But don't swallow the damn thing. It'll scramble your brains. All it takes is a few random changes in a tiny percentage of the RNA."

"We don't have time to send it to Douglass tonight. Can we put it in the freezer?"

"Good. Give it here."

I dropped the pill in a sandwich-size plastic bag, sucked the air out of the top, tied the end, and dropped it in the freezer. Vacuum and cold would help preserve the thing. It was something I should have done last night.

"So much for miracles," Morris said bitterly. "Let's get down to business. We'll have several men outside the place tonight, and a few more in here. You won't know who they are, but go ahead and guess if you like. A lot of your customers will be turned away tonight. They'll be told to watch the newspapers if they want to know why. I hope it won't cost you too much business."

"It may make our fortune. We'll be famous. Were you maybe doing the same thing last night?"

"Yes. We didn't want the place too crowded. The Monks might not like autograph hounds."

"So that's why the place was half empty."

Morris looked at his watch. "Opening time. Are we ready?"

"Take a seat at the bar. And look nonchalant, dammit."

Louise went to turn on the lights.

Morris took a seat to one side of the middle. One big

square hand was closed very tightly on the bar edge. "Another gin and tonic. Weak. After that one, leave out the gin."

"Right."

"Nonchalant. Why should I be nonchalant? Frazer, I had to tell the President of the United States of America that the end of the world is coming unless he does something. I had to talk to him myself!"

"Did he buy it?"

"I hope so. He was so goddam calm and reassuring, I wanted to scream at him. God, Frazer, what if we can't build the laser? What if we try and fail?"

I gave him a very old and classic answer. "Stupidity is always a capital crime."

He screamed in my face, "Damn you and your supercilious attitude and your murdering monsters too!" The next second he was ice-water calm. "Never mind, Frazer. You're thinking like a starship captain."

"I'm what?"

"A starship captain has to be able to make a sun go nova to save the ship. You can't help it. It was in the pill."

Damn, he was right. I could *feel* that he was right. The pill had warped my way of thinking. Blowing up the sun that warms another race *had* to be immoral. Didn't it?

I couldn't trust my own sense of right and wrong!

Four men came in and took one of the bigger tables. Morris's men? No. Real estate men, here to do business.

"Something's been bothering me," said Morris. He grimaced. "Among all the things that have been ruining my composure, such as the impending end of the world, there was one thing that kept nagging at me."

I set his gin and tonic in front of him. He tasted it and said, "Fine. And I finally realized what it was, waiting there in the phone booth for a chain of human snails to put the President on. Frazer, are you a college man?"

"No. Webster High."

"See, you don't really talk like a bartender. You use big words."

"I do?"

"Sometimes. And you talked about 'suns exploding,' but you knew what I meant when I said 'nova.' You talked about 'H-bomb power,' but you knew what fusion was."

"Sure."

"I got the possibly silly impression that you were learning the words the instant I said them. *Parlez-vous français?*"

"No. I don't speak any foreign languages."

"None at all?"

"Nope. What do you think they teach at Webster High?"

"Je parle la langue un peu, Frazer. *Et tu?"*

"Merde de cochon! Morris, *je vous dit*—oops."

He didn't give me a chance to think it over. He said, "What's *fanac?*"

My head had that *clogged* feeling again. I said, "Might be anything. Putting out a zine, writing to the lettercol, helping put on a Con—Morris what *is* this?"

"That language course was more extensive than we thought."

"Sure as hell it was. I just remembered. Those women on the cleaning team were speaking Spanish, but I understood them."

"Spanish, French, Monkish, technical languages, even Fannish. What you got was a generalized course in how to understand languages the instant you hear them. I don't see how it could work without telepathy."

"Reading minds? Maybe." Several times today it had felt like I was guessing with too much certainty at somebody's private thoughts.

"Can you read my mind?"

"That's not quite it. I get the feel of *how* you think, not *what* you're thinking. Morris, I don't like the idea of being a political prisoner."

"Well, we can talk that over later." *When my bargaining position is better,* Morris meant. *When I don't need the bartender's good will to con the Monk.* "What's important is that you might be able to read a Monk's mind. That could be crucial."

"And maybe he can read mine. And yours."

I let Morris sweat over that one while I set drinks on Louise's tray. Already there were customers at four tables. The Long Spoon was filling rapidly; and only two of them were Secret Service.

Morris said, "Any ideas on what Louise Schu ate last night? We've got your professions pretty well pegged down. Finally."

"I've got an idea. It's kind of vague." I looked around. Louise was taking more orders. "Sheer guesswork, in fact. Will you keep it to yourself for a while?"

"Don't tell Louise? Sure—for a while."

I made four drinks, and Louise took them away. I told Morris, "I have a profession in mind. It doesn't have a simple one-or-two-word name, like teleport or starship captain or translator. There's no reason why it should, is there? We're dealing with aliens."

Morris sipped at his drink. Waiting.

"Being a woman," I said, "can be a profession, in a way that being a man can never be. The word is *housewife*, but it doesn't cover all of it. Not nearly."

"Housewife. You're putting me on."

"No. You wouldn't notice the change. You never saw her before last night."

"Just what kind of change have you got in mind? Aside from the fact that she's beautiful, which I did notice."

"Yes, she is, Morris. But last night she was twenty pounds overweight. Do you think she lost it all this morning?"

"She *was* too heavy. Pretty, but also pretty well padded." Morris turned to look over his shoulder, casually turned back. "Damn. She's still well padded. Why didn't I notice before?"

"There's another thing. —By the way, have some pizza."

"Thanks." He bit into a slice. "Good, it's still hot. Well?"

"She's been staring at that pizza for half an hour. She bought it. But she hasn't tasted it. She couldn't possibly have done that yesterday."

"She may have had a big breakfast."

"Yah." I knew she hadn't. She'd eaten diet food. For years she'd kept a growing collection of diet food, but she'd never actively tried to survive on it before. But how could I make such a claim to Morris? I'd never even been in Louise's apartment.

"Anything else?"

"She's gotten good at nonverbal communication. It's a very womanly skill. She can say things just by the tone of her voice or the way she leans on an elbow or—"

"But if mind reading is one of your new skills . . ."

"Damn. Well . . . it used to make Louise nervous if someone touched her. And she never touched anyone else." I felt myself flushing. I don't talk easily of personal things.

Morris radiated skepticism. "It all sounds very subjective. In fact, it sounds like you're making yourself believe it. Frazer, why should Louise Schu want such a capsule course? Because you haven't described a housewife at all. You've described a woman looking to persuade a man to marry her." He saw my face change. "What's wrong?"

"Ten minutes ago we decided to get married."

"Congratulations," Morris said, and waited.

"All right, you win. Until ten minutes ago we'd never even kissed. I'd never made a pass, or vice versa. No, dammit, I don't believe it! I *know* she loves me; I ought to!"

"I don't deny it," Morris said quietly. "That would be why she took the pill. It must have been strong stuff, too, Frazer. We looked up some of your history. You're marriage-shy."

It was true enough. I said, "If she loved me before, I never knew it. I wonder how a Monk could know."

"How would he know about such a skill at all? Why

would he have the pill on him? Come on, Frazer, you're the Monk expert!''

"He'd have to learn from human beings. Maybe by interviews, maybe by—well, the Monks can map an alien memory into a computer space, then interview that. They may have done that with some of your diplomats.''

"Oh, *great.*''

Louise appeared with an order. I made the drinks and set them on her tray. She winked and walked away, swaying deliciously, followed by many eyes.

"Morris. Most of your diplomats, the ones who deal with the Monks—they're men, aren't they?''

"Most of them. Why?''

"Just a thought.''

It was a difficult thought, hard to grasp. It was only that the changes in Louise had been all to the good from a man's point of view. The Monks must have interviewed many men. Well, why not? It would make her more valuable to the man she caught—or to the lucky man who caught her—

"Got it.''

Morris looked up quickly. "Well?''

"Falling in love with me was part of her pill learning. A *set*. They made a guinea pig of her.''

"I wondered what she saw in you.'' Morris's grin faded. "You're serious. Frazer, that still doesn't answer—''

"It's a slave indoctrination course. It makes a woman love the first man she sees, permanently, and it trains her to be valuable to him. The Monks were going to make them in quantity and sell them to men.''

Morris thought it over. Presently he said, "That's awful. What'll we do?''

"Well, we can't tell her she's been made into a domestic slave! Morris, I'll try to get a memory eraser pill. If I can't . . . I'll marry her, I guess. Don't look at me that way,'' I said, low and fierce. "I didn't do it. And I can't desert her now!''

"I know. It's just—oh, put gin in the next one.''

"Don't look now," I said.

In the glass of the door there was darkness and motion. A hooded shape, shadow-on-shadow, supernatural, a human silhouette twisted out of true . . .

He came gliding in with the hem of his robe just brushing the floor. Nothing was to be seen of him but his flowing gray robe, the darkness in the hood and the shadow where his robe parted. The real estate men broke off their talk of land and stared, popeyed, and one of them reached for his heart-attack pills.

The Monk drifted toward me like a vengeful ghost. He took the stool we had saved him at one end of the bar.

It wasn't the same Monk.

In all respects he matched the Monk who had been here these last two nights. Louise and Morris must have been fooled completely. But it wasn't the same Monk.

"Good evening," I said.

He gave an equivalent greeting in the whispered Monk language. His translator was half on, translating my words into a Monk whisper, but letting his own speech alone. He said, "I believe we should begin with the Rock and Rye."

I turned to pour. The small of my back itched with danger.

When I turned back with the shot glass in my hand, he was holding a fist-sized tool that must have come out of his robe. It looked like a flattened softball, grooved deeply for five Monk claws, with two parallel tubes poking out in my direction. Lenses glinted in the ends of the tubes.

"Do you know this tool? It is a——" and he named it.

I knew the name. It was a beaming tool, a multifrequency laser. One tube locked on the target; thereafter the aim was maintained by tiny flywheels in the body of the device.

Morris had seen it. He didn't recognize it, and he didn't know what to do about it, and I had no way to signal him.

"I know that tool," I confirmed.

"You must take two of these pills." The Monk had them ready in another hand. They were small and pink and triangular. He said, "I must be convinced that you have taken them. Otherwise you must take more than two. An overdose may affect your natural memory. Come closer."

I came closer. Every man and woman in the Long Spoon was staring at us, and each was afraid to move. Any kind of signal would have trained four guns on the Monk. And I'd be fried dead by a narrow beam of X-rays.

The Monk reached out with a third hand/foot/claw. He closed the fingers/toes around my throat, not hard enough to strangle me, but hard enough.

Morris was cursing silently, helplessly. I could feel the agony in his soul.

The Monk whispered, "You know of the trigger mechanism. If my hand should relax now, the device will fire. Its target is yourself. If you can prevent four government agents from attacking me, you should do so."

I made a palm-up gesture toward Morris. *Don't do anything.* He caught it and nodded very slightly without looking at me.

"You can read minds," I said.

"Yes," said the Monk—and I knew instantly what he was hiding. He could read everybody's mind, except mine.

So much for Morris's little games of deceit. But the Monk could not read my mind, and I could see into his own soul.

And, reading his alien soul, I saw that I would die if I did not swallow the pills.

I placed the pink pills on my tongue, one at a time, and swallowed them dry. They went down hard. Morris watched it happen and could do nothing. The Monk felt them going down my throat, little lumps moving past his finger.

And when the pills had passed across the Monk's finger, I worked a miracle.

"Your pill-induced memories and skills will be gone

within two hours," said the Monk. He picked up the shot glass of Rock and Rye and moved it into his hood. When it reappeared it was half empty.

I asked, "Why have you robbed me of my knowledge?"

"You never paid for it."

"But it was freely given."

"It was given by one who had no right," said the Monk. He was thinking about leaving. I had to do something. I knew now, because I had reasoned it out with great care, that the Monk was involved in an evil enterprise. But he must stay to hear me or I could not convince him.

Even then, it wouldn't be easy. He was a Monk crewman. His ethical attitudes had entered his brain through an RNA pill, along with his professional skills.

"You have spoken of rights," I said. In Monk. "Let us discuss rights." The whispery words buzzed oddly in my throat; they tickled; but my ears told me they were coming out right.

The Monk was startled. "I was told that you had been taught our speech, but not that you could speak it."

"Were you told what pill I was given?"

"A language pill. I had not known that he carried one in his case."

"He did not finish his tasting of the alcohols of Earth. Will you have another drink?"

I felt him guess at my motives, and guess wrong. He thought I was taking advantage of his curiosity to sell him my wares for cash. And what had he to fear from me? Whatever mental powers I had learned from Monk pills, they would be gone in two hours.

I set a shot glass before him. I asked him, "How do you feel about launching lasers?"

The discussion became highly technical. "Let us take a special case," I remember saying. "Suppose a culture has been capable of starflight for some sixty-fours of years—or even for eight of times that long. Then an asteroid slams into a major ocean, precipitates an ice age . . ." It had happened once, and well he knew it. "A natural disaster can't spell the difference between sentience and nonsentience, can it? Not unless it affects brain tissue directly."

At first it was his curiosity that held him. Later it was me. He couldn't tear himself loose. He never thought of it. He was a sailship crewman, and he was cold sober, and he argued with the frenzy of an evangelist.

"Then take the general case," I remember saying. "A world that cannot build a launching laser is a world of animals, yes? And Monks themselves can revert to animals."

Yes, he knew that.

"Then build your own launching laser. If you cannot, then your ship is captained and crewed by animals."

At the end I was doing all the talking. All in the whispery Monk tongue, whose sounds are so easily distinguished that even I, warping a human throat to my will, need only whisper. It was a good thing. I seemed to have been eating used razor blades.

Morris guessed right. He did not interfere. I could tell him nothing, not if I had had the power, not by word or gesture or mental contact. The Monk would read Morris's mind. But Morris sat quietly drinking his tonic and tonics, waiting for something to happen. While I argued in whispers with the Monk.

"But the ship!" he whispered. "What of the ship?" His agony was mine; for the ship must be protected. . . .

At one-fifteen the Monk was halfway across the bottom row of bottles. He slid from the stool, paid for his drinks in one-dollar bills, and drifted to the door and out.

All he needed was a scythe and hourglass, I thought, watching him go. And what I needed was a long morning's sleep. And I wasn't going to get it.

"Be sure nobody stops him," I told Morris.

"Nobody will. But he'll be followed."

"No point. The Garment to Wear Among Strangers is a lot of things. It's bracing; it helps the Monk hold human shape. It's a shield and an air filter. And it's a cloak of invisibility.''

"Oh?"

"I'll tell you about it if I have time. That's how he got out here, probably. One of the crewmen divided, and then one stayed and one walked. He had two weeks.''

Morris stood up and tore off his sport jacket. His shirt was wet through. He said, "What about a stomach pump for you?"

"No good. Most of the RNA enzyme must be in my blood by now. You'll be better off if you spend your time getting down everything I can remember about Monks while I can remember anything at all. It'll be nine or ten hours before everything goes.'' Which was a flat-out lie, of course.

"Okay. Let me get the dictaphone going again.''

"It'll cost you money.''

Morris suddenly had a hard look. "Oh? How much?''

I'd thought about that most carefully. "One hundred thousand dollars. And if you're thinking of arguing me down, remember whose time we're wasting.''

"I wasn't.'' He was, but he'd changed his mind.

"Good. We'll transfer the money now, while I can still read your mind.''

"All right.''

He offered to make room for me in the booth, but I declined. The glass wouldn't stop me from reading Morris's soul.

He came out silent; for there was something he was afraid to know. Then: "What about the Monks? What about our sun?''

"I talked that one around. That's why I don't want him molested. He'll convince others.''

"Talked him around? How?''

"It wasn't easy.'' And suddenly I would have given my soul to sleep. "The profession pill put it in his genes; he must protect the ship. It's in me too. I know how strong it is.''

"Then—"

"Don't be an ass, Morris. The ship's perfectly safe where it is, in orbit around the moon. A sailship's only in danger when it's between stars, far from help."

"Oh."

"Not that that convinced him. It only let him consider the ethics of the situation rationally."

"Suppose someone else unconvinces him?"

"It could happen. That's why we'd better build the launching laser."

Morris nodded unhappily.

The next twelve hours were rough.

In the first four hours I gave them everything I could remember about the Monk teleport system, Monk technology, Monk family life, Monk ethics, relations between Monks and aliens, details on aliens, directions of various inhabited, and uninhabited worlds . . . everything. Morris and the Secret Service men who had been posing as customers sat around me like boys around a campfire, listening to stories. But Louise made us fresh coffee, then went to sleep in one of the booths.

Then I let myself slack off.

By nine in the morning I was flat on my back, staring at the ceiling, dictating a random useless bit of information every thirty seconds or so. By eleven there was a great black pool of lukewarm coffee inside me, my eyes ached marginally more than the rest of me, and I was producing nothing.

I was convincing, and I knew it.

But Morris wouldn't let it go at that. He believed me. I felt him believing me. But he was going through the routine anyway, because it couldn't hurt. If I was useless to him, if I knew nothing, there was no point in playing soft. What could he lose?

He accused me of making everything up. He accused me of faking the pills. He made me sit up, and damn near caught me that way. He used obscure words and phrases from mathematics and Latin and Fan vocabulary. He got nowhere. There wasn't any way to trick me.

At two in the afternoon he had someone drive me home.

Every muscle in me ached; but I had to fight to maintain my exhausted slump. Else my hindbrain would have lifted me onto my toes and poised me against a possible shift in artificial gravity. The strain was double, and it hurt. It had hurt for hours, sitting with my shoulders hunched and my head hanging. But now, if Morris saw me walking like a trampoline performer . . .

Morris's man got me to my room and left me.

I woke in darkness and sensed someone in my room. Someone who meant me no harm. In fact, Louise. I went back to sleep.

I woke again at dawn. Louise was in my easy chair, her feet propped on a corner of the bed. Her eyes were open. She said, "Breakfast?"

I said, "Yah. There isn't much in the fridge."

"I brought things."

"All right." I closed my eyes.

Five minutes later I decided I was all slept out. I got up and went to see how she was doing.

There was bacon frying, there was bread already buttered for toasting in the Toast-R-Oven, there was a pan hot for eggs, and the eggs scrambled in a bowl. Louise was filling the percolator.

"Give that here a minute," I said. It only had water in it. I held the pot in my hands, closed my eyes and tried to remember. . . .

Ah.

I knew I'd done it right even before the heat touched my hands. The pot held hot, fragrant coffee.

"We were wrong about the first pill," I told Louise. She was looking at me very curiously. "What happened that second night was this. The Monk had a translator gadget, but he wasn't too happy with it. It kept screaming in his ear. Screaming English.

"He could turn off the part that was shouting English at *me*, and it would still whisper a Monk translation of what I was saying. But first he had to teach me the Monk language. He didn't have a pill to do that. He didn't have a generalized language-learning course either, if there is one, which I doubt.

"He was pretty drunk, but he found something that would serve. The profession it taught me was something like yours. I mean, it's an old one, and it doesn't have a one-or-two-word name. But if it did, the word would be *prophet.*"

"Prophet," said Louise. "Prophet?" She was doing a remarkable thing. She was listening with all her concentration, and scrambling eggs at the same time.

"Or *disciple*. Maybe *apostle* comes closer. Anyway, it included the Gift of Tongues, which was what the Monk was after. But it included other talents too."

"Like turning cold water into hot coffee?"

"Miracles, right. I used the same talent to make the little pink amnesia pills disappear before they hit my stomach. But an apostle's major talent is persuasion.

"Last night I convinced a Monk crewman that blowing up suns is an evil thing.

"Morris is afraid that someone might convert him back. I don't think that's possible. The mind-reading talent that goes with the prophet pill goes deeper than just reading minds. I read souls. The Monk is my apostle. Maybe he'll convince the whole crew that I'm right.

"Or he may just curse the *hachiroph shisp*, the little old nova maker. Which is what I intend to do."

"Curse it?"

"Do you think I'm kidding or something?"

"Oh, no." She poured our coffee. "Will that stop it working?"

"Yes."

"Good," said Louise. And I felt the power of her own faith, her faith in me. It gave her the serenity of an idealized nun.

When she turned back to serve the eggs, I dropped a pink triangular pill in her coffee.

She finished setting breakfast and we sat down. Louise said, "Then that's it. It's all over."

"All over." I swallowed some orange juice. Wonderful, what fourteen hours' sleep will do for a man's appetite. "All over. I can go back to my fourth profession, the only one that counts."

She looked up quickly.

"Bartender. First, last, and foremost, I'm a bartender. You're going to marry a bartender."

"Good," she said, relaxing.

In two hours or so the slave sets would be gone from her mind. She would be herself again: free, independent, unable to diet, and somewhat shy.

But the pink pill would not destroy real memories. Two hours from now, Louise would still know that I loved her; and perhaps she would marry me after all.

I said, "We'll have to hire an assistant. And raise our prices. They'll be fighting their way in when the story gets out."

Louise had pursued her own thoughts. "Bill Morris looked awful when I left. You ought to tell him he can stop worrying."

"Oh, no. I *want* him scared. Morris has got to talk the rest of the world into building a launching laser, instead of just throwing bombs at the Monk ship. And we need the launching laser."

"Mmm! That's good coffee. Why do we need a launching laser?"

"To get to the stars."

"That's Morris's bag. You're a bartender, remember? The fourth profession."

I shook my head. "You and Morris. You don't see how *big* the Monk marketplace is, or how thin the Monks are scattered. How many novas have you seen in your lifetime?

"Damn few," I said. "There are damn few trading ships

in a godawful lot of sky. There are things out there besides Monks. Things the Monks are afraid of, and probably others they don't know about.

"Things so dangerous that the only protection is to be somewhere else, circling some other star, when it happens here! The Monk drive is our lifeline and our immortality. It would be cheap at any price—"

"Your eyes are glowing," she breathed. She looked half hypnotized, and utterly convinced. And I knew that for the rest of my life, I would have to keep a tight rein on my tendency to preach.

Larry Niven has made a career of exploring ideas others later hate themselves for missing. He won the Nebula and Hugo awards for his famous novel *Ringworld*.

Goodnight, Children

by
Joe Clifford Faust

They hadn't seen the dust kicked up by the Sandcrab's arrival, nor had they heard as the vehicle clamored into the garage. He thought for sure that they would have heard the pumps as the garage repressurized, but their concentration had been so intense that he had greeted his wife and made it all the way to the solarium door without their noticing. He stood and watched them now, beaming proudly.

Benjamin, who was ten, was displaying a rare moment of patience with his four-year-old sister, Rachel. She was hunched over the eyepiece of the telescope, squinting one eye and then the other. Finally she exclaimed, "I see it!"

Benjamin gently nudged her aside and looked for himself.

"Sorry, Rach," he said softly. "That's Phobos."

"I want to see it," Rachel protested.

Benjamin shrugged. "We just have to keep looking. Remember, what we're looking for is in a diamond shape. You remember the diamond shape?"

Rachel formed a crude diamond with her fingertips.

"It'll be silver. And there'll be flickering lights," Benjamin continued. "Red and green."

"I don't see it," Rachel protested, frustrated.

"Be patient," Benjamin said. "Sometimes you have to wait—"

"Isn't this a welcome scene!"

The pajama-clad children turned. They saw him and their faces lit up.

"Daddy!"

Benjamin was across the room in one deft leap. Rachel made it in two hops and a kick, and he caught them both in midair, spinning to the floor in the light gravity.

"You made it home, you made it home!"

He laughed and exchanged kisses with them. "I promised I would, didn't I?"

"Mom told us not to get our hopes up," Benjamin explained. "She said if the storms got too bad, you'd just have to wait them out."

"Phooey," Rachel said. "I knew he'd be home."

"I don't know. Daddy's boss is a mean old—"

"Hold on," the father said. "You don't know Mr. Smotherman the way I do. He might seem mean, but he's actually very nice. Did you know he was just as anxious to get home as I was?"

They looked at him incredulously.

"He was. He was sure the buildup wave of plants in the Elysium biosphere would be all right for a few days, so he told us all to go home. Then he looked right at me and said, 'You've got to go all the way to Utopia Ridge, and I'm not about to lose my best terraengineer in the rust. You take 'crab number six. It's just been serviced, and it'll get you through the worst this season can throw at you.' "

"Was there a storm?" Benjamin asked.

Father nodded. "It started to get bad around fourteen hundred, so I stopped at the Viking 2 monument and got some lunch. When things calmed I came on home."

"Glad you're home, Daddy," Rachel said, hugging him.

"I'm glad I made it." He patted his children. "What's the big scene with the telescope?" he asked, winking at Benjamin.

"We're looking for the sailer," Rachel said.

"But the next fleet isn't due in for another couple of months yet."

"Not those sailers," she protested. *"The* sailer."

"The sailer?"

Rachel put her hands on her hips. "You know. It's almost Christmas."

"That's right," he confessed. "I'd forgotten."

"You have to read the story," Benjamin said.

Father sat up and looked at his son. After last year, he was surprised to hear him ask for it.

"I don't know . . . I did read it last year . . ."

"But it's been a whole year!" Rachel said.

"Surely you know it by heart . . ."

"C'mon, Dad," Benjamin said, watching the scene with amusement.

"Get the book," Rachel said. She jumped off of her father's lap and bounded out of the solarium, turning the phrase into a song. "Get the book, get the book, get the book . . ."

They started through the house to the library, following Rachel's song.

"She giving you any trouble, son?"

"Naw," Benjamin answered. "She's a pretty good kid."

He put his arm around the boy and hugged him. "So are you."

"Book. Book. Book. Book. Book."

Rachel was bouncing up and down in time to her improvised tune, reaching toward an outsized box on the top shelf of the software case. Father reached up and grabbed it, causing her voice to rise in pitch.

"*Book!*" She latched onto her father's leg, and he started out of the library with an exaggerated limp. "Read it, read it."

"Is the living room ready?" He looked at Benjamin.

The boy grinned. "I'll set the holo," he said, and with a leap, he disappeared.

Father plucked the little girl from his leg and placed her on his shoulder. "Everything needs to be ready."

"Ready," she echoed.

When they arrived in the living room, the western hall was a field of static. Benjamin keyed orders into the controller, and the image of a still, quiet river appeared.

"Nope," he said.

More static. The image changed to a desertscape.

"Nope."

A cornfield in late summer.

"You're playing, Benjamin."

The wall became an image of Currier and Ives. Large flakes of snow were slowly falling on a bare forest, and in the background, in a small clearing, was a small white house with smoke lazily rising from the chimney.

Rachel applauded. The air in the room became still and cool.

"You're sure you don't want the fireplace?" Benjamin asked.

"This is fine." He lifted Rachel off his shoulder and set her on the couch. He put the box in her hands, and she started to work on the latch.

"Wait," he told her. "This isn't like a disk."

He sat, and she crawled into his lap. Benjamin joined them after focusing the holo.

"It's the book," Rachel said.

Father snapped the latch and opened the box. A strange, musty smell rose from inside, stale air left from last year's reading.

"This is how we used to store information," he explained, running his fingers over the hard cloth cover. "We didn't always have disks. We used paper, which wasn't susceptible to erasure by magnetic fields. The problem was, paper tended to age. This is made of acid-free paper, which was the best we had, but it's still getting old. Look."

The book opened with a creak. Rachel's eyes grew wide. On the title page, in Old English lettering, were the words *Goodnight, Children.* Below it, in a more common type style, was *Preservation Press. New York, London, Burroughs City.*

"Tell how it was written, Dad."

He smiled at Benjamin. It wasn't the story itself that the boy was still interested in. It was the history.

"All right." He closed the book. "Almost a hundred

years ago, the first colony ship came to Mars. The job of those on board was to select and clear a site in preparation for the arrival of the Great Silver Fleet, which was bringing more colonists and supplies. They came down at Viking 1, built the monument there, and set up the biosphere that they would live in while doing their work.

"The place would eventually become Burroughs City, but back then it was just a little frontier outpost. The people worked at clearing landing sites for the incoming fleet, made studies of the soil so they could start terraforming, and did all sorts of research on what natural resources were here."

"What about kids?" Rachel asked.

"There were children," Father continued. "They went to school and helped their mothers and fathers, just as you do. The difference was, things weren't as nice as they are now. They didn't have the masterdome complexes or parks full of scrubgreens. Each family had their own dome and the domes were connected by tunnels, so there wasn't an outside to play in. They hadn't even tapped the icecaps yet, so water was strictly rationed and they used bottled or recycled air. But they were all very brave and grew up wanting to make this planet a good place to live. And when they grew up, most of them stayed here and did just that."

"Tell about the story," Benjamin said.

"One of the men who came to Mars had the job of figuring out the best way to free the water trapped in the permafrost while others set up the polar-ice network. He had two children, a girl and a boy, who were both just a little younger than the two of you."

"The girl was older than the boy," Rachel said, glaring at her brother.

"The children had been born on Terra and had slept on the trip out, so this was their first year on Mars. And as Christmas got closer, they started to worry about whether or not their presents were going to arrive because they were so far away from the home world.

"This bothered the father, and he tried to explain that everything would arrive on Christmas Eve, just as it did back home. But his children kept asking questions about how everything was going to get here, so one night he sat down and wrote them this story. And he read it to them every Christmas Eve."

"Like you do," Benjamin said.

Rachel opened the book to the title page. "G'nite, children," she read, pointing at the words.

"Goodnight, children," Father repeated. He turned the page to the first illustration, one of an unlikely-looking vehicle passing through deep space. He cleared his throat and began to read.

> *"For the longest of times we have all heard the tales,*
> *That through space he will come pushed by bright silver sails,*
> *And how what he brings puts a smile on the face,*
> *And brings a warm glow to this desolate place."*

Benjamin pointed at the vehicle's driver. "There he is, sis." Rachel mimicked her older brother. "That's him."
Father turned the page and continued reading.

> *"But it's not been too long since his travel was slow,*
> *And his coming this far has not always been so,*
> *His business has been all on Terra, you see—*
> *Till at last humankind from old Terra broke free.*
>
> *"And he always assumed (in his kindly old way)*
> *That all children remained while their folks were away,*
> *But leave here they did in a glorious ascent!*
> *And on outsystem ships to the planets they went!"*

"Is that what the Great Silver Fleet looked like?" Benjamin asked. They had been studying it in school and he hadn't been able to learn enough about it.

"Yes and no." Father pointed to the lead ship in the illustration. "This one was the first colony ship, the *Utopia Bound*. Behind it is the wave of ships that followed, although they didn't arrive for another three years."

"That's because the sailers are slow," Benjamin said.

Father put his finger to his lips and gestured at Rachel. The boy nodded.

"*Most* of them are slow," he amended.

"The first fleet had about a dozen ships," Father continued. "And while the later ones were bigger, everyone was so excited over that first one that it became known as Great."

"Great Silver Fleet," Rachel said.

He turned the page.

> *"And one day he said as he gazed at the stars,*
> *'Look at all of the children on Luna and Mars,*
> *How can I reach them for one night a year?*
> *My promise was made to the far and the near!' "*

"Far away," Rachel said, waving at the forlorn figure on the page.

"Far away," Benjamin echoed.

> *"So he sat and researched and the experts he called,*
> *Until one gave him blueprints that left him enthralled,*
> *To the workshop he went! And he called up his crew!*
> *And he gave them the task to build something brand-new!*
>
> *"Oh, the clang and the clatter! The noise and the din!*
> *They worked through the year on a Something so thin—*
> *Till that Something was ready they worked night and day,*
> *And with minutes to spare it attached to his sleigh . . ."*

Father paused. This was the problem spot. Last year, Benjamin, who had been near the end of believing in the overnight delivery of specialized payloads from Terra to Mars, began to question how a sleigh could lift off with such a big Something attached to the back. For Rachel's sake, Father had insisted that if it could haul all of those toys, it could certainly haul the Something. The rest of the reading had been interrupted with all sorts of technical questions brought on by a ballistics study in his science class.

"Go on," Rachel said.

Father studied Benjamin's face. "Any questions?"

"Nope." He smiled.

"You're sure?"

"Please," said Rachel. "Read it, Daddy."

"Then his crew watched him leave—and not one of them knew,
What that big Something was—or just what it would do.
Nor would they believe as he went on his rounds,
That the Something would take him beyond Terra's bounds!"

His reading began to slow. The next few lines had produced a myriad of questions about escape velocities.

"He was done in a flash (as he had been for years),
And then upward he flew into thin atmospheres.
With his reindeer cut free a new helmet he donned,
And his upward trajectory took him beyond . . ."

He trailed to a stop.

"Terry Below," Rachel urged. "Poor old Terry Below."

Father looked at Benjamin and smiled, then turned back to the page.

". . . poor old Terra below, and out of the blue—
And in blackness of space that old sleigh became new . . .

The bells were all silenced by the vacuum of space,
So bright red and green lasers were put in their
*   place!*

"From the back of the sleigh, robot arms did de-
*   ploy*
And they shook out a sail of metal alloy—
It was bright, shining Mylar that caught the sun's
*   light—*
And it gave him a push for a Luna-bound flight!"

"Not slow," Rachel said, gesturing at the restructured
sleigh. "Not slow, Benjamin."

Benjamin shrugged. "You're right, sis."

He hadn't believed that his sister doted on every word
that he said. He'd believe it now.

"And when Luna was finished he headed to Mars,
Guided by maps he had made of the stars,
Then when in Mars orbit this sailer arrives,
He makes planetfall and a Sandcrab he drives."

The picture was of an ancient-model Sandcrab topping
a dune, great clouds of rust billowing behind it.

"Is this Daddy's 'crab?" Rachel asked.

"No," Father said.

"Is Daddy's 'crab better?"

"Dad's 'crab is *different.*" Benjamin said. He winked
at his father.

The kid's learning, Father thought.

"Then across all of Mars with a great sack he
*   roams,*
Till he finds sleeping children inside of the domes,
And because there's no chimney (no entrance, it
*   seems),*
He steps through their holo of soft Winter Scenes.

"With a twitch of his nose the great sack will un-
*   fold,*

And he lays out the presents for young and for old,
Then he's off to see others, and when he is done,
It is up to his sleigh that is powered by sun—

"To return him to Terra through the vacuum's tra-
    vails,
Riding home on the solar wind trapped in its sails.
And he says, 'Goodnight, children—sleep in free-
    dom from fear—
Be good little Martians—I'll see you next year."

He sat with them for a moment, leaving the book open.

"G'nite, children," Rachel said, waving. "G'nite, g'nite."

Benjamin smiled at his father. "I liked it better this year."

"For a different reason?"

The boy nodded.

Father closed the book and returned it to the box, sealing it tight and hooking the latch. As he did, his wife appeared in the living room.

"Did you get it all read?" she asked.

"Made it all the way through."

Benjamin made a point to say, "It's a pretty good story, really."

"Fantastic." She clapped her hands. "Now it's time for the two of you to get to bed."

"But I didn't find him," Rachel stressed.

Father plucked her up from his lap and dangled her overhead. "That's a good thing. If you had, he wouldn't come."

"Why won't he come till we're asleep?"

"Because if he stopped to answer all of the questions that all of the boys and girls want to ask him, he wouldn't make it back to Terra in time for next year." He flexed his arm and brought her down for a kiss. "Goodnight, Rachel."

She gave him a wet smack on the cheek. "G'nite, Daddy."

He turned Rachel to her mother and gave a gentle heave. Squealing with delight, she flew across the room, arms outstretched, through winter birches and swirling flakes until she landed in her mother's arms.

Benjamin kissed them both, and they went to the bedroom.

Father rose slowly from the couch and patted his son's shoulder. "That goes for you, too."

"Can't I go see if I can spot the incoming fleet?"

He shook his head. "They won't be visible until after New Year's."

They walked to Benjamin's bedroom, which was lined with posters of popular sail jockeys and the latest designs of sporting sailers. The boy folded back the simulated Mylar comforter and climbed between the sheets.

"By the way," Father said, turning off the lights, "there's something I wanted to tell you."

Benjamin rolled onto his side. "Yeah?"

"Thanks for not spoiling the story for Rachel. She won't be able to enjoy it like that for much longer."

"No problem," he answered. "Everyone's got to have something to dream about, you know?"

"I know." He kissed his forehead. "Goodnight, Benjamin."

"Goodnight, Dad."

He started out the door.

"Dad?"

"Yes, son."

"The solar wind—technically, it's not really wind, is it?"

"Not like we have here. It's more like a stream of light energy."

"Thanks," he said.

"Goodnight."

The voice of his wife singing a carol filled the hall. Slowly, he returned to the living room and settled down in the middle of the snow-covered forest, nose filling with the scent from the small house's chimney. In a little while, when the children were asleep, he would go to his bedroom closet and step back through the soft Winter scenes, laying out disks and fruit and nuts for them both, the Jenny Astro doll that Rachel had wanted, and the scale model of the Great Silver Fleet's flagship that Benjamin had been hinting about since the week after his birthday. And early tomorrow morning, whether they really believed or not, their dreams would come true.

As his son had said, everyone had to have something to dream about.

They were living proof of that.

Joe Clifford Faust is the author of five science fiction novels and a very strange play called *Old Loves Die Hard.* He also scripts stories for *Open Space,* a science fiction title for Marvel Comics, and advertisements for a top-rated FM station in northeast Ohio. He currently lives in Ohio with his wife and two children, and is at work on a new novel.

Solar Sails in an Interplanetary Economy

by
Robert L. Staehle
and Louis Friedman

Liverpool . . . Bombay . . . New York . . . Rio . . . Perth . . . Shanghai . . . Rotterdam. Do your grandparents remember these ports of call for the great ocean liners of the past? They remain focal points of international commerce. Where will the ports of call be in an interplanetary economy? The moon? Phobos? The icy plains of Callisto? Will these and other exotic destinations be served by the new generations of clipper ships? Moreover, might these ships ride a network of powerful, pencil-thin beams, or be gently pushed by natural sunlight?

We must, of course, walk before we can run. In order to locate the ports, much less name them, we will have to explore our solar system in much greater detail, discover the resources, and create the demands which will drive the commerce. And before majestic, city-size sails fill the heavens, playing a part in this great drama, we must develop the rudimentary skills of interplanetary sailing.

Our first tentative steps will be with the smallest sails, no bigger than a football field or two. We will hold a collective "school for solar sailing," where everyone starts as a freshman. Theoretical studies and computer simulations already model basic control laws, but only real flight can teach us the techniques and refinements needed to harness and best use our sun-driven spacecraft.

The Interplanetary Shuttle

Just as with the shores of the seven seas from the sixteenth through the nineteenth centuries, the planets, natural satellites, comets, and asteroids of the solar system are the targets for exploration and, at least for some of them, development in the twenty-first century and beyond.

For a single mission it rarely makes sense to develop a whole new technology. This reasoning has thus far prevented the use of low-thrust (electric- or sail-derived) primary propulsion. But now that we are beyond the initial reconnaissance of the solar system, solar sailing will become really useful for the more intensive exploration and later development, which will follow.

The chief advantage of a solar sail interplanetary vehicle we could build over the next decade is not the amount of speed it gains over ordinary spacecraft. In fact, the minimum energy ballistic trajectories used by chemical rockets take somewhat less time than first-generation sails. (But advanced, metal-only sails built in space can cut trip times far below those using the best chemical rockets.) Nevertheless if we can accept a typical trip time from Earth to Mars of 400 days, or 600 days to Mercury, or 270 days to Venus, then we can reap the benefits of launching a smaller mass from Earth for a given mission, or placing more scientific instruments on a spacecraft for a given launch weight. At $3,000 per kilogram (over $6,500 per pound) for launch costs, the cost savings can be dramatic.

Where the sail really becomes advantageous, because it requires no fuel or other propellant, is for *round-trip* missions, such as sample returns. Rocket-driven missions must not only carry the propellant required to get to the destination, but also fuel and oxidizer for the return journey. All of this along with the useful payload. This results in much more than a doubling of the weight burden. Propellant masses multiply exponentially, even for highly efficient schemes such as electric propulsion. A sail, on the other hand, needn't weigh a single pound more to bring samples back from Mars than if it were simply carrying a scientific orbiter on the one-way trip to the Red Planet. Controlled from Earth, the sail can just turn around and come home.

Sails offer the added option, if you're not in a hurry, of trading trip time for added payload. For example, using the kind of sail designed at JPL during the mid-1970s, over a ton can be delivered to Mars in a 400-day mission; but if we can accept a 500-day trip time, the sail can deliver 2.5 tons! For Mercury, nearly 4 tons can be delivered in 600 days, but this goes to 8 tons for a 900-day mission. Even out to the main belt asteroids, over a ton can be delivered in 600 days. And of course, with the sail each of these journeys comes with a return-trip option.

Current proposals for human exploration of Mars call for numerous automated missions before we send the first crew. Both the United States and Soviet Union contemplate a series of robotic explorers—as many as six rover and sample-return missions might be performed to help select landing sites of greatest scientific interest and practical benefit. One concept for making this series of missions more economical is having a regular interplanetary transport which continuously shuttles back and forth between Earth and Mars. Sails would be ideal for such an "interplanetary shuttle."

A three-quarter million square meter-class solar sail (850 meters or one-half mile on a side, or the equivalent heliogyro) could be used for a high-performance Mars sample-return mission. This is the same size sail designed for the cancelled Halley's Comet Rendezvous Mission at the Jet Propulsion Laboratory. For Mars, the landed mass could be as high as 3 tons, sufficient to include an atmospheric entry vehicle, a lander with sample-gathering equipment, and an ascent rocket to return the sample to the sail for return to Earth. The entire interplanetary shuttle weighs

234 Project Solar Sail

about 1.6 tons, or about as much as a mid-size automobile.

A possible intermediate step between the World Space Foundation's Engineering Development Mission and a true interplanetary shuttle is the proposed Asteroid Rendezvous Mission.

If we select carefully, there are a few opportunities where a single chemically propelled spacecraft can rendezvous with one asteroid, and then leave at a precise time to go on to the next. But such a spacecraft would be so dominated by the need for fuel and oxidizer that it would look like a propellant-tank farm, with little room left for instrumentation. On the other hand, even a modest solar sail can get to any asteroid. And if it can get to one, it is perfectly equipped to go on to another, and another, and so on, stopping at each long enough to perform a thorough reconnaissance. The itinerary can even be changed along the way if new discoveries or changing priorities suggest new targets.

Among the first asteroids to be visited will be those in Earth-approaching orbits around the sun. At just the right times, a few are even easier to reach in propulsive terms than the surface of the moon. Nearly all are accessible to a small solar sail. (Many were discovered through the World Space Foundation's Asteroid Project, in conjunction with the NASA-sponsored Planet Crossing Asteroid Survey and International Near-Earth Asteroid Survey at the Jet Propulsion Laboratory. Principal investigator Eleanor Helin and her team travel nearly every month to Palomar Mountain to search for "fast-moving objects." During 1989 her team discovered five new comets and over 250 new asteroids, including nine of the rare Earth-approachers.)

Originally the Foundation's Engineering Development Mission (EDM) sail design was done with the Asteroid Rendezvous Mission (ARM) in mind. It would measure about 100 feet on a side, giving a sail area of 800 square meters, or 8,600 square feet, sufficient to go to the moon and escape Earth orbit, although its subsystems are not designed for an interplanetary cruise.

Responding to the possible challenge of the Columbus Quincentenary Solar Sail Race (see the chapter "A Rebel Technology Comes Alive"), the foundation upgraded the EDM design to give it greater maneuverability, a 3,000-square-meter (32,000-square-foot) sail area, and interplanetary capability. This sail could go to Mars or a succession of asteroids, trading simplicity for a longer trip time.

In either its original 800-square-meter form, or in its upgraded 3,000-square-meter Race Vehicle form, the Engineering Development Mission could be the first solar sail flown. Either way, the intent is to learn enough to go on and build larger sails for future exploration needs.

Supply Lines for Human Explorers

The first expedition crew to travel to Mars will almost certainly use chemical rockets. For crew members, speed will be essential, because every day requires more oxygen, food, water, and even a "short" trip can last over two years.

However, just as mountaineering expeditions sometimes use air-dropped supplies or caches put in place earlier, the crew of a Mars mission really need not carry with it everything they need. In fact, everything required from the moment the crew arrives at Mars, including the propellant for their return home, should be already there before they even set out—delivered by "slow freighter" prior to their departure from Earth—so they can be sure that essential supplies are waiting there, in good condition.

In research performed for NASA's Lewis Research Center, Dr. Robert Frisbee of the Jet Propulsion Laboratory has shown that dramatic savings can be achieved using solar sail freighters. (This was based on earlier work by Robert Staehle, Eric Drexler, and John Garvey.) In the least complex of these cargo vessels, a sail two miles on a side and weighing 19 tons hauls 32 tons of supplies to Mars in 4.2 years, returning empty in 2 years. This appears to be largest sail which could be assembled on the ground and launched aboard the Shuttle or a Titan IV. The payload mass was selected to match the capability of an upgraded space shuttle, and happens to be about the maximum load carried by an eighteen-wheeler tractor-trailer. And since most of the expense would no longer go into hauling propellant around, many *more* supplies could be sent to Mars, ensuring an adequate safety margin when the crew arrives, in case of any emergency. If the excess isn't used, it can be left on the surface or in orbit above Mars, to tempt forth later visitors from Earth.

A fleet of ten to twenty such vessels would be sufficient to carry the supplies for the first expedition. Then these same spacecraft, continuously shuttling between Earth and Mars, could carry the equipment to build a permanent outpost on the Red Planet. Dramatic improvements in trip time and a reduction in fleet size might also be possible, using the metal-only sails proposed by Eric Drexler and others.

Mars is not the only destination which can be served by such cargo vessels. As pointed out earlier, they might form the basis for early commercial shipping. Higher-temperature metals or highly radiative coatings to provide cooling are necessary for trips to Venus or Mercury. One can even envisage solar sail vessels being used to save Earth from a threatening collision with a small asteroid! If a collision threat were known far enough in advance, only a gentle nudge of a few centimeters per second would be required to avert disaster.

(The last occasion an object large enough to do substantial damage collided with the Earth was 1908, above the remote Tunguska region of Siberia, and we were lucky that time. Heard as far away as London, the explosion leveled a forest. The late Nobel laureate, Luis Alvarez, theorized that a much larger asteroid collision might have resulted in the extinction of the dinosaurs about 67 million years ago. Another Tunguska-like event, next time in a more populated world, could be as devastating as a nuclear bomb.)

The Commercial Clippership

Because a lightsail will use reflected sunlight, or perhaps laser beams, it needs to appear to its light source as a nearly rigid mirror. To our ground-bred intuition, this suggests something fairly heavy, but of course we know a sail must be gossamer-thin to be effective. To rigidize a sail we must either build a supporting structure or spin the sail so that centrifugal force maintains its rigidity.

An obvious shape for a spinning sail would be a flat disk, with the entire surface spinning. Another alternative is the heliogyro, invented by helicopter expert Richard MacNeal, which is appropriate since it is like the blades of a helicopter without the helicopter. Sunlight sets them spinning, which rigidizes an efficient structure to catch more sunlight.

A more critical question than shape is how to control a sail. For a square sail, control is achieved by small sails, called vanes, which act very much like ailerons on an airliner to create differential torques to turn the sail. Disk sails are difficult to control, requiring either gas jets or a very complicated center-of-mass/center-of-pressure offset system in the middle of the sail. The heliogyro is controlled in a better understood manner, similar to a helicopter.

Even more touchy than shape and control is the packaging of a large sail for launch, and then its deployment in space. When large sails can be manufactured in space it will be much simpler to construct and use different types of designs. R. Gilbert Moore has proposed one technique of essentially blowing very large bubbles of thin plastic, coating the inside with reflective aluminum, and then cutting away the excess material. If two bubbles are blown of equal size with a common wall, that common wall will be flat and could serve as a sail. If the bubble substrate is chemically composed to break down into gasses after a week or so of exposure to the sun's ultraviolet radiation, only the metal will be left behind, making a very light-weight sail.

Eric Drexler has proposed various other techniques to build such lightsails in orbit. (See his article in this volume.) And John Garvey of McDonnell Douglas looked at the use of a sail-construction machine running along a tether tied to NASA's space station. There appears to be no theoretical limitation on the size of sails built in space.

Solar Sailing and Environmental Protection in Space*

Virtually every time mankind has entered a new frontier, we've assumed humans are too insignificant to cause widespread harm to the vast reaches spread before us. Imagine early settlers from Europe standing on a gentle rise in the North American Great Plains, contemplating bison as far as the eye could see, or cursing hours of unexpected darkened sky resulting from migrations of passenger pigeons. It must have seemed inconceivable that the actions of people could endanger either species. However, we have found to our chagrin just how fragile the Great Plains and forests were. Do similar hard lessons await us in space?

Awareness of space as a natural environment, which

*Editors Note: This article was originally prepared as a portion of the proposal to the Charles A. Lindbergh Fund which resulted in their support of the Solar Sail Project. One of their criteria for funding projects is that there be a balance between technological development and environmental benefit as a result of the work being supported. We have reprinted it here as we feel its pertinence has increased rather than diminished. Planning for environmental safety must be concurrent with mission and technology development.

could be subject to human damage, is not common in the field of astronautics. Of course we have discovered no nonterrestrial life in the solar system. One may ask, therefore, why anyone should bother to protect the space "desert" environment. The answer is threefold.

First, obviously, we have not actually proven the nonexistence of extraterrestrial life in the solar system. In fact, a close examination has only been made in two very small spots on the surface of Mars, where the results were inconclusive. While the conditions for life on Mars now are not good, they apparently once were. We infer this from the evidence of running water in the past. Thus there may have been past life, and we don't want the evidence destroyed before we can study it properly.

The second answer is that within the next century, people may begin to inhabit space themselves, and it is certainly undesirable to alter the space environment in any way which renders it less habitable for our descendants.

In a third sense, simple prudence demands that we take care, rather than tamper with any natural environment before having a reasonable understanding what the consequences might be. Environmental destruction of newly inhabited frontiers has often resulted from a simple lack of forethought. Frontiersmen often simply do not consider the long-term payoff of environmental protection. Bearing this in mind, solar sails suggest advantages compared to other propulsion techniques, because nearly all other systems require the expulsion of mass from the vehicle. For every 1 kilogram of payload launched out of Earth orbit, say on a trajectory to Mars, approximately 9 kilograms of typical chemical propellants must be expended. For small scientific payloads such as those launched in the last three decades, the quantity of propellant released in low Earth orbit is meaningless.* However, looking twenty to fifty

*The problems become severe, however, when rockets misfire or explode! Just two accidents with booster rockets plus one satellite blown up by the Soviets on purpose are responsible for half the dangerous debris in orbit today.

years ahead, moving the material to manufacture one modest space settlement (such as proposed by Dr. Gerard K. O'Neill of Princeton University) from the asteroid belt to Earth could require on the order of twenty thousand million (2×10^{10}) kilograms (1 kg = 2.2 pounds) of expelled reaction mass.

A propulsion technique frequently suggested for moving massive objects (such as asteroids) is the so-called "mass driver," which operates by accelerating small, solid chunks (pieces of the asteroid, for example) to high velocity with a linear-induction motor. But one unfortunate side-effect would be a vast number of dangerous "pellets" orbiting the sun, each permanent and capable of doing considerable damage in a collision. When we talk of building just one settlement, the disruptions may not be particularly large. (Similar statistics applied to the first few buffalo hunters.) But when we contemplate building 100 settlements, using 1 kilogram pellets, then there are two million million (2×10^{12}) of them.

Solar sails offer an environmentally attractive alternative to rockets and mass drivers. No reaction mass or propellant need be carried. The sail is a totally reusable propulsion system with a useful life of perhaps decades. There is no by-product to remain in orbit as a hazard, and sails are very unlikely to explode.

Bryan Palaszewski's article tells how ion engines share some of these advantages. However, even these "clean" engines might have environmental impact. Routine activities in low Earth orbit could inject quantities of mercury, cesium, argon, or other propellants into the magnetosphere. We don't know if this would be benign, or possibly affect geomagnetic storms or the Van Allen radiation belts, with unknown consequences for the lower atmosphere.

To be fair, it is not clear whether solar sails can function well between 1,000 kilometer and 20,000 kilometer altitudes. Turning rates required to reorient a sail toward the sun during each orbit may prove operationally difficult that low. Experience gained during the first engineering development mission should help answer this question. As Palaszewski points out clearly, solar sailing and ion drives both have definite limitations and trade-offs.

While not a universal space-propulsion technique, solar sailing does seem likely to play a major role in some future space-transportation markets because of its economic attractiveness. When compared with several rocket techniques requiring mass expulsion, solar sailing compares favorably with regard to its impact on the space environment. Environmental impact in space is only a dimly perceived concept at this time, but a historical perspective suggests that considerable long-term regret can be avoided through near-term awareness of possible environmental sensitivities of space itself.

Concluding Remarks

Finally, one of us (Robert Staehle) would like to take a moment for a comment or two.

First, I want to thank all of the contributors to this fundraising volume, whose generosity goes beyond anything I have words for. Bob Cesarone, whose idea this was, David Brin, who made it happen, and Arthur Clarke, who made it a success; all three have our special gratitude.

It was Arthur's inspiration, especially in the story *The Wind from the Sun,* which introduced me to solar sails. His factual writings prepared me for a tough technical curriculum at Purdue University, and all his writing inspired me to follow my strongest calling to contribute whatever I could to the art and science of space exploration.

We would be remiss without acknowledging the support of the Charles A. Lindbergh Fund, which has generously helped the Solar Sail Project. One of their criteria for funding is that there be a potential environment benefit, which we hope has been shown. Other corporate and institutional supporters include the Jet Propulsion Laboratory, Hughes Aircraft Company, Radio Amateur Satellite Corporation (AMSAT), the law firm of Silvestri & Massicot, Morton Thiokol Corp., United Technologies Corporation's Chemical Systems Division, E.I. du Pont de Nemours & Co., the University of California and their California Space Institute, Societé d'Astronomie Populaire de Toulouse, Technische Universität München, and Pasadena City College.

Also critical to our progress have been Solar Sail Project subscribers and associates of the World Space Foundation. All Solar Sail Project staff members deserve mention, though they are simply too numerous. They have graciously donated seemingly endless hours of dedication and expertise beginning in 1979, and many will continue to do so. Among the most important are Jerry Wright, the project's originator and first director, Chauncey Uphoff, Jim French, Mark Bergam, Emerson LaBombard, Hoppy Price, Dallas Legan, and Gabe Gabriel. Sharlyn French was always cheerful and efficient dealing with so many editorial changes. Other key individuals have included Richard Dowling, Phil Hatten, Kristan Lattu, and the artists Julian Baum (for the cover) and Carter Emmart. Many others have supported the foundation in a variety of innovative and dedicated ways—accountants, attorneys, educators, writers, artists, photographers, editors, secretaries, managers, and all the other talents necessary to make an organization run.

(Having said all of this, I must nevertheless offer one important caveat. In any diverse assemblage of talent like the authors contributing to this book, there are bound to be healthy differences of opinion. One should therefore expect that opinions expressed in the individual chapters belong to the authors themselves and do not necessarily represent opinions of other authors, the editors, or officers of the World Space Foundation.)

Things are definitely looking up. Even without the Columbus Regatta (though we hope it flies) and operating on a shoestring, we believe we should be able to fly a test sail soon enough that every person who bought this book will be able to point up into the night sky and say, "I helped make that happen."

Even after that, it will be a long step from this first mission to the interplanetary shuttle, commercial cargo vessels, and interstellar probes. But we believe this is the place to start, within the modest resources available to visionary individuals, corporations, and other sources.

We acknowledge the help of everyone who purchases this book. This *does* make a difference. If you wish to do more, please write to us:

Project Solar Sail,
World Space Foundation,
Post Office Box Y,
South Pasadena, CA 91031-1000, USA.

Thank you.
Robert L. Staehle, President
World Space Foundation

P.S. To all of those who join the foundation by sending in the coupon at the back of the book, this promise: your name will be part of the cargo of our first solar sail.

Robert L. Staehle is president and founder of the World Space Foundation. He began his aerospace career as a high school and college student when his experiment, Bacteria Aboard Skylab, flew twice on America's first space station. With a B.S. in Aeronautical and Astronautical Engineering from Purdue University, Mr. Staehle is currently manager of space station science utilization studies at the NASA/Caltech Jet Propulsion Laboratory. He has been involved in a variety of planetary mission studies and helped to plan observations for the Voyager encounters at Jupiter. The moon and Mars are among his principal fascinations, and Mr. Staehle wrote the first technical paper describing use of solar sails to haul cargo to Mars in support of early expedition crews.

Dr. Louis Friedman is a native of New York City. He received a Ph.D. from the Aeronautics and Astronautics department at M.I.T. in 1971. During the 1970s he worked on several projects while at the Jet Propulsion Laboratory and was the leader of the Halley Comet Rendezvous-Solar Sail Program. He left JPL in 1980 to become executive director of the Planetary Society, a nonprofit, popular society for enhancing the exploration of the planets and the search for extraterrestrial life. Dr. Friedman is the author of *Starsailing: Solar Sails and Interstellar Travel*.

Afterword

In the old days before the World War II, many popular tales about exploring outer space pictured the adventure taking off on a shoestring—perhaps financed by some eccentric millionaire, or put together in the basement laboratory of some brave, lonely visionaries. Few of us ever thought space flight would someday become a monopoly of huge governments, operating on such a mammoth scale.

Perhaps we were naive, underestimating the magnitude of the problems involved. Anyway, don't get me wrong. Much of the work of NASA and ESA and other big space institutions has been marvelous. Even miraculous. Still, isn't it somewhat intimidating and remote? It's so hard for the average citizen to feel he or she is a participant.

Don't you sometimes wish there was a David to cheer for? Not so much to *defeat* Goliath, as to give him a little honest competition?

That is what this volume has been all about. It is the reason so many of us gave our time and creativity, in order to give a little boost to an idea. Perhaps it's only a magnificently crazy idea. On the other hand, it may also be one whose time at last has come.

To those who bought this volume, thank you for your help. But now comes the bonus. There is a way you can contribute even more. Just send in the coupon at the back of this book. (Or send a photocopy if—like me—you can't bring yourself to rip out pages!) With your paid membership in the World Space Foundation, you'll get the foundation's fascinating periodicals concerning the cutting edge

of space exploration, and much more. I am also assured
that the names of all contributors will be inscribed upon a
scroll, which will be the most important cargo carried
aboard the first test mission of the foundation's solar sail.

The planned trajectory? Why, past the moon, of course!
And beyond.

Now if only there were a way to go along in person!

Well, perhaps next time.

Perhaps indeed.

FLY IN SPACE!

We hope you'll be aboard, in name anyway, when Project Solar Sail comes to fruition and our spacecraft reaches orbit.

We would never suggest that you cut something out of this book—we hope you consider it a valuable collector's item. So PLEASE DO NOT CLIP OUT THIS COUPON, but make a copy, jot a note, or whatever, and tell us you want to be aboard.

All contributors will get their name onboard when the sail unfurls in orbit.*

☐ Count me in as a Subscriber to the Solar Sail Project. I understand that for one year, renewable annually if I wish, I will receive quarterly Foundation publications and other benefits accorded Foundation Associates, such as product and conference discounts. I would like to subscribe at the ☐ $25.00 or ☐ $50.00 level.

☐ Please enroll me as a member of the Solar Mariners Group and carry my signature on microfiche aboard your spacecraft. For my $100.00 contribution, renewable annually if I wish, I understand that I will receive the benefits noted above for the $25.00 and $50.00 levels, and that after launch, I will receive a piece of one of your prototype sails no longer required for testing or backup hardware. My signature appears below:

☐ I would like to become a Life Associate of the World Space Foundation. For my $500.00 contribution, I understand that I will receive the benefits of members of the Solar Mariners Group, and that annual renewals will not be required. My signature appears below to be carried on your first solar sail spacecraft.

☐ Other contribution:

☐ $10.00 ☐ $15.00 ☐ $_____

Enclosed is my check or money order for

$_____.

payable to World Space Foundation. (Amounts are shown in US dollars. Please convert at the prevailing rate for Canadian dollars or other convertible currencies.)

Name _____

Address _____

City _____ State/Prov. _____

Country _____ State/Zip _____

Contributions, less value of any articles received, are tax-deductible per Section 501(c) (3) of Internal Revenue Code

EXTRA BONUS

Contributions of $50.00 or more receive a free "Solar Sail Project" T-Shirt. Please specify adult size
☐ S ☐ M ☐ L ☐ XL

Mail to: **Project Solar Sail**
World Space Foundation
P.O. Box Y
South Pasadena, California
91031-1000 USA

My signature _____

_____

* World Space Foundation will make its best effort to build and obtain a launch for the Engineering Development Mission (which may be renamed). As with any advanced scientific research, success cannot be guaranteed. The Foundation has made great strides in getting solar sail technology ready for flight. We need your help to get the rest of the way